ENGLISH HOURS

HENRY JAMES

ENGLISH HOURS

WITH AN INTRODUCTION BY
LEON EDEL

Oxford New York Toronto Melbourne
OXFORD UNIVERSITY PRESS
1981

Oxford University Press, Walton Street, Oxford OX2 6DP

London Glasgow New York Toronto
Delhi Bombay Calcutta Madras Karachi
Kuala Lumpur Singapore Hong Kong Tokyo
Nairobi Dar es Salaam Cape Town
Melbourne Wellington
and associate companies in
Beirut Berlin Ibadan Mexico City

Introduction © Leon Edel 1981

First edition in book form published in the USA by
Houghton Mifflin & Co. 1905
First edition in book form published in the UK by
William Heinemann 1905
This edition first published as an
Oxford University Press paperback 1981

British Library Cataloguing in Publication Data

James, Henry
English hours.
1. England – Description and travel – 1801-1900
I. Title
914.2'04'74   DA625   80-41736
ISBN 0-19-281321-8

Printed in Great Britain by
Cox and Wyman Ltd
Reading, Berks

Contents

Introduction

On the threshold of his old age, Henry James revised and rewrote his novels and tales, and also gave attention to his travel writings which occupy an important place in the entire corpus of his work. These were the lighter essays of four decades in which he had reported to his American readers on England, France and Italy, the international world of his adoption. In his younger years he had described England as 'a good married matron', and Italy as 'a beautiful dishevelled nymph'. He had taken up permanent residence with the matron: she had become a kind of second mother—or motherland—to him; and periodically he visited his continental nymph, or mistress, taking a well-beaten path to the cities he had loved in his early prime, Rome, Florence, Venice and some of the byways of Italy. The result of his late gatherings-in of these fugitive travelogues was two books, perhaps less known today than they should be—*English Hours*, a neat octavo published in 1905 and the large quarto *Italian Hours* of 1910.

English Hours contains James's finest tributes—critical and appreciative—to the land in which he lived for half a century and whose citizenship he finally claimed. There is calculated art in the arrangement of the essays which are essentially painterly and documentary. James is not a Tocqueville or a Brycc; he is certainly not an economist or a social scientist; nor does he attempt a scientific critique of British institutions. He travels for the delight of his senses; he relishes the old, the picturesque, the noble antiquities, the idea of continuity and preservation—the sense of history that lives within the beauties and the uglinesses of the land. He does not turn his eyes completely away from the visible poverty and the slums. He is a very polite and even cautious tourist, and, as he says, a 'grateful alien' who at the same time allows himself to observe closely. In one of his older essays, he wonders whether it is worth while for a traveller to leave home 'only to see new forms of human suffering, only to be reminded that toil and privation, hunger and sorrow and sordid effect, are the portion of the great majority of his fellow-men'. It seemed to him there was something heartless 'in stepping forth into the streets of a foreign town to feast upon novelty when the novelty consists simply of the slightly different costume in which hunger and labour present themselves'.

He could say this more of Italy and of other nations on the continent than of England. In England it was possible for the American traveller to visit castles and abbeys, great houses, old churches and cathedrals and study the architecture which encased the Establishment; he could pause in Oxford or Cambridge and turn his eyes away from the centres of industry and the haunts of poverty. He was writing originally for an American audience. And if he ministered to the curiosity of restless new generations of his countrymen, and England was still, as Hawthorne had called it, 'our old home', he spoke as well to a land where democratic feeling had become deeply rooted. British royalty dazzled America—it does still—but the British class structure and British manners were viewed with a certain distance and chill. It was one way in which the children of New England asserted their independence.

Early in his career, James found that his travel sketches, intended first entirely for the United States, required careful retouching for publication abroad. As demand for his work grew, he sold his first travel book, *Transatlantic Sketches*, to Tauchnitz and quickly changed the title to *Foreign Parts* lest Europeans think he was offering them sketches of America. So in using some of his earlier English essays in *Portraits of Places* in 1883 he had to find—he felt impelled to find—delicate euphemisms and cushion-words for his English readers. He explained his dilemma to American friends saying 'there are some English institutions and idiosyncrasies that it is certainly a great blessing to be outside of' and he added that they could be handled only through 'the happy medium of irony'. That was why, he said, he tried to make his essays 'ironical without being too much so'. And this accounts for the resourceful phrases sown through his text which give him distance and a special character. The reader is always being told that foreign parts are being looked at by foreign eyes. Things appear 'to alien eyes' and to 'the desultory stranger' or to 'the imported consciousness'. The visitor is very urbane and possesses a cool charm. Sometimes he is 'the brooding spectator' when he doesn't become, in a moment of more acute vision, with a certain amount of self-irony, 'a stray savage'. But we know this is a conceit; he is hardly an American primitive. In general he seeks delicately and even fastidiously to be kind to his readers; he wants to be certain he has said nothing that might sound harsh to British ears.

We may see examples of this in the essay 'London at Midsummer' which includes a long paragraph about the outdoor cafés of the continent. In London, James remarks, such haunts of leisure would hardly be frequented by the British upper classes. Indeed in the original version he takes occasion to remark that the upper classes are 'too refined', adding that the lower classes are 'too miserable'. The retouching hand in *Portraits of Places*, and finally in this volume, asks us to read, 'The better sort are too "genteel", and the inferior sort too base.'

So in the earlier version, he alludes to 'the aristocratic constitution of English society'. Even this appears too blunt to the revising James and he substitutes 'the essentially hierarchical' plan of this society. These niceties of expression may seem today excessive: but we must remind ourselves that James's stock-in-trade was fiction which dealt with national traits and international idiosyncrasies; and he had learned early how sensitive local patriotisms could be to even so gentle an ironist as himself. The first version of the essay which we have been examining remarks that the English aristocrats are 'people of fortune and are naturally independent of communistic pleasures'. (Henry James is using the word 'communistic' in the old sense of 'communal'.) At any rate the sentence is changed in *English Hours* to 'They are persons for whom the private machinery of ease has been made to work with extraordinary smoothness.' And James admires the smoothness. As an outsider he experiences neither guilt nor disdain for a society which is organised in this way. Like most great novelists he accepts the world—in such societies 'such things are', as he remarks in *The Ambassadors*. His concern is with concrete and palpable reality. He is not a reformer.

Reading *English Hours*, we discover behind the mask of language three different silhouettes of Henry James engaged in making an art of travel. The first is the young Henry James, who calls himself 'the sentimental tourist' and we find this tourist in the essays of 1872, those that begin with his account of Chester and end with Wells and Salisbury. He was still in his twenties and travelling in England with his sister and an aunt, and his papers were written as part of a series, describing a summer in Europe for the American weekly, the *Nation*.

The second traveller is in his middle thirties; and, from 1877 into the 1880s, much in need of money, he writes the papers that begin with 'An English Easter' and end with 'An English Watering Place'. No longer a tourist of sentiment, he has taken up residence in London and reports on his excursions into the countryside, for he is busy taking the measure of his environment and the people in it. His role is now that of an 'observant stranger'. He looks inevitably through American eyes, even though he is highly cosmopolitanised, and he writes essentially for the readers of the *Galaxy* and *Lippincott's*, the literary journals of New York and Philadelphia. Certain of these papers were reprinted in *Portraits of Places* together with his travel essays on France, Italy and the Low Countries; and to make this volume truly international for European readers he inserts for good measure a few domestic essays—a trip to Niagara Falls, a summer in Saratoga, a return to Newport and a journey to the then-unchangeable Quebec. Abroad, he boasts that he carries England 'in my breeches pocket' and works always to achieve a note of intimacy and charm in his reportage. And he admits readily that there are many things he must treat with reserve. 'One can't say everything when one is settling down to enjoy the hospitality, as it were, of a country.'

The third traveller confronts us with fewer qualifications: James is now in his prime and in full possession of his England. He has lived in London for a decade and a half—long enough to have certain responsibilities as a resident alien, such as jury duty. The four essays of his high maturity are used by him to encase or frame the others in *English Hours*—two at the front of the book and two at the back. Those at the beginning are of 1888 and 1890 and those at the end of 1897 and 1901. He now has a flat in London and a russet brick house in Sussex. Indeed we can discover that he is describing Lamb House, very carefully and impersonally, in his essay on Winchelsea and Rye when he asks us to stand 'on the open, sunny terrace of a dear little old garden—a garden brown-walled, red-walled, rose-covered on its other sides, divided by a width of a quiet street of grass-grown cobbles from the house of its master.' He is in the act of imagining Thackeray writing *Denis Duval* in his Lamb House study, 'a little old glass-fronted panelled pavilion'. And he goes on to describe the furniture, the books, the atmosphere, and to inform us that 'by kind permission' (of himself) he has been allowed to peep into this room and the sight of it brings back memories of his youth when he lay on the grass of some New England meadow reading an old English novel and imagining just such a house and such a scene. His dreams have come true—and he looks into a chamber in which 'there is room for the hard-pressed table and the tilted chair—there is room for a novelist and his friends'. He allows himself to be a little more coy than the sentimental traveller or the observant stranger. But he is no longer an outsider: he is an alien only in name.

In studying the three different figures of Henry James looking at England at three different stages of his life, we become aware of the autobiography within the dispassionate reporting of *English Hours*. James the moralist, the humanist, is well aware that civilisation relies on muted statement and on things unsaid. But between the lines he cannot resist being a soft-voiced commentator on English manners 'from afar'. He sees the Victorian world as organised to preserve and reinforce respect for traditional institutions and that these are accepted on the whole by an entire society as a tacit social contract. He is struck by the rigidly aristocratic constitution of the British Establishment; he protests at the unaesthetic temper of the people, and he likes 'the private character' of most kinds of comfort and entertainment. He examines also—very delicately—the British public character. In a paper not here reproduced he reported on the Oxford–Cambridge boat race; in another he wrote of the British soldier and in still another told of his peregrinations in the suburbs of London. Apparently these papers were too American to be called 'English hours' and they remain un-collected to this day.

In this volume we see him having a day at Epsom, proceeding by a horse-drawn omnibus with a well-liquored company of fellow-passengers and heartily enjoying the general air of festivity and the Dickensian tipsiness that accompanies the Derby. James, coming from an American society in a state of flux, often accepts British standards and values; he finds much merit in hierarchies which give society a sense of diversity. People enjoy the comfort of 'be-longing' where in America—as he has a character say in one of his tales—'every one is Mr Jones, Mr Brown; and everyone looks like Mr Jones and Mr Brown'. But James reserves such explorations for his international stories where he can have different personages air their national prejudices as in a common debate. At moments in his topographical essays he allows himself to speak of human suffering—'that physical and mental degradation which comes from slums and purlieus' in the grey Babylon of London, 'the pallid, stunted, misbegotten and in every way miserable figures'. And he stops aghast when in the gaslight one evening he sees 'a horrible old woman in a smoking bonnet, lying prone in a puddle of whiskey'. He adds, 'She . . . almost frightened me away.'

James was not in reality that easily frightened. He stayed on in England—in this land in which he found so many felicities of land-scape and history, architecture and the 'human picturesque'. British poverty, glimpsed when he was a young sentimental tourist, was later studied less in its pictured stasis than its effect on human conditions, as his novel *The Princess Casamassima*—his 'working class' novel—showed. In the travel papers he is careful to let us know that we read *sotto voce*, and this he achieves most often with his high economic irony. No one can forget, once he has read it, the passage in *English Hours* in which, at Christmas time, James goes with a Lady Bountiful to see a tree she has bestowed upon an orphanage, and to assist in the distribution of toys. His mind turns to his memories of Dickens and he seeks to discover whether, among the hundred and fifty children of charity, there may be an Oliver Twist. What he recognises instead is the hard fact that the children already have the stamp of their condition. They show no sign of resistance; they are frozen little mortals, some clearly damaged, some even 'idiotic'. He faces a crude mixture of Yuletide poetry and 'sordid prose'. The dying wintry day, the big bare stale room, the lady herself extravagantly attired, the twinkling tree—but the picture has its final anguished touch, 'the multitude of staring and wondering, yet perfectly expressionless, faces'. The word 'expressionless' varnishes his tableau.

His contrasts between the poetry and prose of English life are put in terms of the literary imagination in a writer who would be called in the future one of the great poets of prose. We may linger for another moment on this side of the 'observant stranger's' feelings and recognise the power with which he describes the role of English women both in the slums and in the lower middle class:

They are ill-dressed as their betters are well-dressed and their garments have that sooty surface which has nothing in common with the continental costume of labour and privation. It is the hard prose of misery, an ugly and hopeless imitation of respectable attire. This is especially noticeable in the battered and bedraggled bonnets of the women, which look as if their husbands had stamped on them, in hob-nailed boots, as a hint of what may be in store for their wearers.

So too he ventures an opinion about the English women of the higher walks of society. He notices 'the absence of a morbid strain' among such women, and admires their beauty—'the real perfection of feature and colour'. And he gets the sense of an English woman 'being completely and profoundly, without reservation for other uses, at the service of the man she loves'. This might be challenged today by feminists. They could say that James, as a bachelor, wasn't an entirely reliable witness. But we remind ourselves that the American novelist was looking, when he wrote this, at the Victorians. It was a partial truth—but an interesting one, and a reflection of the 'man's world' of that century.

Henry James became, in his later novels and tales, the historian of the 'better sort'. Yet he never lost sight of other sorts—the servants, the governesses, the little shopgirls, the slaveys in the artists' studios, the entire human civilisation that reared itself behind the leisured classes. He felt himself to be somewhere in between. Certainly he belonged to a kind of labouring class during the long hours he spent at his writing desk—where other 'better sort' males lived in idleness, on horseback, or in the salons, or their clubs. Then he would emerge to participate in the higher forms of English life, take tea with grand ladies or dine 'in society'. He had a 'home feeling' for England: the British had most certainly made him feel at home; but the feeling within came from his continuous and mutually consistent impressions. London itself, as the opening essay of *English Hours* shows, was at the heart of these feelings. He had known it from infancy; and he could discern attitudes and details its inhabitants took for granted. 'It takes passionate pilgrims,' James remarks, 'vague aliens and other disinterested persons, to appreciate the "points" of this admirable country.' To that extent he justified his asking the English to read a book about themselves made up of pieces originally written for Americans.

In London he loves 'the congregation of the parks'. He has come to experience a deep familiarity with the rows of mundane dwellings that give certain parts of the city a graveyard effect during periods of holiday; yet the city's atmosphere has for him 'magnificent mystifications'. It 'flatters and superfuses, makes everything brown, rich, dim, vague, magnifies distances and minimises details, confirms the inference of vastness by suggesting that, as the great city makes everything, it makes its own system of weather and its own optical laws'. There was nothing finer in Europe for James than the view from the bridge over the Serpentine. The towers of Westminster were quite the equal of the towers—on the other side of the Channel—of Notre Dame, as he looked at them far beyond the shining stretch of Hyde Park water. Great towers, great memories, great names—but the edge of Westminster made him qualify his picture, saying that this edge had 'as many associations of misery as of Empire'. He was never more conscious of Empire than when he took the boat to Greenwich and looked at the blackness of warehouse backs, the polluted river, the sprawling barges, the wilderness of masts, a dismal series of images which he described as 'smudgy detail', only to pull himself up and add that it was 'anything but trivial'. The river that had witnessed the Romans and the ships of Elizabeth, and now summoned commerce from the four corners of the earth, reminded him of nothing less than 'all the greatness of England ... the great space she has occupied, her tremendous might, her far-stretching rule'. The Thames scene seemed to him (as it would a few years later to the mariner, Joseph Conrad) the full expression of Victorian might and glory and civilisation.

The entire English scene was imaged by him in what we today would describe as Picasso-terms, for he speaks of 'this richly complex English world, where the present is always seen, as it were in profile, and the past presents a full face'. It was not too much to say, after his little journey to Greenwich, that he had travelled an Empire; and after spending twenty-four hours in a house that was 600 years old 'you seem yourself to have lived in it 600 years'. When he looked over these collected papers and revised them he felt (as he said in a prefatory note) that they represented 'a good many wonderments and judgments and emotions whether felicities or mistakes', adding with a rueful touch 'the fine freshness of which the author has—to his misfortune, no doubt—sufficiently outlived'.

If the old freshness of the sentimental tourist was gone, something noble and profound now remained. And it is given to us in the brief essay James added to this book which has little to do with tourism or sightseeing, or the study of British landmarks. This was the eloquent record of the novelist's emotions in Westminster Abbey as he watched the consignment of Robert Browning's ashes to the Poets' Corner. Browning took into the Abbey, James told himself, 'an immense expression of life'. He had possessed 'an unprejudiced intellectual eagerness to put himself in other people's place, to participate in complications and consequences'. This represented, James added, 'a restlessness of psychological research'. In saying this the American writer of prose fiction was characterising his own genius as well as the poet's.

As we ask ourselves what constitutes the relevance, in a book of English pictures and English hours, of a brief image and moment of 'Browning in the Abbey', we perceive that these seven pages contain within them James's high summary of what his own 'English hours' had meant to him personally during his half-century of intense and passionate feeling. In the mounting rhetoric of his little essay, he invokes the qualities of the race that had created the history, the language, the literature, the civilisation reflected in his gathered impressions. Browning stood for 'the things that, as a race, we like best—the fascination of faith, the acceptance of life, the respect for its mysteries, the endurance of its charges, the vitality of the will, the validity of character, the beauty of action, the seriousness, above all, of the great human passion'. Reading this we realise that the author who set down these words in testimony to Browning was also setting them down because they spoke for himself. And in including them in *English Hours* he turned his tribute to Browning into a tribute to all England—his England of the lived decades which contained his 'wonderments and judgments and emotions'.

In our century, since James's death, history and wars have blotted out some of the scenes and erased some of the streets and buildings; but the people remain, and we still recognise them and their land and their language in the magic of an individual voice and style, and the delicate and perceptive observations of a 'brooding spectator'. *English Hours*, within its narrative, is the record of Henry James's prolonged love affair, that of a gallant ageing American bachelor who, however much he flirted abroad with a dishevelled nymph, always returned to the 'good married matron'. His primary loyalty was to England, the land of his race and tongue, as the beautiful memorial tablet placed in the Abbey in 1976 testifies. His own testimony can be read in *English Hours*. We may safely consider it, after the passage of so many decades, a classic among travel books.

LEON EDEL

London

THERE is a certain evening that I count as virtually a first impression—the end of a wet, black Sunday, twenty years ago, about the first of March. There had been an earlier vision, but it had turned to gray, like faded ink, and the occasion I speak of was a fresh beginning. No doubt I had mystic prescience of how fond of the murky modern Babylon I was one day to become; certain it is that as I look back I find every small circumstance of those hours of approach and arrival still as vivid as if the solemnity of an opening era had breathed upon it. The sense of approach was already almost intolerably strong at Liverpool, where, as I remember, the perception of the English character of everything was as acute as a surprise, though it could only be a surprise without a shock. It was expectation exquisitely gratified, superabundantly confirmed. There was a kind of wonder, indeed, that England should be as English as, for my entertainment, she took the trouble to be; but the wonder would have been greater, and all the pleasure absent, if the sensation had not been violent. It seems to sit there again like a visiting presence, as it sat opposite to me at breakfast at a small table in a window of the old coffee-room of the Adelphi Hotel—the unextended (as it then was), the unimproved, the unblushingly local Adelphi. Liverpool is not a romantic city, but that smoky Saturday returns to me as a supreme success, measured by its association with the kind of emotion in the hope of which, for the most part, we betake ourselves to far countries.

It assumed this character at an early hour—or rather, indeed, twenty-four hours before—with the sight, as one looked across the wintry ocean, of the strange, dark, lonely freshness of the coast of Ireland. Better still, before we could come up to the city, were the black steamers knocking about in the yellow Mersey, under a sky so low that they seemed to touch it with their funnels, and in the thickest, windiest light. Spring was already in the air, in the town; there was no rain, but there was still less sun—one wondered what had become, on this side of the world, of the big white splotch in the heavens; and the gray mildness, shading away into black at every pretext, appeared in itself a promise. This was how it hung about me, between the window and the fire, in the coffee-room of the hotel—late in the morning for breakfast, as we had been long disembarking. The other passengers had dispersed, knowingly catching trains for London (we had only been a handful); I had the place to myself, and I felt as if I had an exclusive property in the impression. I prolonged it, I sacrificed to it, and it is perfectly recoverable now, with the very taste of the national muffin, the creak of the waiter's shoes as he came and went (could anything be so English as his intensely professional back? it revealed a country of tradition), and the rustle of the newspaper I was too excited to read.

I continued to sacrifice for the rest of the day; it didn't seem to me a sentient thing, as yet, to inquire into the means of getting away. My curiosity must indeed have languished, for I found myself on the morrow in the slowest of Sunday trains, pottering up to London with an interruptedness which might have been tedious without the conversation of an old gentleman who shared the carriage with me, and to whom my alien as well as comparatively youthful character had betrayed itself. He instructed me as to the sights of London, and impressed upon me that nothing was more worthy of my attention than the great cathedral of St Paul. 'Have you seen St Peter's in Rome? St Peter's is more highly embellished, you know; but you may depend upon it that St Paul's is the better building of the two.' The impression I began with speaking of was, strictly, that of the drive from Euston, after dark, to Morley's Hotel in Trafalgar Square. It was not lovely—it was in fact rather horrible; but as I move again through dusky, tortuous miles, in the greasy four-wheeler to which my luggage had compelled me to commit myself, I recognise the first step in an initiation of which the subsequent stages were to abound in pleasant things. It is a kind of humiliation in a great city not to know where you are going, and Morley's Hotel was then, to my imagination, only a vague ruddy spot in the general immensity. The immensity was the great fact, and that was a charm; the miles of housetops and viaducts, the complication of junction and signals through which the train made its way to the station had already given me the scale. The weather had turned to wet, and we went deeper and deeper into the Sunday night. The sheep in the fields, on the way from Liverpool, had shown in their demeanour a certain consciousness of the day; but this momentous cab-drive was an introduction to the rigidities of custom. The low black houses were as inanimate as so many rows of coal-scuttles, save where at frequent corners, from a gin-shop, there was a flare of light more brutal still than the darkness. The custom of gin—that was equally rigid, and in this first impression the public-houses counted for much.

Morley's Hotel proved indeed to be a ruddy spot; brilliant, in my recollection, is the coffee-room fire, the hospitable mahogany, the sense that in the stupendous city this, at any rate for the hour, was a shelter and a point of view. My remembrance of the rest of the evening—I was probably very tired—is mainly a remembrance of a vast four-poster. My little bedroom-candle, set in its deep basin, caused this monument to project a huge shadow and to make me think, I scarce knew why, of 'The Ingoldsby Legends'. If at a tolerably early hour the next day I found myself approaching St Paul's, it was not wholly in obedience to the old gentleman in the railway-carriage: I had an errand in the City, and the City was doubtless prodigious. But what I mainly recall is the romantic consciousness of passing under the Temple Bar, and the way two lines of 'Henry Esmond' repeated themselves in my mind as I drew near the masterpiece of Sir Christopher Wren. 'The stout, red-faced woman' whom Esmond had seen tearing after the staghounds over the slopes at Windsor was not a bit like the effigy 'which turns its stony back upon St Paul's and faces the coaches struggling up Ludgate Hill'. As I looked at Queen Anne over the apron of my hansom—she struck me as very small and dirty, and the vehicle ascended the mild incline without an effort—it was a thrilling thought that the statue had been familiar to the hero of the incomparable novel. All history appeared to live again, and the continuity of things to vibrate through my mind.

To this hour, as I pass along the Strand, I take again the walk I took there that afternoon. I love the place to-day, and that was the commencement of my passion. It appeared to me to present phenomena, and to contain objects of every kind, of an inexhaustible interest; in particular it struck me as desirable and even indispensable that I should purchase most of the articles in most of the shops. My eyes rest with a certain tenderness on the places where I resisted and on those where I succumbed. The fragrance of Mr Rimmel's establishment is again in my nostrils; I see the slim young lady (I hear her pronunciation) who waited upon me there. Sacred to me to-day is the particular aroma of the hair-wash that I bought of her. I pause before the granite portico of Exeter Hall (it was unexpectedly narrow and wedge-like), and it evokes a cloud of associations which are none the less impressive because they are vague; coming from I don't know where—from *Punch*, from Thackeray, from volumes of the *Illustrated London News* turned over in childhood; seeming connected with Mrs Beecher Stowe and 'Uncle Tom's Cabin'. Memorable is a rush I made into a glover's at Charing Cross—the one you pass, going eastward, just before you turn into the station; that, however, now that I think of it, must have been in the morning, as soon as I issued from the hotel. Keen within me was a sense of the importance of deflowering, of despoiling the shop.

A day or two later, in the afternoon, I found myself staring at my fire, in a lodging of which I had taken possession on foreseeing that I should spend some weeks in London. I had just come in, and, having attended to the distribution of my luggage, sat down to consider my habitation. It was on the ground floor, and the fading daylight reached it in a sadly damaged condition. It struck me as stuffy and unsocial, with its mouldy smell and its decoration of lithographs and wax-flowers—an impersonal black hole in the huge general blackness. The uproar of Piccadilly hummed away at the end of the street, and the rattle of a heartless hansom passed close to my ears. A sudden horror of the whole place came over me, like a tiger-pounce of homesickness which had been watching its moment. London was hideous, vicious, cruel, and above all overwhelming; whether or no she was 'careful of the type', she was as indifferent as Nature herself to the single life. In the course of an hour I should have to go out to my dinner, which was not supplied on the premises, and that effort assumed the form of a desperate and dangerous quest. It appeared to me that I would rather remain dinnerless, would rather even starve, than sally forth into the infernal town, where the natural fate of an obscure stranger would be to be trampled to death in Piccadilly and have his carcass thrown into the Thames. I did not starve, however, and I eventually attached myself by a hundred human links to the dreadful, delightful city. That momentary vision of its smeared face and stony heart has remained memorable to me, but I am happy to say that I can easily summon up others.

II

It is, no doubt, not the taste of every one, but for the real London-lover the mere immensity of the place is a large part of its savour. A small London would be an abomination, as it fortunately is an impossibility, for the idea and the name are beyond everything an expression of extent and number. Practically, of course, one lives in a quarter, in a plot; but in imagination and by a constant mental act of reference the accommodated haunter enjoys the whole—and it is only of him that I deem it worth while to speak. He fancies himself, as they say, for being a particle in so unequalled an aggregation; and its immeasurable circumference, even though unvisited and lost in smoke, gives him the sense of a social, an intellectual margin. There is a luxury in the knowledge that he may come and go without being noticed, even when his comings and goings have no nefarious end. I don't mean by this that the tongue of London is not a very active member; the tongue of London would indeed be worthy of a chapter by itself. But the eyes which at least in some measure feed its activity are fortunately for the common advantage solicited at any moment by a thousand different objects. If the place is big, everything it contains is certainly not so; but this may at least be said, that if small questions play a part there, they play it without illusions about its importance. There are too many questions, small or great; and each day, as it arrives, leads its children, like a kind of mendicant mother, by the hand. Therefore perhaps the most general characteristic is the absence of insistence. Habits and inclinations flourish and fall, but intensity is never one of them. The spirit of the great city is not analytic, and, as they come up, subjects rarely receive at its hands a treatment drearily earnest or tastelessly thorough. There are not many—of those of which London disposes with the assurance begotten of its large experience—that wouldn't lend themselves to a tenderer manipulation elsewhere. It takes a very great affair, a turn of the Irish screw or a divorce case lasting many days, to be fully threshed out. The mind of Mayfair, when it aspires to show what it really can do, lives in the hope of a new divorce case, and an indulgent providence—London is positively in certain ways the spoiled child of the world—abundantly recognises this particular aptitude and humours the whim.

The compensation is that material does arise; that there is a great variety, if not morbid subtlety; and that the whole of the procession of events and topics passes across your stage. For the moment I am speaking of the inspiration there may be in the sense of far frontiers; the London-lover loses himself in this swelling consciousness, delights in the idea that the town which encloses him is after all only a paved country, a state by itself. This is his condition of mind quite as much if he be an adoptive as if he be a matter-of-course son. I am by no means sure even that he need be of Anglo-Saxon race and have inherited the birthright of English speech; though, on the other hand, I make no doubt that these advantages minister greatly to closeness of allegiance. The great city spreads her dusky mantle over innumerable races and creeds, and I believe there is scarcely a known form of worship that has not some temple there (have I not attended at the Church of Humanity, in Lamb's Conduit, in company with an American lady, a vague old gentleman, and several seamstresses?) or any communion of men that has not some club or guild. London is indeed an epitome of the round world, and just as it is a commonplace to say that there is nothing one can't 'get' there, so it is equally true that there is nothing one may not study at first hand.

One doesn't test these truths every day, but they form part of the air one breathes (and welcome, says the London-hater—for there be

6

such perverse reasoners—to the pestilent compound). They colour the thick, dim distances which in my opinion are the most romantic town-vistas in the world; they mingle with the troubled light to which the straight, ungarnished aperture in one's dull, undistinctive housefront affords a passage and which makes an interior of friendly corners, mysterious tones and unbetrayed ingenuities, as well as with the low, magnificent medium of the sky, where the smoke and fog and the weather in general, the strangely undefined hour of the day and season of the year, the emanations of industries and the reflection of furnaces, the red gleams and blurs that may or may not be of sunset—as you never see any *source* of radiance you can't in the least tell—all hang together in a confusion, a complication, a shifting but irremovable canopy. They form the undertone of the deep, perpetual voice of the place. One remembers them when one's loyalty is on the defensive; when it is a question of introducing as many striking features as possible into the list of fine reasons one has sometimes to draw up, that eloquent catalogue with which one confronts the hostile indictment—the array of *other* reasons which may easily be as long as one's arm. According to these other reasons it plausibly and conclusively stands that, as a place to be happy in, London will never do. I don't say it is necessary to meet so absurd an allegation except for one's personal complacency. If indifference, in so gorged an organism, is still livelier than curiosity, you may avail yourself of your own share in it simply to feel that since such and such a person doesn't care for real richness, so much the worse for such and such a person. But once in a while the best believer recognises the impulse to set his religion in order, to sweep the temple of his thoughts and trim the sacred lamp. It is at such hours as this that he reflects with elation that the British capital is the particular spot in the world which communicates the greatest sense of life.

III

The reader will perceive that I do not shrink even from the extreme concession of speaking of our capital as British, and this in a shameless connection with the question of loyalty on the part of an adoptive son. For I hasten to explain that if half the source of one's interest in it comes from feeling that it is the property and even the home of the human race—Hawthorne, that best of Americans, says so somewhere, and places it in this sense side by side with Rome—one's appreciation of it is really a large sympathy, a comprehensive love of humanity. For the sake of such a charity as this one may stretch one's allegiance; and the most alien of the cockneyfied, though he may bristle with every protest at the intimation that England has set its stamp upon him, is free to admit with conscious pride that he has submitted to Londonisation. It is a real stroke of luck for a particular country that the capital of the human race happens to be British. Surely every other people would have it theirs if they could. Whether the English deserve to hold it any longer might be an interesting field of inquiry; but as they have not yet let it slip, the writer of these lines professes without scruple that the arrangement is to his personal taste. For, after all, if the sense of life is greatest there, it is a sense of the life of people of our consecrated English speech. It is the headquarters of that strangely elastic tongue; and I make this remark with a full sense of the terrible way in which the idiom is misused by the populace in general, than whom it has been given to few races to impart to conversation less of the charm of tone. For a man of letters who endeavours to cultivate, however modestly, the medium of Shakespeare and Milton, of Hawthorne and Emerson, who cherishes the notion of what it has achieved and what it may even yet achieve, London must ever have a great illustrative and suggestive value, and indeed a kind of sanctity. It is the single place in which most readers, most possible lovers, are gathered together; it is the most inclusive public and the largest social incarnation of the language, of the tradition. Such a personage may well let it go for this and leave the German and the Greek to speak for themselves, to express the grounds of *their* predilection, presumably very different.

When a social product is so vast and various it may be approached on a thousand different sides, and liked and disliked for a thousand different reasons. The reasons of Piccadilly are not those of Camden Town, nor are the curiosities and discouragements of Kilburn the same as those of Westminster and Lambeth. The reasons of Picca-

dilly—I mean the friendly ones—are those of which, as a general
thing, the rooted visitor remains most conscious; but it must be
confessed that even these, for the most part, do not lie upon the
surface. The absence of style, or rather of the intention of style, is
certainly the most general characteristic of the face of London. To
cross to Paris under this impression is to find one's self surrounded
with far other standards. There everything reminds you that the
idea of beautiful and stately arrangement has never been out of
fashion, that the art of composition has always been at work or at
play. Avenues and squares, gardens and quays, have been distributed for effect, and to-day the splendid city reaps the accumulation
of all this ingenuity. The result is not in every quarter interesting,
and there is a tiresome monotony of the 'fine' and the symmetrical
above all, of the deathly passion for making things 'to match'. On
the other hand the whole air of the place is architectural. On the
banks of the Thames it is a tremendous chapter of accidents—the
London-lover has to confess to the existence of miles upon miles
of the dreariest, stodgiest commonness. Thousands of acres are
covered by low black houses of the cheapest construction, without
ornament, without grace, without character or even identity. In
fact there are many, even in the best quarters, in all the region of
Mayfair and Belgravia, of so paltry and inconvenient, especially of
so dimunitive a type (those that are let in lodgings—such poor
lodgings as they make—may serve as an example), that you wonder
what peculiarly limited domestic need they were constructed to
meet. The great misfortune of London to the eye (it is true that
this remark applies much less to the City) is the want of elevation.
There is no architectural impression without a certain degree of
height, and the London street-vista has none of that sort of pride.

All the same, if there be not the intention, there is at least the
accident, of style, which, if one looks at it in a friendly way, appears
to proceed from three sources. One of these is simply the general
greatness, and the manner in which that makes a difference for the
better in any particular spot; so that, though you may often perceive yourself to be in a shabby corner, it never occurs to you that
this is the end of it. Another is the atmosphere, with its magnificent
mystifications, which flatters and superfuses, makes everything

brown, rich, dim, vague, magnifies distances and minimises details, confirms the inference of vastness by suggesting that, as the great city makes everything, it makes its own system of weather and its own optical laws. The last is the congregation of the parks, which constitute an ornament not elsewhere to be matched and give the place a superiority that none of its uglinesses overcome. They spread themselves with such a luxury of space in the centre of the town that they form a part of the impression of any walk, of almost any view, and, with an audacity altogether their own, make a pastoral landscape under the smoky sky. There is no mood of the rich London climate that is not becoming to them—I have seen them look delightfully romantic, like parks in novels, in the wettest winter—and there is scarcely a mood of the appreciative resident to which they have not something to say. The high things of London, which here and there peep over them, only make the spaces vaster by reminding you that you are, after all, not in Kent or Yorkshire; and these things, whatever they be—rows of 'eligible' dwellings, towers of churches, domes of institutions—take such an effective gray-blue tint that a clever water-colourist would seem to have put them in for pictorial reasons.

The view from the bridge over the Serpentine has an extraordinary nobleness, and it has often seemed to me that the Londoner twitted with his low standard may point to it with every confidence. In all the town-scenery of Europe there can be few things so fine; the only reproach it is open to is that it begs the question by seeming—in spite of its being the pride of five millions of people—not to belong to a town at all. The towers of Notre Dame, as they rise in Paris from the island that divides the Seine, present themselves no more impressively than those of Westminster as you see them looking doubly far beyond the shining stretch of Hyde Park water. Equally delectable is the large river-like manner in which the Serpentine opens away between its wooded shores. Just after you have crossed the bridge (whose very banisters, old and ornamental, of yellowish-brown stone, I am particularly fond of), you enjoy on your left, through the gate of Kensington Gardens as you go towards Bayswater, an altogether enchanting vista—a footpath over the grass, which loses itself beneath the scattered oaks and elms exactly as if the place were a 'chase'. There could be nothing less like London in general than this particular morsel, and yet it takes London, of all cities, to give you such an impression of the country.

IV

It takes London to put you in the way of a purely rustic walk from Notting Hill to Whitehall. You may traverse this immense distance —a most comprehensive diagonal—altogether on soft, fine turf, amid the song of birds, the bleat of lambs, the ripple of ponds, the rustle of admirable trees. Frequently have I wished that, for the sake of such a daily luxury and of exercise made romantic, I were a government-clerk living, in snug domestic conditions, in a Pembridge villa—let me suppose—and having my matutinal desk in Westminster. I should turn into Kensington Gardens at their northwest limit, and I should have my choice of a hundred pleasant paths to the gates of Hyde Park. In Hyde Park I should follow the water-side, or the Row, or any other fancy of the occasion; liking best perhaps, after all, the Row in its morning mood, with the mist hanging over the dark red course, and the scattered early riders taking an identity as the soundless gallop brings them nearer. I am free to admit that in the Season, at the conventional hours, the Row becomes a weariness (save perhaps just for a glimpse once a year, to remind one's self how much it is like Du Maurier); the preoccupied citizen eschews it and leaves it for the most part to the gaping barbarian. I speak of it now from the point of view of the pedestrian; but for the rider as well it is at its best when he passes either too early or too late. Then, if he be not bent on comparing it to its disadvantage with the bluer and boskier alleys of the Bois de Boulogne, it will not be spoiled by the fact that, with its surface that looks like tan, its barriers like those of the ring on which the clown stands to hold up the hoop to the young lady, its empty benches and chairs, its occasional orange-peel, its mounted policemen patrolling at intervals like expectant supernumeraries, it offers points of real contact with a circus whose lamps are out. The sky that bends over it is frequently not a bad imitation of the dingy tent of such an establishment. The ghosts of past cavalcades seem to haunt the foggy arena, and somehow they are better company than the mashers and elongated beauties of current seasons. It is not without interest to remember that most of the salient figures of English society during the present century—and English society means, or rather has hitherto meant, in a large degree English history—have bobbed in the saddle between Apsley House and Queen's Gate. You may call the roll if you care to, and the air will be thick with dumb voices and dead names, like that of some Roman amphitheatre.

It is doubtless a signal proof of being a London-lover *quand même* that one should undertake an apology for so bungled an attempt at a great public place as Hyde Park Corner. It is certain that the improvements and embellishments recently enacted there have only served to call further attention to the poverty of the elements, and to the fact that this poverty is terribly illustrative of general conditions. The place is the beating heart of the great West End, yet its main features are a shabby, stuccoed hospital, the low park-gates in their neat but unimposing frame, the drawing-room windows of Apsley House, and of the commonplace frontages on the little terrace beside it; to which must be added, of course, the only item in the whole prospect that is in the least monumental—the arch spanning the private road beside the gardens of Buckingham Palace. This structure is now bereaved of the rueful effigy which used to surmount it—the Iron Duke in the guise of a tin soldier—and has not been enriched by the transaction as much as might have been expected.* There is a fine view of Piccadilly and Knightsbridge, and of the noble mansions, as the house-agents call them, of Grosvenor Place, together with a sense of generous space beyond the vulgar little railing of the Green Park; but, except for the impression that there would be room for something better, there is nothing in all this that speaks to the imagination: almost as much as the grimy desert of Trafalgar Square the prospect conveys the idea of an opportunity wasted.

None the less has it on a fine day in spring an expressiveness of

---

* The monument in the middle of the square, with Sir Edgar Boehm's four fine soldiers, had not been set up when these words were written.

which I shall not pretend to explain the source further than by saying that the flood of life and luxury is immeasurably great there. The edifices are mean, but the social stream itself is monumental, and to an observer not purely stolid there is more excitement and suggestion than I can give a reason for in the long, distributed waves of traffic, with the steady policemen marking their rhythm, which roll together and apart for so many hours. Then the great dim city becomes bright and kind, the pall of smoke turns into a veil of haze carelessly worn, the air is coloured and almost scented by the presence of the biggest society in the world, and most of the things that meet the eye—or perhaps I should say more of them, for the most in London is, no doubt, ever the realm of the dingy— present themselves as 'well-appointed'. Everything shines more or less, from the window-panes to the dog-collars. So it all looks, with its myriad variations and qualifications, to one who surveys it over the apron of a hansom, while that vehicle of vantage, better than any box at the opera, spurts and slackens with the current.

It is not in a hansom, however, that we have figured our punctual young man, whom we must not desert as he fares to the south-east, and who has only to cross Hyde Park Corner to find his way all grassy again. I have a weakness for the convenient, familiar, tree-less, or almost treeless, expanse of the Green Park, and the friendly part it plays as a kind of encouragement to Piccadilly. I am so fond of Piccadilly that I am grateful to any one or anything that does it a service, and nothing is more worthy of appreciation than the southward look it is permitted to enjoy just after it passes Devon-shire House—a sweep of horizon which it would be difficult to match among other haunts of men, and thanks to which, of a sum-mer's day, you may spy, beyond the browsed pastures of the fore-ground and middle distance, beyond the cold chimneys of Bucking-ham Palace and the towers of Westminster and the swarming river-side and all the southern parishes, the hard modern twinkle of the roof of the Crystal Palace.

If the Green Park is familiar, there is still less of the exclusive in its pendant, as one may call it—for it literally hangs from the other, down the hill—the remnant of the former garden of the queer, shabby old palace whose black, inelegant face stares up St James's

Street. This popular resort has a great deal of character, but I am free to confess that much of its character comes from its nearness to the Westminster slums. It is a park of intimacy, and perhaps the most democratic corner of London, in spite of its being in the royal and military quarter and close to all kinds of stateliness. There are few hours of the day when a thousand smutty children are not sprawling over it, and the unemployed lie thick on the grass and cover the benches with a brotherhood of greasy corduroys. If the London parks are the drawing-rooms and clubs of the poor—that is, of those poor (I admit it cuts down the number) who live near enough to them to reach them—these particular grass-plots and alleys may be said to constitute the very *salon* of the slums.

I know not why, being such a region of greatness—great towers, great names, great memories; at the foot of the Abbey, the Parliament, the fine fragment of Whitehall, with the quarters of the sovereign right and left—but the edge of Westminster evokes as many associations of misery as of empire. The neighbourhood has been much purified of late, but it still contains a collection of specimens—though it is far from unique in this—of the low, black element. The air always seems to me heavy and thick, and here more than elsewhere one hears old England—the panting, smoke-stained Titan of Matthew Arnold's fine poem—draw her deep breath with effort. In fact one is nearer to her heroic lungs, if those organs are figured by the great pinnacled and fretted talking-house on the edge of the river. But this same dense and conscious air plays such everlasting tricks to the eye that the Foreign Office, as you see it from the bridge, often looks romantic, and the sheet of water it overhangs poetic—suggests an Indian palace bathing its feet in the Ganges. If our pedestrian achieves such a comparison as this he has nothing left but to go on to his work—which he will find close at hand. He will have come the whole way from the far-north-west on the green—which is what was to be demonstrated.

V

I feel as if I were taking a tone almost of boastfulness, and no doubt the best way to consider the matter is simply to say—without going into the treachery of reasons—that, for one's self, one likes this part or the other. Yet this course would not be unattended with danger, inasmuch as at the end of a few such professions we might find ourselves committed to a tolerance of much that is deplorable. London is so clumsy and so brutal, and has gathered together so many of the darkest sides of life, that it is almost ridiculous to talk of her as a lover talks of his mistress, and almost frivolous to appear to ignore her disfigurements and cruelties. She is like a mighty ogress who devours human flesh; but to me it is a mitigating circumstance—though it may not seem so to every one—that the ogress herself is human. It is not in wantonness that she fills her maw, but to keep herself alive and do her tremendous work. She has no time for fine discriminations, but after all she is as good-natured as she is huge, and the more you stand up to her, as the phrase is, the better she takes the joke of it. It is mainly when you fall on your face before her that she gobbles you up. She heeds little what she takes, so long as she has her stint, and the smallest push to the right or the left will divert her wavering bulk from one form of prey to another. It is not to be denied that the heart tends to grow hard in her company; but she is a capital antidote to the morbid, and to live with her successfully is an education of the temper, a consecration of one's private philosophy. She gives one a surface for which in a rough world one can never be too thankful. She may take away reputations, but she forms character. She teaches her victims not to 'mind', and the great danger for them is perhaps that they shall learn the lesson too well.

It is sometimes a wonder to ascertain what they do mind, the best-seasoned of her children. Many of them assist, without winking, at the most unfathomable dramas, and the common speech of others denotes a familiarity with the horrible. It is her theory that she both produces and appreciates the exquisite; but if you catch her in flagrant repudiation of both responsibilities and confront her with the shortcoming, she gives you a look, with a shrug of her colossal shoulders, which establishes a private relation with you for evermore. She seems to say: 'Do you really take me so seriously as that, you dear, devoted, voluntary dupe, and don't you know what an immeasurable humbug I am?' You reply that you shall know it henceforth; but your tone is good-natured, with a touch of the cynicism that she herself has taught you; for you are aware that if she makes herself out better than she is, she also makes herself out much worse. She is immensely democratic, and that, no doubt, is part of the manner in which she is salutary to the individual; she teaches him his 'place' by an incomparable discipline, but deprives him of complaint by letting him see that she has exactly the same lash for every other back. When he has swallowed the lesson he may enjoy the rude but unfailing justice by which, under her eye, reputations and positions elsewhere esteemed great are reduced to the relative. There are so many reputations, so many positions, that supereminence breaks down, and it is difficult to be so rare that London can't match you. It is a part of her good-nature and one of her clumsy coquetries to pretend sometimes that she hasn't your equivalent, as when she takes it into her head to hunt the lion or form a ring round a celebrity. But this artifice is so very transparent that the lion must be very candid or the celebrity very obscure to be taken by it. The business is altogether subjective, as the philosophers say, and the great city is primarily looking after herself. Celebrities are convenient—they are one of the things that people are asked to 'meet'—and lion-cutlets, put upon ice, will nourish a family through periods of dearth.

This is what I mean by calling London democratic. You may be in it, of course, without being of it; but from the moment you *are* of it—and on this point your own sense will soon enough enlighten you—you belong to a body in which a general equality prevails. However exalted, however able, however rich, however renowned you may be, there are too many people at least as much so for your own idiosyncrasies to count. I think it is only by being beautiful that you may really prevail very much; for the loveliness of woman it has long been noticeable that London will go most out of her way. It is when she hunts that particular lion that she becomes most dangerous; then there are really moments when you would believe, for all the world, that she is thinking of what she can give, not of what she can get. Lovely ladies, before this, have paid for believing it, and will continue to pay in days to come. On the whole the people who are least deceived are perhaps those who have permitted themselves to believe, in their own interest, that poverty is not a disgrace. It is certainly not considered so in London, and indeed you can scarcely say where—in virtue of diffusion—it would more naturally be exempt. The possession of money is, of course, immensely an advantage, but that is a very different thing from a disqualification in the lack of it.

Good-natured in so many things in spite of her cynical tongue, and easy-going in spite of her tremendous pace, there is nothing in which the large indulgence of the town is more shown than in the liberal way she looks at obligations of hospitality and the margin she allows in these and cognate matters. She wants above all to be amused; she keeps her books loosely, doesn't stand on small questions of a chop for a chop, and if there be any chance of people's proving a diversion, doesn't know or remember or care whether they have 'called'. She forgets even if she herself have called. In matters of ceremony she takes and gives a long rope, wasting no time in phrases and circumvallations. It is no doubt incontestable that one result of her inability to stand upon trifles and consider details is that she has been obliged in some ways to lower rather portentously the standard of her manners. She cultivates the abrupt —for even when she asks you to dine a month ahead the invitation goes off like the crack of a pistol—and approaches her ends not exactly *par quatre chemins*. She doesn't pretend to attach importance to the lesson conveyed in Matthew Arnold's poem of 'The Sick King in Bokhara', that,

> Though we snatch what we desire,
> We may not snatch it eagerly.

London snatches it more than eagerly if that be the only way she can get it. Good manners are a succession of details, and I don't mean to say that she doesn't attend to them when she has time. She has it, however, but seldom—*que voulez-vous?* Perhaps the matter of note-writing is as good an example as another of what certain of the elder traditions inevitably have become in her hands. She lives by notes—they are her very heartbeats; but those that bear her signatures are as disjointed as the ravings of delirium, and have nothing but a postage-stamp in common with the epistolary art.

VI

If she doesn't go into particulars it may seem a very presumptuous act to have attempted to do so on her behalf, and the reader will doubtless think I have been punished by having egregiously failed in my enumeration. Indeed nothing could well be more difficult than to add up the items—the column would be altogether too long. One may have dreamed of turning the glow—if glow it be—of one's lantern on each successive facet of the jewel; but, after all, it may be success enough if a confusion of brightness be the result. One has not the alternative of speaking of London as a whole, for the simple reason that there is no such thing as the whole of it. It is immeasurable—embracing arms never meet. Rather it is a collection of many wholes, and of which of them is it most important to speak? Inevitably there must be a choice, and I know of none more scientific than simply to leave out what we may have to apologise for. The uglinesses, the 'rookeries', the brutalities, the night-aspect of many of the streets, the gin-shops and the hour when they are cleared out before closing—there are many elements of this kind which have to be counted out before a genial summary can be made.

And yet I should not go so far as to say that it is a condition of such geniality to close one's eye upon the immense misery; on the contrary, I think it is partly because we are irremediably conscious of that dark gulf that the most general appeal of the great city remains exactly what it is, the largest chapter of human accidents. I have no idea of what the future evolution of the strangely mingled monster may be; whether the poor will improve away the rich, or the rich will expropriate the poor, or they will all continue to dwell together on their present imperfect terms of intercourse. Certain it is, at any rate, that the impression of suffering is a part of the general vibration; it is one of the things that mingle with all the others to make the sound that is supremely dear to the consistent London-lover—the rumble of the tremendous human mill. This is the note which, in all its modulations, haunts and fascinates and inspires him. And whether or no he may succeed in keeping the misery out of the picture, he will freely confess that the latter is not spoiled for him by some of its duskiest shades. We are far from liking London well enough till we like its defects: the dense darkness of much of its winter, the soot on the chimney-pots and everywhere else, the early lamplight, the brown blur of the houses, the splashing of hansoms in Oxford Street or the Strand on December afternoons.

There is still something that recalls to me the enchantment of children—the anticipation of Christmas, the delight of a holiday walk—in the way the shop-fronts shine into the fog. It makes each of them seem a little world of light and warmth, and I can still waste time in looking at them with dirty Bloomsbury on one side and dirtier Soho on the other. There are winter effects, not intrinsically sweet, it would appear, which somehow, in absence, touch the chords of memory and even the fount of tears; as for instance the front of the British Museum on a black afternoon, or the portico, when the weather is vile, of one of the big square clubs in Pall Mall. I can give no adequate account of the subtle poetry of such reminiscences; it depends upon associations of which we have often lost the thread. The wide colonnade of the Museum, its symmetrical wings, the high iron fence in its granite setting, the sense of the misty halls within, where all the treasures lie—these things loom patiently through atmospheric layers which instead of making them dreary impart to them something of a cheer of red lights in a storm. I think the romance of a winter afternoon in London arises partly from the fact that, when it is not altogether smothered, the general lamplight takes this hue of hospitality. Such is the colour of the interior glow of the clubs in Pall Mall, which I positively like best when the fog loiters upon their monumental staircases.

In saying just now that these retreats may easily be, for the exile, part of the phantasmagoria of homesickness, I by no means alluded simply to their solemn outsides. If they are still more solemn within, that does not make them any less dear, in retrospect at least, to a visitor much bent upon liking his London to the end. What is the solemnity but a tribute to your nerves, and the stillness but a refined proof of the intensity of life? To produce such results as these the balance of many tastes must be struck, and that is only possible in a very high civilisation. If I seem to intimate that this last abstract term must be the cheer of him who has lonely possession of a foggy library, without even the excitement of watching for some one to put down the magazine he wants, I am willing to let the supposition pass, for the appreciation of a London club at one of the empty seasons is nothing but the strong expression of a preference for the great city—by no means so unsociable as it may superficially appear —at periods of relative abandonment. The London year is studded with holidays, blessed little islands of comparative leisure—intervals of absence for good society. Then the wonderful English faculty for 'going out of town for a little change' comes into illimitable play, and families transport their nurseries and their bathtubs to those rural scenes which form the real substratum of the national life. Such moments as these are the paradise of the genuine London-lover, for he then finds himself face to face with the object of his passion: he can give himself up to an intercourse which at other times is obstructed by his rivals. Then every one he knows is out of town, and the exhilarating sense of the presence of every one he doesn't know becomes by so much the deeper.

This is why I pronounce his satisfaction not an unsociable, but a positively affectionate emotion. It is the mood in which he most measures the immense humanity of the place, and in which its limits recede furthest into a dimness peopled with possible illustrations. For his acquaintance, however numerous it may be, is finite; whereas the other, the unvisited London, is infinite. It is one of his pleasures to think of the experiments and excursions he may make in it, even when these adventures don't particularly come off. The friendly fog seems to protect and enrich them—to add both to the mystery and security, so that it is most in the winter months that the imagination weaves such delights. They reach their climax perhaps during the strictly social desolation of Christmas week, when the country-houses are crowded at the expense of the capital. Then it is that I am most haunted with the London of Dickens, feel most as if it were still recoverable, still exhaling its queerness in patches perceptible to the appreciative. Then the big fires blaze in the lone twilight of the clubs, and the new books on the tables say 'Now at last you have time to read me', and the afternoon tea and toast, and the torpid old gentleman who wakes up from a doze to order potash-water, appear to make the assurance good. It is not a small matter either, to a man of letters, that this is the best time for writing, and that during the lamplit days the white page he tries to blacken becomes, on his table, in the circle of the lamp, with the screen of the climate folding him in, more vivid and absorbent. Those to whom it is forbidden to sit up to work in the small hours may, between November and March, enjoy a semblance of this luxury in the morning. The weather makes a kind of sedentary midnight and muffles the possible interruptions. It is bad for the eyesight, but excellent for the image.

VII

Of course it is too much to say that all the satisfaction of life in London comes from literally living there, for it is not a paradox that a great deal of it consists in getting away. It is almost easier to leave it than not to, and much of its richness and interest proceeds from its ramifications, the fact that all England is in a suburban relation to it. Such an affair it is in comparison to get away from Paris or to get into it. London melts by wide, ugly zones into the green country, and becomes pretty insidiously, inadvertently—without stopping to change. It is the spoiling, perhaps, of the country, but it is the making of the insatiable town, and if one is a helpless and shameless cockney that is all one is obliged to look at. Anything is excusable which enlarges one's civic consciousness. It ministers immensely to that of the London-lover that, thanks to the tremendous system of coming and going, to the active, hospitable habits of the people, to the elaboration of the railway-service, the frequency and rapidity of trains, and last, though not least, to the fact that much of the loveliest scenery in England lies within a radius of fifty miles—thanks to all this he has the rural picturesque at his door and may cultivate unlimited vagueness as to the line of division between centre and circumference. It is perfectly open to him to consider the remainder of the United Kingdom, or the British empire in general, or even, if he be an American, the total of the English-speaking territories of the globe, as the mere margin, the fitted girdle.

Is it for this reason—because I like to think how great we all are together in the light of heaven and the face of the rest of the world, with the bond of our glorious tongue, in which we labour to write articles and books for each other's candid perusal, how great we all are and how great is the great city which we may unite fraternally to regard as the capital of our race—is it for this that I have a singular kindness for the London railway-stations, that I like them aesthetically, that they interest and fascinate me, and that I view them with complacency even when I wish neither to depart nor to arrive? They remind me of all our reciprocities and activities, our energies and curiosities, and our being all distinguished together from other people by our great common stamp of perpetual motion, our passion for seas and deserts and the other side of the globe, the secret of the impression of strength—I don't say of social roundness and finish—that we produce in any collection of Anglo-Saxon types. If in the beloved foggy season I delight in the spectacle of Paddington, Euston or Waterloo—I confess I prefer the grave northern stations —I am prepared to defend myself against the charge of puerility; for what I seek and what I find in these vulgar scenes is at bottom simply so much evidence of our larger way of looking at life. The exhibition of variety of type is in general one of the bribes by which London induces you to condone her abominations, and the railway-platform is a kind of compendium of that variety. I think that nowhere so much as in London do people wear—to the eye of observation—definite signs of the sort of people they may be. If you like above all things to know the sort, you hail this fact with joy; you recognise that if the English are immensely distinct from other people they are also socially—and that brings with it, in England, a train of moral and intellectual consequences—extremely distinct from each other. You may see them all together, with the rich colouring of their differences, in the fine flare of one of Mr W. H. Smith's bookstalls—a feature not to be omitted in any enumeration of the charms of Paddington and Euston. It is a focus of warmth and light in the vast smoky cavern; it gives the idea that literature is a thing of splendour, of a dazzling essence, of infinite gas-lit red and gold. A glamour hangs over the glittering booth, and a tantalising air of clever new things. How brilliant must the books all be, how veracious and courteous the fresh, pure journals! Of a Saturday afternoon, as you wait in your corner of the compartment for the starting of the train, the window makes a frame for the glowing picture. I say of a Saturday afternoon because that is the most characteristic time—it speaks most of the constant circulation and in particular of the quick jump, by express, just before dinner, for the Sunday, into the hall of the country-house and the forms of closer friendliness, the prolonged talks, the familiarising walks which London excludes.

There is the emptiness of summer as well, when you may have the town to yourself, and I would discourse of it—counting the summer from the first of August—were it not that I fear to seem ungracious in insisting so much on the negative phases. In truth they become positive in another manner, and I have an endearing recollection of certain happy accidents attached to the only period when London life may be said to admit of accident. It is the most luxurious existence in the world, but of that especial luxury—the unexpected, the extemporised—it has in general too little. In a very tight crowd you can't scratch your leg, and in London the social pressure is so great that it is difficult to deflect from the perpendicular or to move otherwise than with the mass. There is too little of the loose change of time; every half-hour has its preappointed use, written down month by month in a little book. As I intimated, however, the pages of this volume exhibit from August to November an attractive blankness; they represent the season during which you may taste of that highest kind of inspiration, the inspiration of the moment.

This is doubtless what a gentleman had in mind who once said to me, in regard to the vast resources of London and its having something for every taste: 'Oh, yes; when you are bored, or want a little change, you can take the boat down to Blackwall.' I have never had occasion yet to resort to this particular remedy. Perhaps it's a proof that I have never been bored. Why Blackwall? I indeed asked myself at the time; nor have I yet ascertained what distractions the mysterious name represents. My interlocutor probably used it generically, as a free, comprehensive allusion to the charms of the river at large. Here the London-lover goes with him all the way, and indeed the Thames is altogether such a wonderful affair that he feels he has distributed his picture very clumsily not to have put it in the very forefront. Take it up or take it down, it is equally an adjunct of London life, an expression of London manners.

From Westminster to the sea its uses are commercial, but none the less pictorial for that; while in the other direction—taking it properly a little further up—they are personal, social, athletic, idyllic. In its recreative character it is absolutely unique. I know of no other classic stream that is so splashed about for the mere fun of it. There is something almost droll and at the same time almost touching in the way that on the smallest pretext of holiday or fine weather the mighty population takes to the boats. They bump each other in the narrow, charming channel; between Oxford and Richmond they make an uninterrupted procession. Nothing is more suggestive of the personal energy of the people and their eagerness to take, in the way of exercise and adventure, whatever they can get. I hasten to add that what they get on the Thames is exquisite, in spite of the smallness of the scale and the contrast between the numbers and the space. In a word, if the river is the busiest suburb of London it is also by far the prettiest. That term applies to it less, of course, from the bridges down, but it is only because in this part of its career it deserves a larger praise. To be consistent, I like it best when it is all dyed and disfigured with the town, and you look from bridge to bridge—they seem wonderfully big and dim—over the brown, greasy current, the barges and the penny-steamers, the black, sordid, heterogeneous shores. This prospect, of which so many of the elements are ignoble, etches itself to the eye of the lover of 'bits' with a power that is worthy perhaps of a better cause.

The way that with her magnificent opportunity London has neglected to achieve a river-front is, of course, the best possible proof that she has rarely, in the past, been in the architectural mood which at present shows somewhat inexpensive signs of settling upon her. Here and there a fine fragment apologises for the failure which it doesn't remedy. Somerset House stands up higher, perhaps, than anything else on its granite pedestal, and the palace of Westminster reclines—it can hardly be said to stand—on the big parliamentary bench of its terrace. The Embankment, which is admirable if not particularly interesting, does what it can, and the mannered houses of Chelsea stare across at Battersea Park like eighteenth-century ladies surveying a horrid wilderness. On the other hand, the Charing Cross railway-station, placed where it is, is a national crime; Millbank prison is a worse act of violence than any it was erected to punish, and the water-side generally a shameless renunciation of effect. We acknowledge, however, that its very cynicism is expensive; so that if one were to choose again—short of there being a London Louvre—between the usual English irresponsibility in such matters and some particular flight of conscience, one would perhaps do as well to let the case stand. We know what it is, the stretch from Chelsea to Wapping, but we know not what it might be. It doesn't prevent my being always more or less thrilled, of a summer afternoon, by the journey on a penny-steamer to Greenwich.

VIII

But why do I talk of Greenwich and remind myself of one of the unexecuted vignettes with which it had been my plan that these desultory and, I fear, somewhat incoherent remarks should be studded? They will present to the reader no vignettes but those which the artist who has kindly consented to associate himself with my vagaries may be so good as to bestow upon them.* Why should I speak of Hampstead, as the question of summer afternoons just threatened to lead me to do after I should have exhausted the subject of Greenwich, which I may not even touch? Why should I be so arbitrary when I have cheated myself out of the space privately intended for a series of vivid and ingenious sketches of the particular physiognomy of the respective quarters of the town? I had dreamed of doing them all, with their idiosyncrasies and the signs by which you shall know them. It is my pleasure to have learned these signs—a deeply interesting branch of observation—but I must renounce the display of my lore.

I have not the conscience to talk about Hampstead, and what a pleasant thing it is to ascend the long hill which overhangs, as it were, St John's Wood and begins at the Swiss Cottage—you must mount from there, it must be confessed, as you can—and pick up a

* The first edition of *English Hours* was illustrated by Joseph Pennell.

friend at a house of friendship on the top, and stroll with him on the rusty Heath, and skirt the garden-walls of the old square Georgian houses which survive from the time when, near as it is to-day to London, the place was a kind of provincial centre, with Joanna Baillie for its muse, and take the way by the Three Spaniards—I would never miss that—and look down at the smoky city or across at the Scotch firs and the red sunset. It would never do to make a tangent in that direction when I have left Kensington unsung and Bloomsbury unattempted and have said never a word about the mighty eastward region—the queer corners, the dark secrets, the rich survivals and mementoes of the City. I particularly regret having sacrificed Kensington, the once-delightful, the Thackerayan, with its literary vestiges, its quiet, pompous red palace, its square of Queen Anne, its house of Lady Castlewood, its Greyhound tavern, where Henry Esmond lodged.

But I can reconcile myself to this when I reflect that I have also sacrificed the Season, which doubtless, from an elegant point of view, ought to have been the central *morceau* in the panorama. I have noted that the London-lover loves everything in the place, but I have not cut myself off from saying that his sympathy has degrees, or from remarking that the sentiment of the author of these pages has never gone all the way with the dense movement of the British carnival. That is really the word for the period from Easter to midsummer; it is a fine, decorous, expensive, Protestant carnival, in which the masks are not of velvet or silk, but of wonderful deceptive flesh and blood, the material of the most beautiful complexions in the world. Holding that the great interest of London is the sense the place gives us of multitudinous life, it is doubtless an inconsequence not to care most for the phase of greatest intensity. But there is life and life, and the rush and crush of these weeks of fashion is after all but a tolerably mechanical expression of human forces. Nobody would deny that it is a more universal, brilliant, spectacular one than can be seen anywhere else; and it is not a defect that these forces often take the form of women extremely beautiful. I risk the declaration that the London season brings together year by year an unequalled collection of handsome persons. I say nothing of the ugly ones; beauty has at the best been allotted to a small minority, and it is never, at the most, anywhere, but a question of the number by which that minority is least insignificant.

There are moments when one can almost forgive the follies of June for the sake of the smile which the sceptical old city puts on for the time and which, as I noted in an earlier passage of this disquisition, fairly breaks into laughter where she is tickled by the vortex of Hyde Park Corner. Most perhaps does she seem to smile at the end of the summer days, when the light lingers and lingers, though the shadows lengthen and the mists redden and the belated riders, with dinners to dress for, hurry away from the trampled arena of the Park. The population at that hour surges mainly westward and sees the dust of the day's long racket turned into a dull golden haze. There is something that has doubtless often, at this particular moment, touched the fancy even of the bored and the *blasés* in such an emanation of hospitality, of waiting dinners, of the festal idea, of the whole spectacle of the West End preparing herself for an evening six parties deep. The scale on which she entertains is stupendous, and her invitations and 'reminders' are as thick as the leaves of the forest.

For half an hour, from eight to nine, every pair of wheels presents the portrait of a diner-out. To consider only the rattling hansoms, the white neckties and 'dressed' heads which greet you from over the apron in a quick, interminable succession, conveys the overwhelming impression of a complicated world. Who are they all, and where are they all going, and whence have they come, and what smoking kitchens and gaping portals and marshalled flunkeys are prepared to receive them, from the southernmost limits of a loosely interpreted, an almost transpontine Belgravia, to the hyperborean confines of St John's Wood? There are broughams standing at every door, and carpets laid down for the footfall of the issuing if not the entering reveller. The pavements are empty now, in the fading light, in the big sallow squares and the stuccoed streets of gentility, save for the groups of small children holding others that are smaller—Ameliar-Ann intrusted with Sarah Jane—who collect, wherever the strip of carpet lies, to see the fine ladies pass from the carriage or the house. The West End is dotted with these pathetic little gazing groups; it is the party of the poor—*their* Season and way of dining out, and a happy illustration of 'the sympathy that prevails between classes'. The watchers, I should add, are by no means all children, but the lean mature also, and I am sure these wayside joys are one of the reasons of an inconvenience much deplored—the tendency of the country poor to flock to London. They who dine only occasionally or never at all have plenty of time to contemplate those with whom the custom has more amplitude. However, it was not my intention to conclude these remarks in a melancholy strain, and goodness knows that the diners are a prodigious company. It is as moralistic as I shall venture to be if I drop a very soft sigh on the paper as I confirm that truth. Are they all illuminated spirits and is their conversation the ripest in the world? This is not to be expected, nor should I ever suppose it to be desired that an agreeable society should fail to offer frequent opportunity for intellectual rest. Such a shortcoming is not one of the sins of the London world in general, nor would it be just to complain of that world, on any side, on grounds of deficiency. It is not what London fails to do that strikes the observer, but the general fact that she does everything in excess. Excess is her highest reproach, and it is her incurable misfortune that there is really too much of her. She overwhelms you by quantity and number—she ends by making human life, by making civilisation, appear cheap to you. Wherever you go, to parties, exhibitions, concerts, 'private views', meetings, solitudes, there are already more people than enough on the field. How it makes you understand the high walls with which so much of English life is surrounded, and the priceless blessing of a park in the country, where there is nothing animated but rabbits and pheasants and, for the worst, the importunate nightingales! And as the monster grows and grows for ever, she departs more and more—it must be acknowledged—from the ideal of a convenient society, a society in which intimacy is possible, in which the associated meet often and sound and select and measure and inspire each other, and relations and combinations have time to form themselves. The substitute for this, in London, is the momentary concussion of a million of atoms. It is the difference between seeing a great deal of a few and seeing a little of every one. 'When did you come—are you "going on"?' and it is over; there is no time even for the answer. This may seem a perfidious arraignment, and I should not make it were I not prepared, or rather were I not eager, to add two qualifications. One of these is that, cumbrously vast as the place may be, I would not have had it smaller by a hair's-breadth, or have missed one of the fine and fruitful impatiences with which it inspires you and which are at bottom a heartier tribute, I think, than any great city receives. The other is that out of its richness and its inexhaustible good humour it belies the next hour any generalisation you may have been so simple as to make about it.

Browning in Westminster Abbey

THE lovers of a great poet are the people in the world who are most to be forgiven a little wanton fancy about him, for they have before them, in his genius and work, an irresistible example of the application of the imaginative method to a thousand subjects. Certainly, therefore, there are many confirmed admirers of Robert Browning to whom it will not have failed to occur that the consignment of his ashes to the great temple of fame of the English race was exactly one of those occasions in which his own analytic spirit would have rejoiced, and his irrepressible faculty for looking at human events in all sorts of slanting coloured lights have found a signal opportunity. If he had been taken with it as a subject, if it had moved him to the confused yet comprehensive utterance of which he was the great professor, we can immediately guess at some of the sparks he would have scraped from it, guess how splendidly, in the case, the pictorial sense would have intertwined itself with the metaphysical. For such an occasion would have lacked, for the author of 'The Ring and the Book', none of the complexity and convertibility that were dear to him. Passion and ingenuity, irony and solemnity, the impressive and the unexpected, would each have forced their way through; in a word, the author would have been sure to take the special, circumstantial view (the inveterate mark of all his speculation) even of so foregone a conclusion as that England should pay her greatest honour to one of her greatest poets. As they stood in the Abbey, at any rate, on Tuesday last, those of his admirers and mourners who were disposed to profit by his warrant for inquiring curiously may well have let their fancy range, with its muffled step, in the direction which *his* fancy would probably not have shrunk from following, even perhaps to the dim corners where humour and the whimsical lurk. Only, we hasten to add, it would have taken Robert Browning himself to render the multifold impression.

One part of it on such occasion is, of course, irresistible—the sense that these honours are the greatest that a generous nation has to confer and that the emotion that accompanies them is one of the high moments of a nation's life. The attitude of the public, of the multitude, at such hours, is a great expansion, a great openness to ideas of aspiration and achievement; the pride of possession and of bestowal, especially in the case of a career so complete as Mr Browning's, is so present as to make regret a minor matter. We possess a great man most when we begin to look at him, through the glass plate of death; and it is a simple truth, though containing an apparent contradiction, that the Abbey never takes us so benignantly as when we have a valued voice to commit to silence there. For the silence is articulate after all, and in worthy instances the preservation great. It is the other side of the question that would pull most the strings of irresponsible reflection—all those conceivable postulates and hypotheses of the poetic and satiric mind to which we owe the picture of how the bishop ordered his tomb in St Praxed's. Macaulay's 'temple of silence and reconciliation'—and none the less perhaps because he himself is now a presence there—strikes us, as we stand in it, not only as local but as social—a sort of corporate company; so thick, under its high arches, its dim transepts and chapels, is the population of its historic names and figures. They are a company in possession, with a high standard of distinction, of immortality, as it were; for there is something serenely inexpugnable even in the position of the interlopers. As they look out, in the rich dusk, from the cold eyes of statues and the careful identity of tablets, they seem, with their converging faces, to scrutinise decorously the claims of each new recumbent glory, to ask each other how he is to be judged as an accession. How difficult to banish the idea that Robert Browning would have enjoyed prefiguring and playing with the mystifications, the reservations, even perhaps the slight buzz of scandal, in the Poet's Corner, to which his own obsequies might give rise! Would not his great relish, in so characteristic an interview with his crucible, have been his perception of the bewildering modernness, to much of the society, of the new candidate for a niche? That is the interest and the fascination, from what may be termed the inside point of view, of Mr Browning's having received, in this direction of becoming a classic, the only official assistance that is ever conferred upon English writers.

It is as classics on one ground and another—some members of it perhaps on that of not being anything else—that the numerous assembly in the Abbey holds together, and it is as a tremendous and incomparable modern that the author of 'Men and Women' takes his place in it. He introduces to his predecessors a kind of contemporary individualism which surely for many a year they had not been reminded of with any such force. The tradition of the poetic character as something high, detached and simple, which may be assumed to have prevailed among them for a good while, is one that Browning has broken at every turn; so that we can imagine his new associates to stand about him, till they have got used to him, with rather a sense of failing measures. A good many oddities and a good many great writers have been entombed in the Abbey; but none of the odd ones have been so great and none of the great ones so odd. There are plenty of poets whose right to the title may be contested, but there is no poetic head of equal power—crowned and recrowned by almost importunate hands—from which so many people would withhold the distinctive wreath. All this will give the marble phantoms at the base of the great pillars and the definite personalities of the honorary slabs something to puzzle out until, by the quick operation of time, the mere fact of his lying there among the classified and protected makes even Robert Browning lose a portion of the bristling surface of his actuality.

For the rest, judging from the outside and with his contemporaries, we of the public can only feel that his very modernness—by which we mean the all-touching, all-trying spirit of his work, permeated with accumulations and playing with knowledge—achieves a kind of conquest, or at least of extension, of the rigid pale. We cannot enter here upon any account either of that or of any other element of his genius, though surely no literary figure of our day seems to sit more unconsciously for the painter. The very imperfections of this original are fascinating, for they never present themselves as weaknesses; they are boldnesses and overgrowths, rich roughnesses and humours, and the patient critic need not despair of digging to the primary soil from which so many disparities and contradictions spring. He may finally even put his finger on some explanation of the great mystery, the imperfect conquest of the poetic form by a genius in which the poetic passion had such volume and range. He may successfully say how it was that a poet without a lyre—for that is practically Browning's deficiency: he had the scroll, but not often the sounding strings—was nevertheless, in his best hours, wonderfully rich in the magic of his art, a magnificent master of poetic emotion. He will justify on behalf of a multitude of devotees the great position assigned to a writer of verse of which the nature or the fortune has been (in proportion to its value and quantity) to be treated rarely as quotable. He will do all this and a great deal more besides; but we need not wait for it to feel that something of our latest sympathies, our latest and most restless selves, passed the other day into the high part—the show-part, to speak vulgarly—of our literature. To speak of Mr Browning only as he was in the last twenty years of his life, how quick such an imagination as his would have been to recognise all the latent or mystical suitabilities that, in the last resort, might link to the great Valhalla by the Thames a figure that had become so conspicuously a figure of London! He had grown to be intimately and inveterately of the London world; he was so familiar and recurrent, so responsive to all its solicitations, that, given the endless incarnations he stands for to-day, he would have been missed from the congregation of worthies whose memorials are the special pride of the Londoner. Just as his great sign to those who knew him was that he was a force of health, of temperament, of tone, so what he takes into the Abbey is an immense expression of life—of life rendered with large liberty and free experiment, with an unprejudiced intellectual eagerness to put himself in other people's place, to participate in complications and consequences; a restlessness of psychological research that might well alarm any pale company for their formal orthodoxies.

But the illustrious whom he rejoins may be reassured, as they will not fail to discover: in so far as they are representative it will clear itself up that, in spite of a surface unsuggestive of marble and a reckless individualism of form, he is quite as representative as any of them. For the great value of Browning is that at bottom, in all the deep spiritual and human essentials, he is unmistakably in the great tradition—is, with all his Italianisms and cosmopolitanisms, all his victimisation by societies organised to talk about him, a magnificent example of the best and least dilettantish English spirit. That constitutes indeed the main chance for his eventual critic, who will have to solve the refreshing problem of how, if subleties be not what the English spirit most delights in, the author of, for instance, 'Any Wife to any Husband' made them his perpetual pasture, and yet remained typically of his race. He was indeed a wonderful mixture of the universal and the alembicated. But he played with the curious and the special, they never submerged him, and it was a sign of his robustness that he could play to the end. His voice sounds loudest, and also clearest, for the things that, as a race, we like best—the fascination of faith, the acceptance of life, the respect for its mysteries, the endurance of its charges, the vitality of the will, the validity of character, the beauty of action, the seriousness, above all, of the great human passion. If Browning had spoken for us in no other way, he ought to have been made sure of, tamed and chained as a classic, on account of the extra-ordinary beauty of his treatment of the special relation between man and woman. It is a complete and splendid picture of the matter, which somehow places it at the same time in the region of conduct and responsibility. But when we talk of Robert Browning's speaking 'for us' we go to the end of our privilege, we say all. With a sense of security, perhaps even a certain complacency, we leave our sophisticated modern conscience, and perhaps even our hetero-geneous modern vocabulary, in his charge among the illustrious. There will possibly be moments in which these things will seem to us to have widened the allowance, made the high abode more com-fortable, for some of those who are yet to enter it.

Chester

IF the Atlantic voyage be counted, as it certainly may, even with the ocean in a fairly good humour, an emphatic zero in the sum of one's better experience, the American traveller arriving at this venerable town finds himself transported, without a sensible gradation, from the edge of the New World to the very heart of the Old. It is almost a misfortune, perhaps, that Chester lies so close to the threshold of England; for it is so rare and complete a specimen of an antique town that the later-coming wonders of its sisters in renown—of Shrewsbury, Coventry, and York—suffer a trifle by comparison, and the tourist's appetite for the picturesque just loses its finer edge. Yet the first impressions of an observant American in England—of our old friend the sentimental tourist—stir up within him such a cloud of sensibility that while the charm is still unbroken he may perhaps as well dispose mentally of the greater as of the less. I have been playing at first impressions for the second time, and have won the game against a cynical adversary. I have been strolling and restrolling along the ancient wall—so perfect in its antiquity—which locks this dense little city in its stony circle, with a certain friend who has been treating me to a bitter lament on the decay of his relish for the picturesque. 'I have turned the corner of youth,' is his ceaseless plaint; 'I suspected it, but now I know it—now that my heart beats but once where it beat a dozen times before, and that where I found sermons in stones and pictures in meadows, delicious revelations and intimations ineffable, I find nothing but the hard, heavy prose of British civilisation.' But little by little I have grown used to my friend's sad monody, and indeed feel half indebted to it as a warning against cheap infatuations.

I defied him, at any rate, to argue sucessfully against the effect of the brave little walls of Chester. There could be no better example of that phenomenon so delightfully frequent in England—an ancient property or institution lovingly readopted and consecrated to some modern amenity. The good Cestrians may boast of their walls without a shadow of that mental reservation on grounds of modern ease which is so often the tax paid by the romantic; and I can easily imagine that, though most modern towns contrive to get on comfortably without this stony girdle, these people should have come to regard theirs as a prime necessity. For through it, surely, they may know their city more intimately than their unbuckled neighbours—survey it, feel it, rejoice in it as many times a day as they please. The civic consciousness, sunning itself thus on the city's rim and glancing at the little swarming towered and gabled town within, and then at the blue undulations of the near Welsh border, may easily deepen to delicious complacency. The wall enfolds the place in a continuous ring, which, passing through innumerable picturesque vicissitudes, often threatens to snap, but never fairly breaks the link; so that, starting at any point, an hour's easy stroll will bring you back to your station. I have quite lost my heart to this charming creation, and there are so many things to be said about it that I hardly know where to begin. The great fact, I suppose, is that it contains a Roman substructure, rests for much of its course on foundations laid by that race of master-builders. But in spite of this sturdy origin, much of which is buried in the well-trodden soil of the ages, it is the gentlest and least offensive of ramparts; it completes its long irregular curve without a frown or menace in all its disembattled stretch. The earthy deposit of time has, indeed, in some places climbed so high about its base that it amounts to no more than a causeway of modest dimensions. It has everywhere, however, a rugged outer parapet and a broad hollow flagging, wide enough for two strollers abreast. Thus equipped, it wanders through its adventurous circuit; now sloping, now bending, now broadening into a terrace, now narrowing into an alley, now swelling into an arch, now dipping into steps, now passing some thorn-screened garden, and now reminding you that it was once a more serious matter than all this by the extrusion of a rugged, ivy-smothered tower. Its final hoary humility is enhanced, to your mind, by the freedom with which you may approach it from any point in the town. Every few steps, as you go, you see some little court or alley boring toward it through the close-pressed houses.

It is full of that delightful element of the crooked, the accidental, the unforeseen, which, to American eyes, accustomed to our eternal straight lines and right angles, is the striking feature of European street scenery. An American strolling in the Chester streets finds a perfect feast of crookedness—of those random corners, projections and recesses, odd domestic interspaces charmingly saved or lost, those innumerable architectural surprises and caprices and fantasies which lead to such refreshing exercise a vision benumbed by brown-stone fronts. An American is born to the idea that on his walks abroad it is perpetual level wall ahead of him, and such a revelation as he finds here of infinite accident and infinite effect gives a wholly novel zest to the use of his eyes. It produces, too, the reflection—a superficial and fallacious one perhaps—that amid all this cunning chiaroscuro of its *mise en scène*, life must have more of a certain homely entertainment. It is at least no fallacy to say that childhood —or the later memory of childhood—must borrow from such a background a kind of anecdotical wealth. We all know how in the retrospect of later moods the incidents of early youth 'compose', visibly, each as an individual picture, with a magic for which the greatest painters have no corresponding art. There is a vivid re-flection of this magic in some of the early pages of Dickens' 'Copper-field' and of George Eliot's 'Mill on the Floss', the writers having had the happiness of growing up among old, old things. Two or three of the phases of this rambling wall belong especially to the class of things fondly remembered. In one place it skirts the edge of the cathedral graveyard, and sweeps beneath the great square tower and behind the sacred east window of the choir. Of the cathedral there is more to say; but just the spot I speak of is the best standpoint for feeling how fine an influence in the architectural line—where theoretically, at least, influences are great—is the massive tower of an English abbey, dominating the homes of men; and for watching the eddying flight of swallows make vaster still to the eye the large calm fields of stonework. At another point, two battered and crumbling towers, decaying in their winding-sheets of ivy, make a prodigiously designed diversion. One inserted in the body of the wall and the other connected with it by a short crumb-ling ridge of masonry, they contribute to a positive jumble of local colour. A shaded mall wanders at the foot of the rampart; beside this passes a narrow canal, with locks and barges and burly water-men in smocks and breeches; while the venerable pair of towers, with their old red sandstone sides peeping through the gaps in their green mantles, rest on the soft grass of one of those odd frag-ments of public garden, a crooked strip of ground turned to social account, which one meets at every turn, apparently, in England—a tribute to the needs of the 'masses'. *Stat magni nominis umbra.* The quotation is doubly pertinent here, for this little garden-strip is adorned with mossy fragments of Roman stonework, bits of pave-ment, altars, baths, disinterred in the local soil. England is the land of small economies, and the present rarely fails to find good use for the odds and ends of the past. These two hoary shells of masonry are therefore converted into 'museums', receptacles for the dustiest and shabbiest of tawdry back-parlour curiosities. Here preside a couple of those grotesque creatures, *à la* Dickens, whom one finds squeezed into every cranny of English civilisation, scraping a thin subsistence, like mites in a mouldy cheese.

Next after its wall—possibly even before it—Chester values its Rows, an architectural idiosyncrasy which must be seen to be appre-ciated. They are a sort of Gothic edition of the blessed arcades and porticoes of Italy, and consist, roughly speaking, of a running public passage tunnelled through the second storey of the houses. The low basement is thus directly on the drive-way, to which a flight of steps descends, at frequent intervals, from this superincum-bent verandah. The upper portion of the houses projects to the outer line of the gallery, where they are propped with pillars and posts and parapets. The shop-fronts face along the arcade and admit you to little caverns of traffic, more or less dusky according to their opportunities for illumination in the rear. If the picturesque be measured by its hostility to our modern notions of convenience, Chester is probably the most romantic city in the world. This arrangement is endlessly rich in opportunities for amusing effect, but the full charm of the architecture of which it is so essential a part must be observed from the street below. Chester is still an antique town, and mediaeval England sits bravely under her gables. Every third house is a 'specimen'—gabled and latticed, timbered and carved, and wearing its years more or less lightly. These ancient dwellings present every shade and degree of historical colour and expression. Some are dark with neglect and deformity, and the horizontal slit admitting light into the lurking Row seems to collapse on its dislocated props like a pair of toothless old jaws. Others stand there square-shouldered and sturdy, with their beams painted and straightened, their plaster whitewashed, their carvings polished, and the low casement covering the breadth of the frontage adorned with curtains and flower-pots. It is noticeable that the actual townsfolk have bravely accepted the situation bequeathed by the past, and the large number of rich and intelligent restorations of the old façades makes an effective jumble of their piety and their policy. These elaborate and ingenious repairs attest a highly informed consciousness of the pictorial value of the city. I indeed suspect much of this revived innocence of having recovered a freshness that never can have been, of having been restored with usurious interest. About the genuine antiques there would be properly a great deal to say, for they are really a theme for the philosopher; but the theme is too heavy for my pen, and I can give them but the passing tribute of a sigh. They are cruelly quaint, dreadfully expressive. Fix one of them with your gaze, and it seems fairly to reek with mortality. Every stain and crevice seems to syllable some human record—a record of lives airless and unlighted. I have been trying hard to fancy them animated by the children of 'Merry England', but I am quite unable to think of them save as peopled by the victims of dismal old-world pains and fears. Human life, surely, packed away behind those impenetrable lattices of lead and bottle-glass, just above which the black outer beam marks the suffocating nearness of the ceiling, can have expanded into scant freedom and bloomed into small sweetness.

Nothing has struck me more in my strolls along the Rows than the fact that the most zealous observation can keep but uneven pace with the fine differences in national manners. Some of the most sensible of these differences are yet so subtle and indefinable that one must give up the attempt to express them, though the omission leave but a rough sketch. As you pass with the bustling current from shop to shop, you feel local custom and tradition—

another tone of things—pressing on you from every side. The tone of things is somehow heavier than with us; manners and modes are more absolute and positive; they seem to swarm and to thicken the atmosphere about you. Morally and physically it is a denser air than ours. We seem loosely hung together at home as compared with the English, every man of whom is a tight fit in his place. It is not an inferential but a palpable fact that England is a crowded country. There is stillness and space—grassy, oak-studded space—at Eaton Hall, where the Marquis of Westminster dwells (or I believe can afford to humour his notion of not dwelling), but there is a crowd and a hubbub in Chester. Wherever you go the population has overflowed. You stroll on the walls at eventide and you hardly find elbow-room. You haunt the cathedral shades, and a dozen sauntering mortals temper your solitude. You glance up an alley or side-street, and discover populous windows and doorsteps. You roll along country roads and find countless humble pedestrians dotting the green waysides. The English landscape is always a 'landscape with figures'. And everywhere you go you are accompanied by a vague consciousness of the British child hovering about your knees and coat-skirts, naked, grimy, and portentous. You reflect with a sort of physical relief on Australia, Canada, India. Where there are many men, of course, there are many needs; which helps to justify to the philosophic stranger the vast number and the irresistible coquetry of the little shops which adorn these low-browed Rows. The shop-fronts have always seemed to me the most elegant things in England; and I waste more time than I should care to confess to in covetous contemplation of the vast, clear panes behind which the nether integuments of gentlemen are daintily suspended from glittering brass rods. The manners of the dealers in these comfortable wares seldom fail to confirm your agreeable impression. You are thanked with effusion for expending twopence— a fact of deep significance to the truly analytic mind, and which always seems to me a vague reverberation from certain of Miss Edgeworth's novels, perused in childhood. When you think of the small profits, the small jealousies, the long waiting, and the narrow margin for evil days implied by this redundancy of shops and shop-men, you hear afresh the steady rumble of that deep keynote of

English manners, overscored so often, and with such sweet beguilement, by finer harmonies, but never extinguished—the economic struggle for existence.

The Rows are as 'scenic' as one could wish, and it is a pity that before the birth of their modern consciousness there was no English Balzac to introduce them into a realistic romance with a psychological commentary. But the cathedral is better still, modestly as it stands on the roll of English abbeys. It is of moderate dimensions, and rather meagre in form and ornament; but to an American it expresses and answers for the type, producing thereby the proper vibrations. Among these is a certain irresistible regret that so much of its hoary substance should give place to the fine, fresh-coloured masonry with which Mr Gilbert Scott, ruthless renovator, is so intelligently investing it. The red sandstone of the primitive structure, darkened and devoured by time, survives at many points in frowning mockery of the imputed need of tinkering. The great tower, however—completely restored—rises high enough to seem to belong, as cathedral towers should, to the far-off air that vibrates with the chimes and the swallows, and to square serenely, east and west and south and north, its embossed and fluted sides. English cathedrals, within, are apt at first to look pale and naked; but after a while, if the proportions be fair and the spaces largely distributed, when you perceive the light beating softly down from the cold clerestory and your eye measures caressingly the tallness of columns and the hollowness of arches, and lingers on the old genteel inscriptions of mural marbles and brasses; and, above all, when you become conscious of that sweet, cool mustiness in the air which seems to haunt these places as the very climate of Episcopacy, you may grow to feel that they are less the empty shells of a departed faith than the abodes of a faith which may still affirm a presence and awaken echoes. Catholicism has gone, but Anglicanism has the next best music. So at least it seemed to me, a Sunday or two since, as I sat in the choir at Chester awaiting a discourse from Canon Kingsley. The Anglican service had never seemed to my profane sense so much an affair of magnificent intonations and cadences—of pompous effects of resonance and melody. The vast oaken architecture of the stalls among which we nestled—somewhat stiffly and with a due apprehension of wounded ribs and knees—climbing vainly against the dizzier reach of the columns; the beautiful English voices of certain officiating canons; the little rosy 'king's scholars' sitting ranged beneath the pulpit, in white-winged surplices, which made their heads, above the pew-edges, look like rows of sleepy cherubs: every element in the scene gave it a great spectacular beauty. They suggested too what is suggested in England at every turn, that conservatism here has all the charm and leaves dissent and democracy and other vulgar variations nothing but their bald logic. Conservatism has the cathedrals, the colleges, the castles, the gardens, the traditions, the associations, the fine names, the better manners, the poetry; Dissent has the dusky brick chapels in provincial by-streets, the names out of Dickens, the uncertain tenure of the *h*, and the poor *mens sibi conscia recti*. Differences which in other countries are slight and varying, almost metaphysical, as one may say, are marked in England by a gulf. Nowhere else does the degree of one's respectability involve such solid consequences, and I am sure I don't wonder that the sacramental word which with us (and, in such correlatives as they possess, more or less among the continental races) is pronounced lightly and facetiously and as a quotation from the Philistines, is uttered here with a perfectly grave face. To have the courage of one's mere convictions is in short to have a prodigious deal of courage, and I think one must need as much to be a Dissenter as one needs patience not to be a duke. Perhaps the Dissenters (to limit the question to them) manage to stay out of the church by letting it all hang on the sermon. Canon Kingsley's discourse was one more example of the familiar truth— not without its significance to minds zealous for the good old fashion of 'making an effort'—that there is an odd link between large forms and small emanations. The sermon, beneath that triply consecrated vault, should have had a builded majesty. It had not; and I confess that a tender memory of ancient obligations to the author of 'Westward Ho!' and 'Hypatia' forbids my saying more of it. An American, I think, is not incapable of taking a secret satisfaction in an incongruity of this kind. He finds with relief that even mortals reared as in the ring of a perpetual circus are only mortals. His constant sense of the beautiful scenic properties of English life is apt to beget a habit of melancholy reference to the dead-blank wall which forms the background of our own life-drama; and from doubting in this fantastic humour whether we have even that modest value in the scale of beauty that he has sometimes fondly hoped, he lapses into a moody scepticism as to our place in the scale of 'importance', and finds himself wondering vaguely whether this be not a richer race as well as a lovelier land. That of course will never do; so that when after being escorted down the beautiful choir in what, from the American point of view, is an almost gorgeous ecclesiastical march, by the Dean in a white robe trimmed with scarlet and black-robed sacristans carrying silver wands, the officiating canon mounts into a splendid canopied and pinnacled pulpit of Gothic stonework and proves—not an 'acting' Jeremy Taylor, our poor sentimental tourist begins to hold up his head again and to reflect that so far as we *have* opportunities we mostly rise to them. I am not sure indeed that in the excess of his reaction he is not tempted to accuse his English neighbours of being impenetrable and uninspired, to affirm that they do not half discern their good fortune, and that it takes passionate pilgrims, vague aliens and other disinherited persons to appreciate the 'points' of this admirable country.

Lichfield and Warwick

To write at Oxford of anything but Oxford requires, on the part of the sentimental tourist, no small power of mental abstraction. Yet I have it at heart to pay to three or four other scenes recently visited the debt of an enjoyment hardly less profound than my relish for this scholastic paradise. First among these is the cathedral city of Lichfield—the city, I say, because Lichfield has a character of its own apart from its great ecclesiastical feature. In the centre of its little market-place—dullest and sleepiest of provincial market-places—rises a huge effigy of Dr Johnson, the *genius loci*, who was constructed, humanly, with very nearly as large an architecture as the great abbey. The Doctor's statue, which is of some inexpensive composite painted a shiny brown, and of no great merit of design, fills out the vacant dulness of the little square in much the same way as his massive personality occupies—with just a margin for Garrick—the record of his native town. In one of the volumes of Croker's 'Boswell' is a steel plate of the old Johnsonian birth-house, by the aid of a vague recollection of which I detected the dwelling beneath its modernised frontage. It bears no mural inscription and, save for a hint of antiquity in the receding basement, with pillars supporting the floor above, seems in no especial harmony with Johnson's time or fame. Lichfield in general appeared to me indeed to have little to say about her great son beyond the fact that the smallness and the sameness and the dulness, amid which it is so easy to fancy a great intellectual appetite turning sick with inanition, may help to explain the Doctor's subsequent almost ferocious fondness for London. I walked about the silent streets, trying to repeople them with wigs and short-clothes, and, while I lingered near the cathedral, endeavoured to guess the message of its Gothic graces to Johnson's ponderous classicism. But I achieved but a colourless picture at the best, and the most vivid image in my mind's eye was that of the London coach facing towards Temple

Bar with the young author of 'Rasselas' scowling near-sightedly from the cheapest seat. With him goes the interest of Lichfield town. The place is stale without being really antique. It is as if that prodigious temperament had absorbed and appropriated its original vitality.

If every dull provincial town, however, formed but a girdle of quietude to a cathedral as rich as that of Lichfield, one would thank it for letting one alone. Lichfield Cathedral is great among churches, and bravely performs the prime duty of objects of its order—that of seeming for the time (to minds unsophisticated by architectural culture) the finest, on the whole, of all such objects. This one is rather oddly placed, on the slope of a hill, the particular spot having been chosen, I believe, because sanctified by the sufferings of certain primitive martyrs; but it is fine to see how its upper portions surmount any crookedness of posture and its great towers overtake in mid-air the conditions of perfect symmetry. The close is extraordinarily attractive; a long sheet of water expands behind it and, besides leading the eye off into a sweet green landscape, renders the inestimable service of reflecting the three spires as they rise above the great trees which mask the Palace and the Deanery. These august abodes edge the northern side of the slope, and behind their huge gate-posts and close-wrought gates the atmosphere of the Georgian era seems to abide. Before them stretches a row of huge elms, which must have been old when Johnson was young; and between these and the long-buttressed wall of the cathedral, you may stroll to and fro among as pleasant a mixture of influences (I imagine) as any in England. You can stand back here, too, from the west front further than in many cases, and examine at your ease its lavish decoration. You are perhaps a trifle too much at your ease; for you soon discover what a more cursory glance might not betray, that the immense façade has been covered with stucco and paint, that an effigy of Charles II, in wig and plumes and trunk-hose, of almost Gothic grotesqueness, surmounts the middle window; that the various other statues of saints and kings have but recently climbed into their niches; and that the whole expanse is in short an imposture. All this was done some fifty years ago, in the taste of that day as to restoration, and yet it but partially mitigates the impressiveness of the high façade, with its brace of spires, and the great embossed and image-fretted surface, to which the lowness of the portals (the too frequent reproach of English abbeys) seems to give a loftier reach. Passing beneath one of these low portals, however, I found myself gazing down as noble a church vista as any you need desire. The cathedral is of magnificent length, and the screen between nave and choir has been removed, so that from stem to stern, as one may say, of the great vessel of the church, it is all a mighty avenue of multitudinous slender columns, terminating in what seems a great screen of ruby and sapphire and topaz—one of the finest east windows in England. The cathedral is narrow in proportion to its length; it is the long-drawn aisle of the poet in perfection, and there is something grandly elegant in the unity of effect produced by this unobstructed perspective. The charm is increased by a singular architectural fantasy. Standing in the centre of the doorway, you perceive that the eastern wall does not directly face you, and that from the beginning of the choir the receding aisle deflects slightly to the left, in reported suggestion of the droop of the Saviour's head on the cross. Here again Mr Gilbert Scott has lately laboured to no small purpose of *un*doing, it would appear— undoing the misdeeds of the last century. This extraordinary period expended an incalculable amount of imagination in proving that it had none. Universal whitewash was the least of its offences. But this has been scraped away and the solid stonework left to speak for itself, the delicate capitals and cornices disencrusted and discreetly rechiselled and the whole temple aesthetically rededicated. Its most beautiful feature, happily, has needed no repair, for its perfect beauty has been its safeguard. The great choir window of Lichfield is the noblest glass-work before the spell of which one's soul has become simple. I remember nowhere colours so chaste and grave, and yet so rich and true, or a cluster of designs so piously decorative and yet so vivified. Such a window as this seems to me the most scared ornament of a great church; to be, not like vault and screen and altar, the dim contingent promise to the spirit, but the very redemption of the whole vow. This Lichfield glass is not the less interesting for being visibly of foreign origin. Exceeding so obviously as it does the range of English genius in this line, it indicates at least the heavenly treasure stored up in continental churches. It dates from the early sixteenth century, and was transferred hither sixty years ago from a decayed Belgian abbey. This, however, is not all of Lichfield. You have not seen it till you have strolled and re-strolled along the close on every side, and watched the three spires constantly change their relation as you move and pause. Nothing can well be finer than the combination of the two lesser ones soaring equally in front with the third riding tremendously the magnifi-cently sustained line of the roof. At a certain distance against the sky this long ridge seems something infinite and the great spire to sit astride of it like a giant mounted on a mastodon. Your sense of the huge mass of the building is deepened by the fact that though the central steeple is of double the elevation of the others, you see it, from some points, borne back in a perspective which drops it to half their stature and lifts them into immensity. But it would take long to tell all that one sees and fancies and thinks in a lingering walk about so great a church as this.

To walk in quest of any object that one has more or less tenderly dreamed of, to find your way, to steal upon it softly, to see at last, if it be church or castle, the tower-tops peeping above elms or beeches—to push forward with a rush, and emerge and pause and draw that first long breath which is the compromise between so many sensations: this is a pleasure left to the tourist even after the broad glare of photography has dissipated so many of the sweet mysteries of travel; even in a season when he is fatally apt to meet a dozen fellow pilgrims returning from the shrine, each as big a fool, so to speak, as he ever was, or to overtake a dozen more tele-graphing their impressions down the line as they arrive. Such a pleasure I lately enjoyed quite in its perfection, in a walk to Haddon Hall, along a meadow-path by the Wye, in this interminable English twilight which I am never weary of admiring watch in hand. Had-don Hall lies among Derbyshire hills, in a region infested, I was about to write, by Americans. But I achieved my own sly pilgrimage in perfect solitude; and as I descried the gray walls among the rook-haunted elms I felt not like a dusty tourist, but like a successful adventurer. I have certainly had, as a dusty tourist, few more charming moments than some—such as any one, I suppose, is free to have—that I passed on a little ruined gray bridge which spans, with its single narrow arch, a trickling stream at the base of the eminence from which those walls and trees look down. The twilight deepened, the ragged battlements and the low, broad oriels glanced duskily from the foliage, the rooks wheeled and clamoured in the glowing sky; and if there had been a ghost on the premises I certainly ought to have seen it. In fact I did see it, as we see ghosts nowadays. I felt the incommunicable spirit of the scene with the last, the right intensity. The old life, the old manners, the old figures seemed present again. The great *coup de théâtre* of the young woman who shows you the Hall—it is rather languidly done on her part—is to point out a little dusky door opening from a turret to a back terrace as the aperture through which Dorothy Vernon eloped with Lord John Manners. I was ignorant of this episode, for I was not to enter the place till the morrow, and I am still unversed in the history of the actors. But as I stood in the luminous dusk weaving the romance of the spot, I recognised the inevitability of a Dorothy Vernon and quite understood a Lord John. It was of course on just such an evening that the romantic event came off, and by listening with the proper credulity, I might surely hear on the flags of the castle court ghostly footfalls and feel in their movements the old heart-beats. The only football I can conscientiously swear to, however, is the far from spectral tread of the damsel who led me through the mansion in the prosier light of the next morning. Haddon Hall, I believe, is one of the sights in which it is the fashion to be 'disappointed'; a fact explained in a great measure by the absence of a formal approach to the house, which shows its low, gray front to every trudger on the high-road. But the charm of the spot is so much less that of grandeur than that of melancholy, that it is rather deepened than diminished by this attitude of obvious survival and decay. And for that matter, when you have entered the steep little outer court through the huge thickness of the low gateway, the present seems effectually walled out and the past walled in, even as a dead man in a sepulchre. It is very dead, of a fine June morning, the genius of Haddon Hall; and the silent courts and chambers, with their hues of ashen gray and faded brown, seem as time-bleached as the dry bones of any mouldering mortality. The comparison is odd, but Haddon Hall reminded me perversely of some of the larger houses at Pompeii. The private life of the past is revealed in each case with very much the same distinctness and on a scale small enough not to stagger the imagination. This old dwelling, indeed, has so little of the mass and expanse of the classic feudal castle that it almost suggests one of those miniature models of great buildings which lurk in dusty corners of museums. But it is large enough to be delectably complete and to contain an infinite store of the poetry of grass-grown courts looked into by wide, jutting windows and climbed out of by crooked stone stairways mounting against the walls to little high-placed doors. The 'tone' of Haddon Hall, of all its walls and towers and stonework, is the gray of unpolished silver, and the reader who has been in England need hardly be reminded of the sweet accord—to eye and mind alike—existing between all stony surfaces covered with the pale corrosions of time and the deep living green of the strong ivy which seems to feed on their slow decay. Of this effect and of a hundred others—from those that belong to low-browed, stone-paved empty rooms where life was warm and atmospheres thick, to those one may note where the dark tower stairway emerges at last, on a level with the highest beech-tops, against the cracked and sun-baked parapet which flaunted the castle standard over the castle woods—of every form of sad desuetude and picturesque decay Haddon Hall contains some delightful example. Its finest point is undoubtedly a certain court from which a stately flight of steps ascends to the terrace where that daughter of the Vernons whom I have mentioned took such happy thought for our requiring, as the phrase is, a reference. These steps, with the terrace, its balustrade topped with great ivy-muffled knobs of stone and its high background of massed woods, form the ideal *mise en scène* for portions of Shakespeare's comedies. 'It's exactly Elizabethan,' said my companion. Here the Countess Olivia may have listened to the fantastic Malvolio, or Beatrix, superbest of flirts, have come to summon Benedick to dinner.

The glories of Chatsworth, which lies but a few miles from Haddon, serve as a marked offset to its more delicate merits, just as they are supposed to gain, I believe, in the tourist's eyes, by contrast with its charming, its almost Italian shabbiness. But the glories

of Chatsworth, incontestable as they are, were so effectually eclipsed
to my mind, a couple of days later, that in future, when I think of
an English mansion, I shall think only of Warwick, and when I
think of an English park, only of Blenheim. Your run by train
through the gentle Warwickshire land does much to prepare you
for the great spectacle of the castle, which seems hardly more than
a sort of massive symbol and synthesis of the broad prosperity and
peace and leisure diffused over this great pastoral expanse. The
Warwickshire meadows are to common English scenery what this
is to that of the rest of the world. For mile upon mile you can see
nothing but broad sloping pastures of velvet turf, overbrowsed by
sheep of the most fantastic shagginess, and garnished with hedges
out of the trailing luxury of whose verdure great ivy-tangled oaks
and elms arise with a kind of architectural regularity. The landscape
indeed sins by excess of nutritive suggestion; it savours of larder
and manger; it is too ovine, too bovine, it is almost asinine; and if
you were to believe what you see before you this rugged globe
would be a sort of boneless ball covered with some such plush-like
integument as might be figured by the down on the cheek of a
peach. But a great thought keeps you company as you go and gives
character to the scenery. Warwickshire—you say it over and over—
was Shakespeare's country. Those who think that a great genius is
something supremely ripe and healthy and human may find comfort
in the fact. It helps greatly to enliven my own vague conception of
Shakespeare's temperament, with which I find it no great shock to
be obliged to associate ideas of mutton and beef. There is something as final, as disillusioned of the romantic horrors of rock and
forest, as deeply attuned to human needs in the Warwickshire
pastures as there is in the underlying morality of the poet.

With human needs in general Warwick Castle may be in no great
accord, but few places are more gratifying to the sentimental tourist.
It is the only great residence he may have coveted as a home. The
fire that we heard so much of last winter in America appears to have
consumed but an inconsiderable and easily spared portion of the
house, and the great towers rise over the great trees and the town
with the same grand air as before. Picturesquely, Warwick gains
from not being sequestered, after the common fashion, in acres of

park. The village street winds about the garden walls, though its hum expires before it has had time to scale them. There can be no better example of the way in which stone walls, if they do not of necessity make a prison, may on occasions make a palace, than the prodigious privacy maintained thus about a mansion whose windows and towers form the main feature of a bustling town. At Warwick the past joins hands so stoutly with the present that you can hardly say where one begins and the other ends, and you rather miss the various crannies and gaps of what I just now called the Italian shabbiness of Haddon. There is a Caesar's tower and a Guy's tower and half a dozen more, but they are so well-conditioned in their ponderous antiquity that you are at a loss whether to consider them parts of an old house revived or of a new house picturesquely superannuated. Such as they are, however, plunging into the grassed and gravelled courts from which their battlements look really feudal, and into gardens large enough for all delight and too small, as they should be, to be amazing; and with ranges between them of great apartments at whose hugely recessed windows you may turn from Vandyck and Rembrandt to glance down the cliff-like pile into the Avon, washing the base like a lordly moat, with its bridge, and its trees and its memories, they mark the very model of a great hereditary dwelling—one which amply satisfies the imagination without irritating the democratic conscience. The pictures at Warwick reminded me afresh of an old conclusion on this matter; that the best fortune for good pictures is not to be crowded into public collections—not even into the relative privacy of Salons Carrés and Tribunes—but to hang in largely spaced half-dozens on the walls of fine houses. Here the historical atmosphere, as one may call it, is almost a compensation for the often imperfect light. If this be true of most pictures it is especially so of the works of Vandyck, whom you think of, wherever you may find him, as having, with that thorough good-breeding which is the stamp of his manner, taken account in his painting of the local conditions and predestined his picture to just the spot where it hangs. This is in fact an illusion as regards the Vandycks at Warwick, for none of them represent members of the house. The very finest perhaps after the great melancholy, picturesque Charles I—death, or at least the presentiment of death on the pale horse—is a portrait from the Brignole palace at Genoa; a beautiful noble matron in black, with her little son and heir. The last Vandycks I had seen were the noble company this lady had left behind her in the Genoese palace, and as I looked at her I thought of her mighty change of circumstance. Here she sits in the mild light of midmost England; there you could almost fancy her blinking in the great glare sent up from the Mediterranean. Intensity for intensity—intensity of situation constituted—I hardly know which to choose.

North Devon

FOR those fanciful observers to whom broad England means chiefly the perfection of the rural picturesque, Devonshire means the perfection of England. I, at least, had so complacently taken for granted here all the characteristic graces of English scenery, had built so boldly on their rank orthodoxy, that before we fairly crossed the border I had begun to look impatiently from the carriage window for the veritable landscape in water-colours. Devonshire meets you promptly in all its purity, for the course of ten minutes you have been able to glance down the green vista of a dozen Devonshire lanes. On huge embankments of moss and turf, smothered in wild flowers and embroidered with the finest lace-work of trailing ground-ivy, rise solid walls of flowering thorn and glistening holly and golden broom, and more strong, homely shrubs than I can name, and toss their blooming tangle to a sky which seems to look down between them, in places, from but a dozen inches of blue. They are oversown with lovely little flowers with names as delicate as their petals of gold and silver and azure— bird's-eye and king's-finger and wandering-sailor—and their soil, a superb dark red, turns in spots so nearly to crimson that you almost fancy it some fantastic compound purchased at the chemist's and scattered there for ornament. The mingled reflection of this rich-hued earth and the dim green light which filters through the hedge is a masterpiece of produced beauty. A Devonshire cottage is no less striking an outcome of the ages and the seasons and the manners. Crushed beneath its burden of thatch, coated with a rough white stucco of a tone to delight a painter, nestling in deep foliage and garnished at door-step and wayside with various forms of chubby infancy, it seems to have been stationed there for no more obvious purpose than to keep a promise to your fancy, though it covers, I suppose, not a little of the sordid side of life which the fancy likes to slur over.

I rolled past lanes and cottages to Exeter, where I had counted upon the cathedral. When one has fairly tasted of the pleasure of cathedral-hunting the approach to each new possible prize of the chase gives a peculiarly agreeable zest to the curiosity. You are making a collection of great impressions, and I think the process is in no case so delightful as applied to cathedrals. Going from one fine picture to another is certainly good; but the fine pictures of the world are terribly numerous, and they have a troublesome way of crowding and jostling each other in the memory. The number of cathedrals is small, and the mass and presence of each specimen great, so that as they rise in the mind in individual majesty they dwarf all the commoner impressions of calculated effect. They form indeed but a gallery of vaster pictures; for when time has dulled the recollection of details you retain a single broad image of the vast gray edifice, with its head and shoulders, its vessel and its towers, its tone of colour, and its still green precinct. All this is especially true perhaps of one's sense of English sacred piles, which are almost alone in possessing, as pictures, a spacious and harmonious setting. The cathedral stands supreme, but the close makes, always, the *scene*. Exeter is not one of the grandest, but, in common with great and small, it has certain points in favour of which local learning discriminates. Exeter indeed does itself injustice by a low, dark front, which not only diminishes the apparent altitude of the nave, but conceals, as you look eastward, two noble Norman towers. The front, however, which has a gloomy impressiveness, is redeemed by two fine features: a magnificent rose-window, whose vast stone ribs (inclosing some very pallid last-century glass) are disposed with the most charming intricacy; and a long sculptured screen—a sort of stony band of images—which traverses the façade from side to side. The little broken-visaged effigies of saints and kings and bishops, niched in tiers along this hoary wall, are prodigiously black and quaint and primitive in expression; and as you look at them with whatever contemplative tenderness your trade of hard-working tourist may have left at your disposal, you fancy that they are broodingly conscious of their names, histories and misfortunes; that, sensitive victims of time, they feel the loss of their noses, their toes, and their crowns; and that, when the long June twilight turns at last to a deeper gray and the quiet of the close to a deeper stillness, they begin to peer sidewise out of their narrow recesses and to converse in some strange form of early English, as rigid, yet as candid, as their features and postures, moaning, like a company of ancient paupers round a hospital fire, over their aches and infirmities and losses, and the sadness of being so terribly old. The vast square transeptal towers of the church seem to me to have the same sort of personal melancholy. Nothing in all architecture expresses better, to my imagination, the sadness of survival, the resignation of dogged material continuance, than a broad expanse of Norman stonework, roughly adorned with its low relief of short columns and round arches and almost barbarous hatchet-work, and lifted high into that mild English light which accords so well with its dull gray surface. The especial secret of the impressiveness of such a Norman tower I cannot pretend to have discovered. It lies largely in the look of having been proudly and sturdily built—as if the masons had been urged by a trumpet-blast, and the stones squared by a battle-axe—contrasted with this mere idleness of antiquity and passive lapse into quaintness. A Greek temple preserves a kind of fresh immortality in its concentrated refinement, and a Gothic cathedral in its adventurous exuberance; but a Norman tower stands up like some simple strong man in his might, bending a melancholy brow upon an age which demands that strength shall be cunning.

The North Devon coast, whither it was my design on coming to Exeter to proceed, has the primary merit of being, as yet, virgin soil as to railways. I went accordingly from Barnstaple to Ilfracombe on the top of a coach, in the fashion of elder days; and, thanks to my position, I managed to enjoy the landscape in spite of the two worthy aboriginals before me who were reading aloud together, with a natural glee which might have passed for fiendish malice, the *Daily Telegraph*'s painfully vivid account of the defeat of the Atalanta crew. It seemed to me, I remember, a sort of pledge and token of the invincibility of English muscle that a newspaper record of its prowess should have power to divert my companions' eyes from the bosky flanks of Devonshire combes. The little watering-place of Ilfracombe is seated at the lower verge of one of these seaward-plunging valleys, between a couple of magnificent headlands which hold it in a hollow slope and offer it securely to the caress of the Bristol Channel. It is a very finished little specimen of its genus, and I think that during my short stay there I expended as much attention on its manners and customs and its social physiognomy as on its cliffs and beach and great coast-view. My chief conclusion perhaps, from all these things, was that the terrible 'summer question' which works annual anguish in so many American households would rage less hopelessly if we had a few Ilfracombes scattered along our Atlantic coast; and furthermore that the English are masters of the art of not losing sight of ease and convenience in the pursuit of the pastoral life—unlike our own people, who, when seeking rural beguilement, are apt but to find a new rudeness added to nature. It is just possible that at Ilfracombe ease and convenience weigh down the scale; so very substantial are they, so very officious and business-like. On the left of the town (to give an example) one of the great cliffs I have mentioned rises in a couple of massive peaks and presents to the sea an almost vertical face, all muffled in tufts of golden broom and mighty fern. You have not walked fifty yards away from the hotel before you encounter half a dozen little sign-boards, directing your steps to a path up the cliff. You follow their indications and you arrive at a little gatehouse, with photographs and various local gimcracks exposed for sale. A most respectable person appears, demands a penny and, on receiving it, admits you with great civility to commune with nature. You detect, however, various little influences hostile to perfect communion. You are greeted by another sign-board threatening legal pursuit if you attempt to evade the payment of the sacramental penny. The path, winding in a hundred ramifications over the cliff, is fastidiously solid and neat, and furnished at intervals of a dozen yards with excellent benches, inscribed by knife and pencil with the names of such visitors as do not happen to have been the elderly maiden ladies who now chiefly occupy them. All this is prosaic, and you have to subtract it in a lump from the total impression before the sense of the beguilement of nature becomes distinct. Your subtraction made, a great deal assuredly remains; quite enough, I found, to give me an ample day's refreshment; for English scenery, like most other English commodities, resists and rewards familiar use. The cliffs are superb, the play of light and shade upon them is a perpetual study, and the air a particular mixture of the breath of the hills and moors and the breath of the sea. I was very glad, at the end of my climb, to have a good bench to sit upon—as one must think twice in England before measuring one's length on the grassy earth; and to be able, thanks to the smooth footpath, to get back to the hotel in a quarter of an hour. But it occurred to me that if I were an Englishman of the period, and, after ten months of a busy London life, my fancy were turning to a holiday, to rest and change and oblivion of the ponderous social burden, it might find rather less inspiration than needful in a vision of the little paths of Ilfracombe, of the sign-boards and the penny fee and the solitude tempered by old ladies and sheep. I wondered whether change perfect enough to be salutary does not imply something more pathless, more idle, more unreclaimed from that deep-bosomed nature to which the overwrought mind reverts with passionate longing; something after all attainable at a moderate distance from New York and Boston. I must add that I cannot find in my heart to object, even on grounds the most aesthetic, to the very beautiful and excellent inn at Ilfracombe, where such of my readers as are perchance actually wrestling with the question of 'where to go' may be interested to learn that they may live *en pension*, very well indeed, at a cost of ten shillings a day. I have paid the American hotel-clerk a much heavier tax on a much lighter entertainment. I made the acquaintance at this establishment of that strange fruit of time the insular *table d'hôte*, but I confess that, faithful to the habit of a tourist open to the *arrière-pensée*, I have retained a more vivid impression of the talk and the faces than of our joints and side-dishes. I noticed here what I have often noticed before (the truth perhaps has never been duly recognised), that no people profit so eagerly as the English by the suspension of a common social law. A *table d'hôte*, being something abnormal and experimental, as it were, resulted apparently in a complete reversal of the supposed national characteristics. Conversation was universal—uproarious almost; old legends and ironies about the insular *morgue* seemed to see their ground crumble away. What social, what psychologic earthquake, in our own time, had occurred?

These are meagre memories, however, compared with those which cluster about that place of pleasantness which is locally known as Lynton. I am afraid I may seem a mere professional gusher when I declare how common almost any term appears to me applied to Lynton with descriptive intent. The little village is perched on the side of one of the great mountain cliffs with which this whole coast is adorned, and on the edge of a lovely gorge through which a broad hill-torrent foams and tumbles from the great moors whose heather-crested waves rise purple along the inland sky. Below it, close beside the beach where the little torrent meets the sea, is the sister village of Lynmouth. Here—as I stood on the bridge that spans the stream and looked at the stony backs and foundations and overclambering garden verdure of certain little gray old houses which plunge their feet into it, and then up at the tender green of scrub-oak and fern, at the colour of gorse and broom and bracken climbing the sides of the hills and leaving them bare-crowned to the sun like miniature mountains—I read an unnatural blueness into the northern sea, and the village below put on the grace of one of the hundred hamlets of the Riviera. The little Castle Hotel at Lynton is a spot so consecrated to supreme repose —to sitting with a book in the terrace-garden, among blooming plants of aristocratic magnitude and rarity, and watching the finest piece of colour in all nature, the glowing red and green of the great cliffs beyond the little harbour-mouth, as they shift and change and melt, the livelong day, from shade to shade and ineffable tone to tone—that I feel as if in helping it to publicity I were doing it rather a disfavour than a service. It is in fact a very deep and sure retreat, and I have never known one where purchased hospitality wore a more disinterested smile. Lynton is of course a capital centre for excursions, but two or three of which I had time to make. None is more beautiful than a simple walk along the running face of the cliffs to a singular rocky eminence whose curious abutments and pinnacles of stone have caused it to be named the Castle. It has a fantastic resemblance to some hoary feudal ruin, with crumbling towers and gaping chambers tenanted by wild sea-birds. The late afternoon light had a way, at this season, of lingering on until within a couple of hours of midnight; and I remember among the charmed moments of English travel none of a more vividly poetical tinge than a couple of evenings spent on the summit of this all but legendary pile in company with the slow-coming darkness and the short, sharp cry of the sea-mews. There are places whose very aspect is a story or a song. This jagged and pinnacled coast-wall, with the rock-strewn valley behind it, the sullen calmness of the unbroken tide at the dreadful base of the cliffs (where they divide into low sea-caves, making pillars and pedestals for the fantastic imagery of their summits), prompted one to wanton reminiscence and outbreak, to a recall of some drawing of Gustave Doré's (of his good time), which was a divination of the place and made one look for his signature under a stone, or, better still, to respouting, for sympathy and relief, some idyllic Tennysonian line that haunted one's destitute past and that seemed to speak of the conditions in spite of being false to them geographically.

The last stage in my visit to North Devon was the long drive along the beautiful remnant of coast and through the rich pastoral scenery of Somerset. The whole broad spectacle that one dreams of viewing in a foreign land to the homely music of a postboy's whip I beheld on this admirable drive—breezy highlands clad in the warm blue-brown of heather-tufts as if in mantles of rusty velvet, little bays and coves curving gently to the doors of clustered fishing-huts, deep pastures and broad forests, villages thatched and trellised as if to take a prize for improbability, manor-tops peeping over rook-haunted avenues. I ought to make especial note of an hour I spent at midday at the village of Porlock in Somerset. Here the thatch seemed steeper and heavier, the yellow roses on the cottage walls more cunningly mated with the crumbling stucco, the dark interiors within the open doors more quaintly pictorial, than elsewhere; and as I loitered, while the horses rested, in the little cool old timber-steepled, yew-shaded church, betwixt the high-backed manorial pew and the battered tomb of a crusading knight and his lady, and listened to the simple prattle of a blue-eyed old sexton, who showed me where, as a boy, in scantier corduroys, he had scratched his name on the recumbent lady's breast, it seemed to me that this at last was old England indeed, and that in a moment more I should see Sir Roger de Coverley marching up the aisle. Certainly, to give a proper account of it all, I should need nothing less than the pen of Mr Addison.

Wells and Salisbury

THE pleasantest thing in life is doubtless ever the pleasantness that has found one off one's guard—though if I was off my guard in arriving at Wells it could only have been by the effect of a frivolous want of information. I knew in a general way that this ancient little town had a great cathedral to produce, but I was far from suspecting the intensity of the impression that awaited me. The immense predominance of the Minster towers, as you see them from the approaching train over the clustered houses at their feet, gives you indeed an intimation of its character, suggests that the city is nothing if not sanctified; but I can wish the traveller no better fortune than to stroll forth in the early evening with as large a reserve of ignorance as my own, and treat himself to an hour of discoveries. I was lodged on the edge of the Cathedral lawn and had only to pass beneath one of the three crumbling Priory gates which enclose it, and cross the vast grassy oval, to stand before a minster-front which ranks among the first three or four in England. Wells Cathedral is extremely fortunate in being approached by this wide green level, on which the spectator may loiter and stroll to and fro and shift his standpoint to his heart's content. The spectator who does not hesitate to avail himself of his privilege of unlimited fastidiousness might indeed pronounce it too isolated for perfect picturesqueness—too uncontrasted with the profane architecture of the human homes for which it pleads to the skies. But Wells is in fact not a city with a cathedral for central feature; it is a cathedral with a little city gathered at the base and forming hardly more than an extension of the spacious close. You feel everywhere the presence of the beautiful church; the place seems always to savour of a Sunday afternoon; and you imagine every house tenanted by a canon, a prebendary or a precentor, with 'backs' providing for choristers and vergers.

The great façade is remarkable not so much for its expanse as for its elaborate elegance. It consists of two great truncated towers, divided by a broad centre bearing, beside its rich fretwork of statues, three narrow lancet windows. The statues on this vast front are the great boast of the cathedral. They number, with the lateral figures of the towers, no less than three hundred; it seems densely embroidered by the chisel. They are disposed, in successive niches, along six main vertical shafts; the central windows are framed and divided by narrower shafts, and the wall above them rises into a pinnacled screen traversed by two superb horizontal rows. Add to these a close-running cornice of images along the line corresponding with the summit of the aisles and the tiers which complete the decoration of the towers on either side, and you have an immense system of images governed by a quaint theological order and most impressive in its completeness. Many of the little high-lodged effigies are mutilated, and not a few of the niches are empty, but the injury of time is not sufficient to diminish the noble serenity of the building. The injury of time is indeed being actively repaired, for the front is partly masked by a slender scaffolding. The props and platforms are of the most delicate structure, and look in fact as if they were meant to facilitate no more ponderous labour than a fitting-on of noses to disfeatured bishops and a rearrangement of the mantle-folds of straitlaced queens discomposed by the centuries. The main beauty of Wells Cathedral, to my mind, is not its more or less visible wealth of detail, but its singularly charming tone of colour. An even, sober, mouse-coloured gray invests it from summit to base, deepening nowhere to the melancholy black of your truly romantic Gothic, but showing as yet none of the spotty brightness of renovation. It is a wonderful fact that the great towers, from their lofty outlook, see never a factory chimney—those cloud-compelling spires which so often break the charm of the softest English horizons; and the general atmosphere of Wells seemed to me, for some reason, peculiarly luminous and sweet. The cathedral has never been discoloured by the moral malaria of a city with an independent secular life. As you turn back from its portal and glance at the open lawn before it, edged by the mild gray seventeenth-century deanery and the other dwellings, hardly less stately, which seem to reflect in their comfortable fronts the rich respectability of the church, and then up again at the beautiful clear-hued pile, you may fancy it less a temple for man's needs than a monument of his pride—less a fold for the flock than for the shepherds; a visible token that, besides the actual assortment of heavenly thrones, there is constantly on hand a 'full line' of cushioned cathedral stalls. Within the cathedral this impression is not diminished. The interior is vast and massive, but it lacks incident—the incident of monuments, sepulchres and chapels —and it is too brilliantly lighted for picturesque, as distinguished from strictly architectural, interest. Under this latter head it has, I believe, great importance. For myself, I can think of it only as I saw it from my place in the choir during afternoon service of a hot Sunday. The Bishop sat facing me, enthroned in a stately Gothic alcove and clad in his crimson band, his lawn sleeves and his lavender gloves; the canons, in their degree, with still other priestly forms, reclined comfortably in the carven stalls, and the scanty congregation fringed the broad aisle. But though scanty, the congregation was select; it was unexceptionably black-coated, bonneted and gloved. It savoured intensely in short of that inexorable gentility which the English put on with their Sunday bonnets and beavers and which fills me—as a mere taster of produced tastes— with a sort of fond reactionary remembrance of those animated bundles of rags which one sees kneeling in the churches of Italy. But even here, as taster of tastes, I found my account. You always do if you throw yourself confidently enough, in England, on the chapter of accidents. Before me and beside me sat a row of the comeliest young men, clad in black gowns and wearing on their shoulders long hoods trimmed with white fur. Who and what they were I know not, for I preferred not to learn, lest by chance they should not be so mediaeval as they looked.

My fancy found its account even better in the singular quaintness of the little precinct known as the Vicars' Close. It directly adjoins the Cathedral Green, and you enter it beneath one of the solid old gatehouses which form so striking an element in the ecclesiastical furniture of Wells. It consists of a narrow, oblong court, bordered on each side with thirteen small dwellings, and terminating in a ruinous little chapel. Here formerly dwelt a congregation of minor priests, established in the thirteenth century to do curates' work for the canons. The little houses are very much modernised; but they retain their tall chimneys, with carven tablets in the face, their antique compactness and neatness, and a certain little sanctified air as of cells in a cloister. The place is adorably of another world and time, and, approaching it as I did in the first dimness of twilight, it looked to me, in its exaggerated perspective, like one of those conventional streets represented on the stage, down whose impossible vista the heroes and confidants of romantic comedies come swaggering arm-in-arm and hold amorous converse with heroines perched at second-story windows. But though the Vicars' Close is a curious affair enough, the great boast of Wells is its episcopal Palace. The Palace loses nothing from being seen for the first time in the kindly twilight, and from being approached with an uncautioned mind. To reach it (unless you go from within the cathedral by the cloisters), you pass out of the Green by another ancient gateway into the market-place, and thence back again through its own peculiar portal. My own first glimpse of it had all the felicity of a *coup de théâtre*. I saw within the dark archway an enclosure bedimmed at once with the shadows of trees and heightened with the glitter of water. The picture was worthy of this agreeable promise. Its main feature is the little gray-walled island on which the Palace stands, rising in feudal fashion out of a broad, clear moat, flanked with round towers and approached by a proper drawbridge. Along the outer side of the moat is a short walk beneath a row of picturesquely stunted elms; swans and ducks disport themselves in the current and ripple the bright shadows of the overclambering plants from the episcopal gardens and masses of wallflower lodged on the hoary battlements. On the evening of my visit the haymakers were at work on a great sloping field in the rear of the Palace, and the sweet perfume of the tumbled grass in the dusky air seemed all that was wanting to fix the scene for ever in the memory. Beyond the moat and within the gray walls dwells my lord Bishop, in the finest seat of all his order. The mansion dates from the thirteenth century; but, stately dwelling though it is, it occupies but a subordinate place in its own grounds. Their great ornament, picturesquely speaking, is the massive ruin of a banqueting-hall erected by a free-living mediaeval bishop and more or less demolished at the Reformation. With its still perfect towers and beautiful shapely windows, hung with those green tapestries so stoutly woven by the English climate, it is a relic worthy of being locked away behind an embattled wall. I have among my impressions of Wells, besides this picture of the moated Palace, half a dozen memories of the romantic sort, which I lack space to transcribe. The clearest impression perhaps is that of the beautiful church of St Cuthbert, of the same date as the cathedral, and in very much the same style of elegant, temperate Early English. It wears one of the high-soaring towers for which Somersetshire is justly celebrated, as you may see from the window of the train in rolling past its almost top-heavy hamlets. The beautiful old church, surrounded with its green graveyard, and large enough to be impressive, without being too large (a great merit, to my sense) to be easily compassed by a deplorably unarchitectural eye, wore a native English expression to which certain humble figures in the foreground gave additional point. On the edge of the churchyard was a low-gabled house, before which four old men were gossiping in the eventide. Into the front of the house was inserted an antique alcove in stone, divided into three shallow little seats, two of which were occupied by extraordinary specimens of decrepitude. One of these ancient paupers had a huge protuberant forehead, and sat with a pensive air, his head gathered painfully upon his twisted shoulders and his legs resting across his crutch. The other was rubicund, blear-eyed and frightfully besmeared with snuff. Their voices were so feeble and senile that I could scarcely understand them, and only just managed to make out the answer to my inquiry of who and what they were—'We're Still's Almshouse, sir.'

One of the lions, almost, of Wells (whence it is but five miles distant) is the ruin of the famous Abbey of Glastonbury, on which Henry VIII, in the language of our day, came down so heavily. The ancient splendour of the architecture survives but in scattered and scanty fragments, among influences of a rather inharmonious sort. It was cattle-market in the little town as I passed up the main street, and a savour of hoofs and hide seemed to accompany me through the easy labyrinth of the old arches and piers. These occupy a large back yard, close behind the street, to which you are most prosaically admitted by a young woman who keeps a wicket and sells tickets. The continuity of tradition is not altogether broken, however, for the little street of Glastonbury has rather an old-time aspect, and one of the houses at least must have seen the last of the abbots ride abroad on his mule. The little inn is a capital bit of character, and as I waited for the 'bus under its low dark archway (in something of the mood, possibly, in which a train was once waited for at Coventry), and watched the barmaid flirting her way to and fro out of the heavy-browed kitchen and among the lounging young appraisers of colts and steers and barmaids, I might have imagined that the Merry England of the Tudors had not utterly passed away. A beautiful England this must have been as well, if it contained many such abbeys as Glastonbury. Such of the ruined columns and portals and windows as still remain are of admirable design and finish. The doorways are rich in marginal ornament—ornament within ornament, as it often is; for the dainty weeds and wild flowers overlace the antique tracery with their bright arabesques and deepen the gray of the stone-work as it brightens their bloom. The thousand flowers which grow among English ruins deserve a chapter to themselves. I owe them, as an observer, a heavy debt of satisfaction, but I am too little of a botanist to pay them in their own coin. It has often seemed to me in England that the purest enjoyment of architecture was to be had among the ruins of great buildings. In the perfect building one is rarely sure that the impression is simply architectural: it is more or less pictorial and romantic; it depends partly upon association and partly upon various accessories and details which, however they may be wrought into harmony with the architectural idea, are not part of its essence and spirit. But in so far as beauty of structure is beauty of line and curve, balance and harmony of masses and dimensions, I have seldom relished it as deeply as on the grassy nave of some crumbling church, before lonely columns and empty windows where the wild flowers were a cornice and the sailing clouds a roof. The arts certainly hang together in what they do for us. These hoary relics of Glastonbury reminded me in their broken eloquence of one of the other great ruins of the world—the *Last Supper* of Leonardo. A beautiful shadow, in each case, is all that remains; but that shadow is the soul of the artist.

Salisbury Cathedral, to which I made a pilgrimage on leaving Wells, is the very reverse of a ruin, and you take your pleasure there on very different grounds from those I have just attempted to define. It is perhaps the best-known typical church in the world, thanks to its shapely spire; but the spire is so simply and obviously fair that when you have respectfully made a note of it you have anticipated aesthetic analysis. I had seen it before and admired it heartily, and perhaps I should have done as well to let my admiration rest. I confess that on repeated inspection it grew to seem to me the least bit *banal*, or even *bête*, since I am talking French, and I began to consider whether it does not belong to the same range of art as the Apollo Belvedere or the Venus de' Medici. I am inclined to think that if I had to live within sight of a cathedral and encounter it in my daily comings and goings I should grow less weary of the rugged black front of Exeter than of the sweet perfection of Salisbury. There are people by temperament easily sated with beauties specifically fair, and the effect of Salisbury Cathedral architecturally is equivalent to that of flaxen hair and blue eyes physiognomically. The other lions of Salisbury, Stonehenge and Wilton House, I revisited with undiminished interest. Stonehenge is rather a hackneyed shrine of pilgrimage. At the time of my former visit a picnic-party was making libations of beer on the dreadful altar-sites. But the mighty mystery of the place has not yet been stared out of countenance; and as on this occasion there were no picnickers we were left to drink deep of all its ambiguities and intensities. It stands as lonely in history as it does on the great plain whose many-tinted green waves, as they roll away from it, seem to symbolise the ebb of the long centuries which have left it so portentously unexplained. You may put a hundred questions to these rough-hewn giants as they bend in grim contemplation of their fallen companions; but your curiosity falls dead in the vast sunny stillness that enshrouds them, and the strange monument, with all its unspoken memories, becomes simply a heart-stirring picture in a land of pictures. It is indeed immensely vague and immensely deep. At a distance you see it standing in a shallow dell of the plain, looking hardly larger than a group of ten-pins on a bowling-green. I can fancy sitting all a summer's day watching its shadows shorten and lengthen again, and drawing a delicious contrast between the world's duration and the feeble span of individual experience. There is something in Stonehenge almost reassuring to the nerves; if you are disposed to feel that the life of man has rather a thin surface and, that we soon get to the bottom of things, the immemorial gray pillars may serve to represent for you the pathless vaults beneath the house of history. Salisbury is indeed rich in antiquities. Wilton House, a delightful old residence of the Earls of Pembroke, contains a noble collection of Greek and Roman marbles. These are ranged round a charming cloister occupying the centre of the house, which is exhibited in the most liberal fashion. Out of the cloister opens a series of drawing-rooms hung with family portraits, chiefly by Vandyck, all of superlative merit. Among them hangs supreme, as the Vandyck *par excellence*, the famous and magnificent group of the whole Pembroke family of James I's time. This splendid work has every pictorial merit—design, colour, elegance, force and finish, and I have been vainly wondering to this hour what it needs to be the finest piece of portraiture, as it surely is one of the most ambitious, in the world. What it lacks, characteristically, in a certain uncompromising veracity, it recovers in the beautiful dignity of its position—unmoved from the stately house in which its author sojourned and wrought, familiar to the descendants of its noble originals.

An English Easter

I

I T may be said of the English, as is said of the council of war in Sheridan's farce of *The Critic* by one of the spectators of the rehearsal, that when they *do* agree, their unanimity is wonderful. They differ among themselves greatly just now as regards the machinations of Russia, the derelictions of Turkey, the merits of the Reverend Arthur Tooth, the genius of Mr Henry Irving, and a good many other matters; but neither just now nor at any other time do they fail to conform to those social observances on which respectability has set her seal. England is a country of curious anomalies, and this has much to do with her being so interesting to foreign observers. The national, the individual character is very positive, very independent, very much made up according to its own sentiment of things, very prone to startling eccentricities; and yet at the same time it has beyond any other this peculiar gift of squaring itself with fashion and custom. In no other country, I imagine, are so many people to be found doing the same thing in the same way at the same time—using the same slang, wearing the same hats and neckties, collecting the same china-plates, playing the same game of lawn-tennis or of polo, admiring the same professional beauty. The monotony of such a spectacle would soon become oppressive if the foreign observer were not conscious of this latent capacity in the performers for great freedom of action; he finds a good deal of entertainment in wondering how they reconcile the traditional insularity of the private person with this perpetual tribute to usage. Of course in all civilised societies the tribute to usage is constantly paid; if it is less apparent in America than elsewhere the reason is not, I think, because individual independence is greater, but because usage is more sparsely established. Where custom can be ascertained people certainly follow it; but for one definite precedent in American life there are fifty in English. I am very far from having discovered the secret; I have not in the least learned what becomes of that explosive personal force in the English character which is compressed and corked down by social conformity. I look with a certain awe at some of the manifestations of the conforming spirit, but the fermenting idiosyncrasies beneath it are hidden from my vision. The most striking example, to foreign eyes, of the power of custom in England is certainly the universal church-going. In the sight of the English people getting up from its tea and toast of a Sunday morning and brushing its hat, and drawing on its gloves, and taking its wife on its arm, and making its offspring march before, and so, for decency's, respectability's, propriety's sake, wending its way to a place of worship appointed by the State, in which it repeats the formulas of a creed to which it attaches no positive sense and listens to a sermon over the length of which it explicitly haggles and grumbles—in this exhibition there is something very impressive to a stranger, something which he hardly knows whether to estimate as a great force or as a great futility. He inclines on the whole to pronounce the spectacle sublime, because it gives him the feeling that whenever it may become necessary for a people trained in these manoeuvres to move all together under a common direction, they will have it in them to do so with tremendous weight and cohesiveness. We hear a good deal about the effect of the Prussian military system in consolidating the German people and making them available for a particular purpose; but I really think it not fanciful to say that the military punctuality which characterises the English observance of Sunday ought to be appreciated in the same fashion. A nation which has passed through such a mill will certainly have been stamped by it. And here, as in the German military service, it is really the whole nation. When I spoke just now of paterfamilias and his *entourage* I did not mean to limit the statement to him. The young unmarried men go to church, the gay bachelors, the irresponsible members of society. (That last epithet must be taken with a grain of allowance. No one in England is literally irresponsible; that perhaps is the shortest way of expressing a stranger's, certainly an American's, sense of their cohesion. Every one is free and every one is responsible. To say what it is people are responsible *to* is of

course a great extension of the question: briefly, to social expectation, to propriety, to morality, to 'position', to the conventional
English conscience, which is, after all, such a powerful factor.
With us there is infinitely less responsibility; but there is also, I
think, less freedom.)

The way in which the example of the more luxurious classes im-
poses itself upon the less luxurious may of course be noticed in
smaller matters than church-going; in a great many matters which
it may seem trivial to mention. If one is bent upon observation
nothing, however, is trivial. So I may cite the practice of banishing
the servants from the room at breakfast. It is the fashion, and accordingly, through the length and breadth of England, every one
who has the slightest pretension to standing high enough to feel
the way the social breeze is blowing conforms to it. It is awkward,
unnatural, troublesome for those at table, it involves a vast amount
of leaning and stretching, of waiting and perambulating, and it has
just that vice against which, in English history, all great movements have been made—it is arbitrary. But it flourishes for all that,
and all genteel people, looking into each other's eyes with the des-
peration of gentility, agree to endure it for gentility's sake. My instance may seem feeble, and I speak honestly when I say I might
give others, forming part of an immense body of prescriptive usage,
to which a society possessing in the largest manner, both by temperament and education, the sense of the 'inalienable' rights and
comforts of the individual, contrives to accommodate itself. I do
not mean to say that usage in England is always uncomfortable and
arbitrary. On the contrary, few strangers can be unfamiliar with
that sensation (a most agreeable one) which consists in perceiving
in the rigidity of a tradition which has struck one at first as mechanical a reason existing in the historic 'good sense' of the English race.
The sensation is frequent, though in saying so I do not mean to
imply that even superficially the presumption is against the usages
of English society. It is not, for instance, necessarily against the
custom of which I had it more especially in mind to speak in writing
these lines. The stranger in London is forewarned that at Easter all
the world goes out of town, and that if he have no mind to be left
to some fate the universal terror of which half allures half appals

his curiosity, he too had better make arrangements for a temporary absence. It must be admitted that there is a sort of unexpectedness in this prompt re-emigration of a body of people who but a week before were apparently devoting much energy to settling down for the season. Half of them have but lately come back from the country, where they have been spending the winter, and they have just had time, it may be supposed, to collect the scattered threads of town-life. Presently, however, the threads are dropped and society is dispersed as if it had taken a false start. It departs as Holy Week draws to a close, and remains absent for the following ten days. Where it goes is its own affair: a good deal of it goes to Paris. Spending last winter in that city, I remember how, when I woke up on Easter Monday and looked out of my window, I found the street covered overnight with a sort of snow-fall of disembarked Britons. They made for other people an uncomfortable week of it. One's customary table at the restaurant, one's habitual stall at the Théâtre Français, one's usual fiacre on the cab-stand, were very apt to have suffered estrangement. I believe the pilgrimage to Paris was this year of the usual proportions; and you may be sure that people who did not cross the Channel were not without invitations to quiet old places in the country, where the pale fresh primroses were beginning to light up the dark turf and the purple bloom of the bare tree-masses to be freckled here and there with verdure. In England country-life is the obverse of the medal, town-life the reverse, and when an occasion comes for quitting London there are few members of what the French call the 'easy class' who have not a collection of dull, moist, verdant resorts to choose from. Dull I call them, and I fancy not without reason, though at the moment I speak of their dulness must have been mitigated by the unintermittent presence of the keenest and liveliest of east winds. Even in mellow English country homes Easter-tide is a period of rawness and atmospheric acridity—the moment at which the frank hostility of winter, which has at last to give up the game, turns to peevishness and spite. This is what makes it arbitrary, as I said just now, for 'easy' people to go forth to the wind-swept lawns and the shivering parks. But nothing is more striking to an American than the frequency of English holidays and the large way in which occasions for a 'little change' are made use of. All this speaks to Americans of three things which they are accustomed to see allotted in scantier measure. The English have more time than we, they have more money, and they have a much higher relish for active leisure. Leisure, fortune, and the love of sport are felicities encountered in English society at every turn. It was a very small number of weeks before Easter that Parliament met, and yet a ten days' recess was already, from the luxurious Parliamentary point of view, a necessity. A short time hence we shall be having the Whitsuntide holidays, which I am told are even more of a season of revelry than Easter, and from this point to midsummer, when everything stops, is an easy journey. The men of business and the professional men partake in equal measure of these agreeable diversions, and I was interested in hearing a lady whose husband was an active member of the bar say that, though he was leaving town with her for ten days, and though Easter was a very nice 'little break', they really amused themselves more during the later festival, which would come on toward the end of May. I thought this highly probable, and admired in their career such an effect of breeze-blown light and shade. If my phrase has a slightly ironical sound, this is purely accidental. A large appetite for holidays, the ability not only to take them but to know what to do with them when taken, is the sign of a robust people, and judged by this measure we Americans are sadly inexpert. Such holidays as we take are taken very often in Europe, where it is sometimes noticeable that our privilege is rather heavy on our hands. Acknowledgment made of English industry, however (our own stands in no need of compliments), it must be added that for those same easy classes I just spoke of things are very easy indeed. The number of persons obtainable for purely social purposes at all times and seasons is infinitely greater than among ourselves; and the ingenuity of the arrangements permanently going forward to disembarrass them of their superfluous leisure is as yet in America an undeveloped branch of civilisation. The young men who are preparing for the stern realities of life among the gray-green cloisters of Oxford are obliged to keep their terms but half the year; and the rosy little cricketers of Eton and Harrow are let loose upon the parental home for an embarrassing number of months. Happily the parental home is apt to be an affair of gardens, lawns and parks.

II

Passion Week, in London, is distinctly an ascetic period; there is really an approach to sackcloth and ashes. Private dissipation is suspended; most of the theatres and music-halls are closed; the huge dusky city seems to take on a still sadder colouring and a half-hearted hush steals over its mighty uproar. At such a moment, for a stranger, London is not cheerful. Arriving there, during the past winter, about Christmas-time, I encountered three British Sundays in a row—a spectacle to strike terror into the stoutest heart. A Sunday and a 'bank-holiday', if I remember aright, had joined hands with a Christmas Day and produced the portentous phenomenon to which I allude. I betrayed, I suppose, some apprehension of its oppressive character, for I remember being told in a consolatory way that I needn't fear; it would not come round again for another year. This information was given me on the occasion of that surprising interruption of one's relations with the laundress which is apparently characteristic of the period. I was told that all the washer-women were intoxicated and that, as it would take them some time to revive, I must not count upon a relay of 'fresh things'. I shall not forget the impression made upon me by this statement; I had just come from Paris and it almost sent me spinning back. One of the incidental *agréments* of life in the latter city had been the knock at my door on Saturday evenings of a charming young woman with a large basket protected by a snowy napkin on her arm, and on her head a frilled and fluted muslin cap which was an irresistible advertisement of her art. To say that my admirable *blanchisseuse* was not in liquor is altogether too gross a compliment; but I was always grateful to her for her russet cheek, her frank expressive eye, her talkative smile, for the way her charming cap was poised upon her crisp, dense hair and her well-made dress adjusted and worn. I talked with her; I *could* talk with her; and as she talked she moved about and laid out her linen with a delightful modest ease. Then her light step carried her off again, talking, to the door, and with a brighter smile and an 'Adieu, monsieur!' she closed it behind her, leaving one to think how stupid is prejudice and how poetic a creature a washerwoman may be. London, in December, was livid with sleet and fog, and against this dismal background was offered me the vision of a horrible old woman in a smoky bonnet, lying prone in a puddle of whisky! She seemed to assume a kind of symbolic significance and almost frightened me away.

I mention this trifle, which is doubtless not creditable to my fortitude, because I found that the information given me was not strictly accurate and that at the end of three months I had another array of London Sundays to face. On this occasion, however, nothing occurred to suggest again the dreadful image I have just sketched, though I devoted a good deal of time to observing the manners of the lower orders. From Good Friday to Easter Monday, inclusive, they were very much *en évidence*, and it was an excellent occasion for getting an impression of the British populace. Gentility had retired to the background, and in the West End all the blinds were lowered; the streets were void of carriages, and well-dressed pedestrians were rare; but the 'masses' were all abroad and making the most of their holiday, so that I strolled about and watched them at their gambols. The heavens were most unfavourable, but in an English 'outing' there is always a margin left for a drenching, and throughout the vast smoky city, beneath the shifting gloom of the sky, the grimy crowds wandered with a kind of weather-proof stolidity. The parks were full of them, the railway stations overflowed, the Thames embankment was covered. The 'masses', I think, are usually an entertaining spectacle, even when observed through the distorting medium of London bad weather. There are indeed few things in their way more impressive than a dusky London holiday; it suggests so many and such interestingly related reflections. Even looked at superficially the capital of the Empire is one of the most appealing of cities, and it is perhaps on such occasions as this that I have most felt its appeal. London is ugly, dusky, dreary, more destitute than any European city of graceful and decorative incident; and though on festal days, like those I speak of, the populace is massed in large numbers at certain points, many of the streets are empty enough of human life to enable you to perceive their intrinsic want of charm. A Christmas Day or a Good Friday uncovers the ugliness of London. As you walk along the streets, having no fellow pedestrians to look at, you look up at the brown brick house-walls, corroded with soot and fog, pierced with their straight stiff window-slits, and finished, by way of a cornice, with a little black line resembling a slice of curbstone. There is not an accessory, not a touch of architectural fancy, not the narrowest concession to beauty. If I were a foreigner it would make me rabid; being an Anglo-Saxon I find in it what Thackeray found in Baker Street—a delightful proof of English domestic virtue, of the sanctity of the British home. There are miles and miles of these edifying monuments, and it would seem that a city made up of them should have no claim to that larger effectiveness of which I just now spoke. London, however, is not made up of them; there are architectural combinations of a statelier kind, and the impression moreover does not rest on details. London is pictorial in spite of details—from its dark green, misty parks, the way the light comes down leaking and filtering from its cloud-ceiling, and the softness and richness of tone which objects put on in such an atmosphere as soon as they begin to recede. Nowhere is there such a play of light and shade, such a struggle of sun and smoke, such aerial gradations and confusions. To eyes addicted to such contemplations this is a constant diversion, and yet this is only part of it. What completes the effect of the place is its appeal to the feelings, made in so many ways, but made above all by agglomerated immensity. At any given point London looks huge; even in narrow corners you have a sense of its hugeness, and petty places acquire interest from their being parts of so mighty a whole. Nowhere else is so much human life gathered together, and nowhere does it press upon you with so many suggestions. These are not all of an exhilarating kind; far from it. But they are of every possible kind, and that is the interest of London. Those that were most forcible during the showery Easter season were certain of the more perplexing and depressing ones; but even with these was mingled a brighter strain.

I walked down to Westminster Abbey on Good Friday afternoon

—walked from Piccadilly across the Green Park and through that of St James. The parks were densely filled with the populace—the elder people shuffling about the walks and the poor little smutty-faced children sprawling over the dark damp turf. When I reached the Abbey I found a dense group of people about the entrance, but I squeezed my way through them and succeeded in reaching the threshold. Beyond this it was impossible to advance, and I may add that it was not desirable. I put my nose into the church and promptly withdrew it. The crowd was terribly compact, and beneath the Gothic arches the odour was not that of incense. I gradually gave it up, with that very modified sense of disappointment that one feels in London at being crowded out of a place. This is a frequent form of philosophy, for you soon learn that there are, selfishly speaking, too many people. Human life is cheap; your fellow mortals are too numerous. Wherever you go you make the observation. At the theatre, at a concert, an exhibition, a reception, you always find that, before you arrive, there are people enough in the field. You are a tight fit in your place, wherever you find it; you have too many companions and competitors. You feel yourself at times in danger of thinking meanly of the human personality; numerosity, as it were, swallows up quality, and the perpetual sense of other elbows and knees begets a yearning for the desert. This is the reason why the perfection of luxury in England is to own a 'park'—an artificial solitude. To get one's self into the middle of a few hundred acres of oak-studded turf and to keep off the crowd by the breadth, at least, of the grassy shade, is to enjoy a comfort which circumstances make peculiarly precious. But I walked back through the profane pleasure-grounds of London, in the midst of 'superfluous herds', and I found the profit of vision that I never fail to derive from a great English assemblage. The English are, on the whole, to my eyes so appreciably the handsomest people in Europe—remembering always, of course, that when we talk of the frequency of beauty anywhere we talk of a minor quantity, more small or less small—that it takes some effort of the imagination to believe that the appearance requires demonstration. I never see a large number of them without feeling this impression confirmed; though I hasten to add that I have sometimes felt it to be much shaken in the presence of a limited group. I suspect that a great English crowd would yield a larger percentage of *regular* faces and tall figures than any other. With regard to the upper class I suppose this is generally granted; but, with all abatements, I should extend it to the people at large. Certainly, if the English populace strike the observer as regular, nature, in them, must have clung hard to the higher ideal. They are as ill-dressed as their betters are well-dressed, and their garments have that sooty surface which has nothing in common with the continental costume of labour and privation. It is the hard prose of misery—an ugly and hopeless imitation of respectable attire. This is especially noticeable in the battered and bedraggled bonnets of the women, which look as if their husbands had stamped on them, in hob-nailed boots, as a hint of what may be in store for their wearers. Then it is not too much to say that two-thirds of the London faces, as the streets present them, bear in some degree or other the traces of alcoholic action. The proportion of flushed, empurpled, eruptive masks is considerable; a source of depression, for the spectator, not diminished by the fact that many of the faces thus disfigured have evidently been planned on lines of high superficial decency. A very large allowance is to be made, too, for the people who bear the distinctive stamp of that physical and mental degradation which comes from the slums and purlieus of this duskiest of modern Babylons—the pallid, stunted, misbegotten and in every way miserable figures. These people swarm in every London crowd, and I know of none in any other place that suggest an equal depth of degradation. But when such exceptions are taken the observer still notes the quantity and degree of facial finish, the firmness of type, if not always its fineness, the clearnesses and symmetries, the modelled brows and cheeks and chins, the immense contribution made to his impression, above all, by the elements of complexion and stature. The question of expression is another matter, and one must admit at the outset, to have done with it, that expression here in general lacks, even to strangeness, any perceptible intensity, though it often has among the women, and adorably among the children, an indescribable shy delicacy. I have it at heart, however, to add that if the English are handsomer than ourselves they are also very much uglier. Indeed I think all the European peoples more richly ugly than the American: we are far from producing those magnificent types of facial eccentricity which flourish on soils socially more rank. American ugliness is on the side of physical poverty and meanness; English on that of redundancy and monstrosity. In America there are few grotesques; in England there are many—and some of them have a high plastic, historic, romantic value.

III

The element of the grotesque was very noticeable to me in the most marked collection of the shabbier English types that I had seen since I came to London. The occasion of my seeing them was the funeral of Mr George Odger, which befell some four or five weeks before the Easter period. Mr George Odger, it will perhaps be remembered, was an English Radical agitator of humble origin, who had distinguished himself by a perverse desire to get into Parliament. He exercised, I believe, the useful profession of shoemaker, and he knocked in vain at the door that opens but to the refined. But he was a useful and honourable man, and his own people gave him an honourable burial. I emerged accidentally into Piccadilly at the moment they were so engaged, and the spectacle was one I should have been sorry to miss. The crowd was enormous, but I managed to squeeze through it and to get into a hansom cab that was drawn up beside the pavement, and here I looked on as from a box at the play. Though it was a funeral that was going on I will not call it a tragedy; but it was a very serious comedy. The day happened to be magnificent—the finest of the year. The ceremony had been taken in hand by the classes who are socially unrepresented in Parliament, and it had the character of a great popular manifestation. The hearse was followed by very few carriages, but the *cortège* of pedestrians stretched away in the sunshine, up and down the classic decorum of Piccadilly, on a scale highly impressive. Here and there the line was broken by a small brass band—apparently one of those bands of itinerant Germans that play for coppers beneath lodging-house windows; but for the rest it was compactly made up of what the newspapers call the dregs of the population. It was the London rabble, the metropolitan mob, men and women, boys and girls, the decent poor and the indecent, who had scrambled into the ranks as they gathered them up on their passage, and were making a sort of solemn 'lark' of it. Very solemn it all was—perfectly proper and undemonstrative. They shuffled along in an interminable line, and as I looked at them out of the front of my hansom I seemed to be having a sort of panoramic view of the under side, the wrong side, of the London world. The procession was filled with figures which seemed never to have 'shown out', as the English say, before; of strange, pale, mouldy paupers who blinked and stumbled in the Piccadilly sunshine. I have no space to describe them more minutely, but I found the whole affair vaguely yet portentously suggestive. My impression rose not simply from the radical, or, as I may say for the sake of colour, the revolutionary, emanation of this dingy concourse, lighted up by the ironic sky; but from the same causes I had observed a short time before, on the day the Queen went to open Parliament, when in Trafalgar Square, looking straight down into Westminster and over the royal procession, were gathered a group of banners and festoons inscribed in big staring letters with mottoes and sentiments which might easily have given on the nerves of a sensitive police department. They were mostly in allusion to the Tichborne claimant, whose release from his dungeon they peremptorily demanded and whose cruel fate was taken as a pretext for several sweeping reflections on the social arrangements of the time and country. These signals of unreason were allowed to sun themselves as freely as if they had been the manifestoes of the Irish Giant or the Oriental Dwarf at a fair. I had lately come from Paris, where the authorities have a shorter patience and where revolutionary placards at the base of the obelisk in the Place de la Concorde fall in with no recognised scheme—such is the effect of the whirligig of time—of the grand style or of monumental decorum. I was therefore the more struck on both of the occasions I speak of with the admirable English practice of letting people alone—with the frank good sense and the frank good humour and even the frank good taste of it. It was this that I found impressive as I watched the manifestation of Mr Odger's underfed partisans—the fact that the mighty mob could march along and do its errand while the excellent

quiet policemen—eternal, imperturbable, positively lovable reminders of the national temperament—stood by simply to see that
the channel was kept clear and comfortable.

When Easter Monday came it was obvious that every one (save
Mr Odger's friends—three or four million or so) had gone out of
town. There was hardly a pair of shutters in the West End that was
not closed; there was not a bell that it was any use to pull. The
weather was detestable, the rain incessant, and the fact that all your
friends were away gave you plenty of leisure to reflect that the
country must be the reverse of enlivening. But all your friends had
gone thither (this is the unanimity I began by talking about), and
to restrict as much as possible the proportions of that game of
hide-and-seek of which, at the best, so much of London social life
consists, it seemed wise to bring within the limits of the dull season
any such excursion as might have been projected in commemoration
of the first days of spring. After due cogitation I paid a little visit
to Canterbury and Dover, taking Rochester by the way, and it was
of this momentous journey that I proposed, in beginning these remarks, to give an account. But I have dallied so much by the way
that I have come almost to my rope's end without reaching my first
stage. I should have begun, artistically, by relating that I put myself
in the humour for remote adventure by going down the Thames
on a penny steamboat to the towers of Julius. This was on the
Saturday before Easter, and the City was as silent as the grave.
'London's lasting shame' was a memory of my childhood, and,
having a theory that from such memories the dust of the ages had
better not be shaken, I had not retraced my steps to its venerable
walls. But the Tower—*the* Tower—is very good, and much less
cockneyfied than I supposed it would seem to my maturer vision;
very gray and historical, with the look that vivifies (rather lividly
indeed) the past. I could not get into it, as it had been closed for
Passion Week, but I was consequently relieved from the obligation
to march about with a dozen fellow starers in the train of a didactic
beefeater, and I strolled at will through the courts and the garden,
sharing them only with the lounging soldiers of the garrison, who
seemed to connect the place, for the backward-reaching fancy, with
important events.

IV

At Rochester I stopped for the sake of its castle, which I espied from the railway-train as it perched on a grassy bank beside the widening Medway. There were other beguilements as well; the place has a small cathedral, and, leaving the creators of Falstaff and of the tale-telling Pilgrims out of the question, one had read about it in Dickens, whose house of Gadshill was a couple of miles from the town. All this Kentish country, between London and Dover, figures indeed repeatedly in Dickens; he expresses to a certain extent, for our later age, the spirit of the land. I found this to be quite the case at Rochester. I had occasion to go into a little shop kept by a talkative old woman who had a photograph of Gadshill lying on her counter. This led to my asking her whether the illustrious master of the house had often, to her old-time vision, made his appearance in the town. 'Oh, bless you, sir,' she said, 'we every one of us knew him to speak to. He was in this very shop on the Tuesday with a party of foreigners—as he was dead in his bed on the Friday.' (I should remark that I probably do not repeat the days of the week as she gave them.) 'He 'ad on his black velvet suit, and it always made him look so 'andsome. I said to my 'usband, "I *do* think Charles Dickens looks so nice in that black velvet suit." But he said he couldn't see as he looked any way particular. He was in this very shop on the Tuesday, with a party of foreigners.' Rochester consists of little more than one long street, stretching away from the castle and the river toward neighbouring Chatham, and edged with low brick houses, of intensely provincial aspect, most of which have some small, dull smugness or quaintness of gable or window. Nearly opposite to the shop of the old lady with the snubby husband is a little dwelling with an inscribed slab set into its face, which must often have provoked a smile in the great master of the comic. The slab relates that in the year 1579 Richard Watts here established a charity which should furnish 'six poor travellers, not rogues or proctors', one night's lodging and entertainment gratis, and fourpence in the morning to go on their way withal, and that in memory of his 'munificence' the stone has lately been renewed. The inn at Rochester had small hospitality, and I felt strongly tempted to knock at the door of Mr Watts's asylum, under plea of being neither a rogue nor a proctor. The poor traveller who avails himself of the testamentary fourpence may easily resume his journey as far as Chatham without breaking his treasure. Is not this the place where little Davy Copperfield slept under a cannon on his journey from London to Dover to join his aunt Miss Trotwood? The two towns are really but one, which forms an interminable crooked thoroughfare, lighted up in the dusk, as I measured it up and down, with the red coats of the vespertinal soldier quartered at the various barracks of Chatham.

The cathedral of Rochester is small and plain, hidden away in rather an awkward corner, without a verdant close to set it off. It is dwarfed and effaced by the great square Norman keep of the adjacent castle. But within it is very charming, especially beyond the detestable wall, the vice of almost all the English cathedrals, which shuts in the choir and breaks the sacred perspective of the aisle. Here, as at Canterbury, you ascend a high range of steps, to pass through the small door in the wall. When I speak slightingly, by the way, of the outside of Rochester cathedral, I intend my faint praise in a relative sense. If we were so happy as to have this secondary pile within reach in America we should go barefoot to see it; but here it stands in the great shadow of Canterbury, and that makes it humble. I remember, however, an old priory gateway which leads you to the church, out of the main street; I remember a kind of haunted-looking deanery, if that be the technical name, at the base of the eastern walls; I remember a fluted tower that took the afternoon light and let the rooks and the swallows come circling and clamouring around it. Better still than these things I remember the ivy-muffled squareness of the castle, a very noble and imposing ruin. The old walled precinct had been converted into a little public garden, with flowers and benches and a pavilion for a band, and the place was not empty, as such places in England never are. The result is agreeable, but I believe the process was barbarous, involving the destruction and dispersion of many interesting portions of the ruin. I lingered there for a long time, looking in the fading light at what was left. This rugged pile of Norman masonry will be left when a great many solid things have departed; it mocks, ever so monotonously, at destruction, at decay. Its walls are fantastically thick; their great time-bleached expanses and all their rounded roughnesses, their strange mixture of softness and grimness, have an undefinable fascination for the eye. English ruins always come out peculiarly when the day begins to fail. Weather-bleached, as I say they are, they turn even paler in the twilight and grow consciously solemn and spectral. I have seen many a mouldering castle, but I remember in no single mass of ruin more of the helpless, bereaved, amputated look.

It is not the absence of a close that damages Canterbury; the cathedral stands amid grass and trees, with a cultivated margin all round it, and is placed in such a way that, as you pass out from under the gatehouse, you appreciate immediately its grand feature—its extraordinary and magnificent length. None of the English cathedrals seems to sit more gravely apart, to desire more to be shut up to itself. It is a long walk, beneath the walls, from the gateway of the close to the farther end of the last chapel. Of all that there is to observe in this upward-gazing stroll I can give no detailed account; I can, in my fear to pretend to dabble in the esoteric constructional question—often so combined with an absence of other felt relations —speak only of the picture, the mere builded *scene*. This is altogether delightful. None of the rivals of Canterbury has a more complicated and elaborate architecture, a more perplexing intermixture of periods, a more charming jumble of Norman arches and English points and perpendiculars. What makes the side-view superb, moreover, is the double transepts, which produce the finest agglomeration of gables and buttresses. It is as if two great churches had joined forces toward the middle—one giving its nave and the other its choir, and each keeping its own great cross-aisles. Astride of the roof, between them, sits a huge Gothic tower, which is one of the latest portions of the building, though it looks like one of the earliest, so tempered and tinted, so thumb-marked and rubbed smooth is it, by the handling of the ages and the breath of the elements. Like the rest of the structure it has a magnificent colour—a sort of rich dull yellow, a sort of personal accent of tone that is neither brown nor gray. This is particularly appreciable from the cloisters on the further side of the church—the side, I mean, away from the town and the open garden-sweep I spoke of; the side that looks toward a damp old clerical house, lurking behind a brown archway through which you see young ladies in Gainsborough hats playing something on a patch of velvet turf; the side, in short, that is somehow intermingled with a green quadrangle—a quadrangle serving as a playground to a King's School and adorned externally with a very precious and picturesque old fragment of Norman staircase. This cloister is not 'kept up'; it is very dusky and mouldy and dilapidated, and of course very sketchable. The old black arches and capitals are various and handsome, and in the centre are tumbled together a group of crooked gravestones, themselves almost buried in the deep soft grass. Out of the cloister opens the chapter-house, which is not kept up either, but which is none the less a magnificent structure; a noble lofty hall, with a beautiful wooden roof, simply arched like that of a tunnel, without columns or brackets. The place is now given up to dust and echoes; but it looks more like a banqueting-hall than a council-room of priests, and as you sit on the old wooden bench, which, raised on two or three steps, runs round the base of the four walls, you may gaze up and make out the faint ghostly traces of decorative paint and gold upon the brown ceiling. A little patch of this has been restored 'to give an idea'. From one of the angles of the cloister you are recommended by the verger to take a view of the great tower, which indeed detaches itself with tremendous effect. You see it base itself upon the roof as broadly as if it were striking roots in earth, and then pile itself away to a height which seems to make the very swallows dizzy as they drop from the topmost shelf. Within the cathedral you hear a great deal, of course, about poor great Thomas A'Becket, and the special sensation of the place is to stand on the spot where he was murdered and look down at a small fragmentary slab which the verger points out to you as a bit of the pavement that caught the blood-drops of the struggle. It was late in the afternoon when I first entered the church; there had been a service in the choir, but that was well over, and I had the place to myself. The verger, who had some pushing-about of benches to attend to, turned me into the locked gates and left me to wander through the side-aisles of the choir and into the great chapel beyond it. I say I had the place to myself; but it would be more decent to affirm that I shared it, in particular, with another gentleman. This personage was stretched upon a couch of stone, beneath a quaint old canopy of wood; his hands were crossed upon his breast, and his pointed toes rested upon a little griffin or leopard. He was a very handsome fellow and the image of a gallant knight. His name was Edward Plantagenet, and his sobriquet was the Black Prince. '*De la mort ne pensai-je mye*', he says in the beautiful inscription embossed upon the bronze base of his image; and I too, as I stood there, lost the sense of death in a momentary impression of personal nearness to him. One had been further off, after all, from other famous knights. In this same chapel, for many a year, stood the shrine of St Thomas of Canterbury, one of the richest and most potent in Christendom. The pavement which lay before it has kept its place, but Henry VIII swept away everything else in his famous short cut to reform. Becket was originally buried in the crypt of the church; his ashes lay there for fifty years, and it was only little by little that his martyrdom was made a 'draw'. Then he was transplanted into the Lady Chapel; every grain of his dust became a priceless relic, and the pavement was hallowed by the knees of pilgrims. It was on this errand of course that Chaucer's story-telling cavalcade came to Canterbury. I made my way down into the crypt, which is a magnificent maze of low, dark arches and pillars, and groped about till I found the place where the frightened monks had first shuffled the inanimate victim of Moreville and Fitzurse out of the reach of further desecration. While I stood there a violent thunderstorm broke over the cathedral; great rumbling gusts and rain-drifts came sweeping through the open sides of the crypt and, mingling with the darkness which seemed to deepen and flash in corners and with the potent mouldy smell, made me feel as if I had descended into the very bowels of history. I emerged again, but the rain had settled down and spoiled the evening, and I splashed back to my inn and sat, in an uncomfortable chair by the coffee-room fire, reading Dean Stanley's agreeable 'Memorials of Canterbury' and wondering over the musty appointments and meagre resources of so many English hostels. This establishment had entitled itself in (compliment to the Black Prince, I suppose) the 'Fleur-de-Lis'. The name was very pretty (I had been foolish enough to let it attract me to the inn), but the lily was sadly deflowered.

London at Midsummer

I BELIEVE it is supposed to require a good deal of courage to confess that one has spent the month of so-called social August in London; and I will therefore, taking the bull by the horns, plead guilty at the very outset to this poorness of spirit. I might attempt some ingenious extenuation of it; I might say that my remaining in town had been the most unexpected necessity or the merest inadvertence; I might pretend I liked it—that I had done it in fact for the perverse love of the thing; I might claim that you don't really know the charms of London until on one of the dog-days you have imprinted your boot-sole in the slumbering dust of Belgravia, or, gazing along the empty vista of the Drive, in Hyde Park, have beheld, for almost the first time in England, a landscape without figures. But little would remain of these specious apologies save the bald circumstance that I had distinctly failed to pack and be off—either on the first of August with the ladies and children, or on the thirteenth with the members of Parliament, or on the twelfth when the grouse-shooting began. (I am not sure that I have got my dates right to a day, but these were about the proper opportunities.) I have, in fact, survived the departure of everything genteel, and the three millions of persons who remained behind with me have been witnesses of my shame.

I cannot pretend, on the other hand, that, having lingered in town, I have found it a very odious or painful experience. Being a stranger, I have not felt it necessary to incarcerate myself during the day and steal abroad only under cover of the darkness—a line of conduct imposed by public opinion, if I am to trust the social criticism of the weekly papers (which I am far from doing), upon the native residents who allow themselves to be overtaken by the unfashionable season. I have indeed always held that few things are pleasanter, during very hot weather, than to have a great city, and a large house within it, quite to one's self. Yet these majestic con-

ditions have not embellished my own metropolitan sojourn, and I
have received an impression that in London it would be rather
difficult for a visitor not having the command of a good deal of
powerful machinery to find them united. English summer weather
is rarely hot enough to make it necessary to darken one's house
and denude one's person. The present year has indeed in this respect been 'exceptional', as any year is, for that matter, that one
spends anywhere. But the manners of the people are, to alien eyes,
a sufficient indication that at the best (or the worst) even the highest
flights of the thermometer in the United Kingdom betray a broken
wing. People live with closed windows in August very much as
they do in January, and there is to the eye no appreciable difference
in the character—that is in the thickness and stiffness—of their coats
and boots. A 'bath' in England, for the most part, all the year
round, means a little portable tin tub and a sponge. Peaches and
pears, grapes and melons, are not a more obvious ornament of the
market at midsummer than at Christmas. This matter of peaches
and melons, by the way, offers one of the best examples of that fact
to which a commentator on English manners from afar finds himself constantly recurring, and to which he grows at last almost
ashamed of alluding—the fact that the beauty and luxury of the
country, that elaborate system known and revered all over the
world as 'English comfort', is a limited and restricted, an essentially
private, affair. I am not one of those irreverent strangers who talk
of English fruit as a rather audacious *plaisanterie*, though I could
see very well what was meant a short time since by an anecdote related to me in a tone of contemptuous generalisation by a couple of
my fellow countrywomen. They had arrived in London in the dog-
days, and, lunching at their hotel, had asked to be served with
some fruit. The hotel was of the stateliest pattern, and they were
waited upon by a functionary whose grandeur was proportionate.
This personage bowed and retired, and, after a long delay, reappear-
ing, placed before them with an inimitable gesture a dish of goose-
berries and currants. It appeared upon investigation that these acrid
vegetables were the only things of succulence that the establishment
could undertake to supply; and it seemed to increase the irony of
the situation that the establishment was as near as possible to

Buckingham Palace. I say that the heroines of my anecdote seemed disposed to generalise: this was sufficiently the case, I mean, to give me a pretext for assuring them that on a thousand fine properties the most beautiful peaches and melons were at that moment ripening either under glass or in warm old walled gardens. My auditors tossed their heads of course at the fine properties, the glass and the walled gardens; and indeed at their place of privation close to Buckingham Palace such a piece of knowledge was but scantily consoling.

It is to a more public fund of entertainment that the desultory stranger in any country chiefly appeals, especially in summer weather; and as I have implied that there is little encouragement in England to such an appeal it may appear remarkable that I should not have felt London, at this season, void of all beguilement. But one's liking for London—a stranger's liking at least—has at the best a kind of perversity and infirmity often rather difficult to reduce to a statement. I am far from meaning by this that there are not in this mighty metropolis a thousand sources of interest, entertainment and delight: what I mean is that, for one reason and another, with all its social resources, the place lies heavy on the imported consciousness. It seems grim and lurid, fierce and unmerciful. And yet the imported consciousness accepts it at last with an active satisfaction and finds something warm and comfortable, something that if removed would be greatly missed, in its portentous pressure. It must be admitted, however, that, granting that every one is out of town, your choice of pastimes is not embarrassing. If you have happened to spend a certain amount of time in places where public manners have more frankness London will seem to you but scantily provided with innocent diversions. This indeed brings us back simply to that question of the absence of a 'public fund' of amusement to which reference was just now made. You must give up the idea of going to sit somewhere in the open air, to eat an ice and listen to a band of music. You will find neither the seat, the ice, nor the band; but on the other hand, faithful at once to your interest and your detachment, you may supply the place of these delights by a little private meditation on the deep-lying causes of the English indifference to them. In such reflections nothing is idle—every grain of testimony counts; and one need therefore not be accused of jumping too suddenly from small things to great if one traces a connection between the absence of ices and music and the essentially hierarchical plan of English society. This hierarchical plan of English society is the great and ever-present fact to the mind of a stranger; there is hardly a detail of life that does not in some degree betray it. It is really only in a country in which a good deal of democratic feeling prevails that people of 'refinement', as we say in America, will be willing to sit at little round tables, on a pavement or a gravel-walk, at the door of a café. The better sort are too 'genteel' and the inferior sort too base. One must hasten to add too, in justice, that the better sort are, as a general thing, quite too well furnished with entertainments of their own; they have those special resources to which I alluded a moment since. They are persons for whom the private machinery of ease has been made to work with extraordinary smoothness. If you can sit on a terrace overlooking gardens and have your *café noir* handed you in old Worcester cups by servants who are models of consideration, you have hardly a decent pretext for going to a public-house. In France and Italy, in Germany and Spain, the count and countess will sally forth and encamp for the evening, under a row of coloured lamps, upon the paving-stones, but it is ten to one that the count and countess live on a single floor and up several pair of stairs. They are, however, I think, not appreciably affected by considerations which operate potently in England. An Englishman who should propose to sit down, in his own country, at a café door would find himself remembering that he is pretending to participations, contacts, fellowships the absolute impracticability of which is expressed in all the rest of his doings.

The study of these reasons, however, would lead us very far from the potential little tables for ices in—where shall I say?—in Oxford Street. But, after all, there is no reason why our imagination should hover about any such articles of furniture. I am afraid they would not strike us as at the best happily situated. In such matters everything hangs together, and I am certain that the customs of the Boulevard des Italiens and the Piazza Colonna would not harmonise with the scenery of the great London thoroughfare. A gin-palace right and left and a detachment of the London rabble in an admiring semicircle—these strike one as some of the more obvious features of the affair. Yet at the season of which I write one's social studies must at the least be studies of low life, for wherever one may go for a stroll or to spend the summer afternoon the comparatively sordid side of things is uppermost. There is no one in the parks save the rough characters who are lying on their faces in the sheep-polluted grass. These people are always tolerably numerous in the Green Park, through which I frequently pass, and are always an occasion for deep wonder. But your wonder will go far if it begins to bestir itself on behalf of the recumbent British tramp. You perceive among them some rich possibilities. Their velveteen legs and their colossal high-lows, their purple necks and ear-tips, their knotted sticks and little greasy hats, make them look like stage-villains of realistic melodrama. I may do them injustice, but consistent character in them mostly requires that they shall have had a taste of penal servitude—that they shall have paid the penalty of stamping on some weaker human head with those huge square heels that are turned up to the summer sky. Actually, however, they are innocent enough, for they are sleeping as peacefully as the most accomplished philanthropist, and it is their look of having walked over half England, and of being pennilessly hungry and thirsty, that constitutes their romantic attractiveness. The six square feet of brown grass are their present sufficiency; but how long will they sleep, whither will they go next, and whence did they come last? You permit yourself to wish that they might sleep for ever and go nowhere else at all.

The month of August is so uncountenanced in London that, going a few days since to Greenwich, that famous resort, I found it possible to get but half a dinner. The celebrated hotel had put out its stoves and locked up its pantry. But for this discovery I should have mentioned the little expedition to Greenwich as a charming relief to the monotony of a London August. Greenwich and Richmond are, classically, the two suburban dining-places. I know not how it may be at this time with Richmond, but the Greenwich incident brings me back (I hope not once too often) to the element of what has lately been called 'particularism' in English pleasures. It was in obedience to a perfectly logical argument that the Greenwich hotel had, as I say, locked up its pantry. All well-bred people leave London after the first week in August, *ergo* those who remain behind are not well-bred, and cannot therefore rise to the conception of a 'fish dinner'. Why then should we have anything ready? I had other impressions, fortunately, of this interesting suburb, and I hasten to declare that during the period of good-breeding the dinner at Greenwich is the most amusing of all dinners. It begins with fish and it continues with fish; what it ends with—except songs and speeches and affectionate partings—I hesitate to affirm. It is a kind of mermaid reversed; for I do know, in a vague way, that the tail of the creature is elaborately and interminably fleshy. If it were not grossly indiscreet I should risk an allusion to the particular banquet which was the occasion of my becoming acquainted with the Greenwich *cuisine*. I would try to express how pleasant it may be to sit in a company of clever and distinguished men before the large windows that look out upon the broad brown Thames. The ships swim by confidently, as if they were part of the entertainment and put down in the bill; the light of the afternoon fades ever so slowly. We eat all the fish of the sea, and wash them down with liquids that bear no resemblance to salt water. We partake of any number of those sauces with which, according to the French adage, one could swallow one's grandmother with a good conscience. To touch on the identity of my companions would indeed be indiscreet, but there is nothing indelicate in marking a high appreciation of the frankness and robustness of English conviviality. The stranger—the American at least—who finds himself in the company of a number of Englishmen assembled for a convivial purpose becomes conscious of an indefinable and delectable something which, for want of a better name, he is moved to call their superior richness of temperament. He takes note of the liberal share of the individual in the magnificent temperament of the people. This seems to him one of the finest things in the world, and his satisfaction will take a keener edge from such an incident as the single one I may permit myself to mention. It was one of those little incidents which can occur only in an old society—a society in which every one that a newly arrived observer meets strikes him as having in some degree or other a sort of historic identity, being connected with some one or something that he has heard of, that he has wondered about. If they are not the rose they have lived more or less near it. There is an old English song-writer whom we all know and admire—whose songs are sung wherever the language is spoken. Of course, according to the law I just hinted at, one of the gentlemen sitting opposite must needs be his great-grandson. After dinner there are songs, and the gentleman trolls out one of his ancestral ditties with the most charming voice and the most finished art.

I have still other memories of Greenwich, where there is a charming old park, on a summit of one of whose grassy undulations the famous observatory is perched. To do the thing completely you must take passage upon one of the little grimy sixpenny steamers that ply upon the Thames, perform the journey by water, and then, disembarking, take a stroll in the park to get up an appetite for dinner. I find an irresistible charm in any sort of river-navigation, but I scarce know how to speak of the little voyage from Westminster Bridge to Greenwich. It is in truth the most prosaic possible form of being afloat, and to be recommended rather to the inquiring than to the fastidious mind. It initiates you into the duskiness, the blackness, the crowdedness, the intensely commercial character of London. Few European cities have a finer river than the Thames, but none certainly has expended more ingenuity in producing a sordid river-front. For miles and miles you see nothing but the sooty backs of warehouses, or perhaps they are the sooty faces: in buildings so utterly expressionless it is impossible to distinguish. They stand massed together on the banks of the wide turbid stream, which is fortunately of too opaque a quality to reflect the dismal image. A damp-looking, dirty blackness is the universal tone. The river is almost black, and is covered with black barges; above the black housetops, from among the far-stretching docks and basins, rises a dusky wilderness of masts. The little puffing steamer is dingy and gritty—it belches a sable cloud that keeps you company as you go. In this carboniferous shower your companions, who belong chiefly, indeed, to the classes bereft of lustre, assume an harmonious grayness; and the whole picture, glazed over with the glutinous London mist, becomes a masterly composition. But it is very impressive in spite of its want of lightness and brightness, and though it is ugly it is anything but trivial. Like so many of the aspects of English civilisation that are untouched by elegance or grace, it has the merit of expressing something very serious. Viewed in this intellectual light the polluted river, the sprawling barges, the dead-faced warehouses, the frowsy people, the atmospheric impurities become richly suggestive. It sounds rather absurd, but all this smudgy detail may remind you of nothing less than the wealth and power of the British Empire at large; so that a kind of metaphysical magnificence hovers over the scene, and supplies what may be literally wanting. I don't exactly understand the association, but I know that when I look off to the left at the East India Docks, or pass under the dark hugely piled bridges, where the railway trains and the human processions are for ever moving, I feel a kind of imaginative thrill. The tremendous piers of the bridges, in especial, seem the very pillars of the Empire aforesaid.

It is doubtless owing to this habit of obtrusive and unprofitable reverie that the sentimental tourist thinks it very fine to see the Greenwich observatory lifting its two modest little brick towers. The sight of this useful edifice gave me a pleasure which may at first seem extravagant. The reason was simply that I used to see it as a child, in woodcuts, in school geographies, and in the corners of large maps which had a glazed, sallow surface and which were suspended in unexpected places, in dark halls and behind doors. The maps were hung so high that my eyes could reach only to the lower corners, and these corners usually contained a print of a strange-looking house perched among trees upon a grassy bank that swept down before it with the most engaging steepness. I used always to think of the joy it must be to roll at one's length down this curved incline. Close at hand was usually something printed about something being at such and such a number of degrees 'east of Greenwich'. Why east of Greenwich? The vague wonder that the childish mind felt on this point gave the place a mysterious importance and seemed to put it into relation with the difficult and fascinating parts of geography—the countries of unintentional outline and the lonely looking pages of the atlas. Yet there it stood the other day, the precise point from which the great globe is measured; there was the plain little façade with the old-fashioned cupolas;

there was the bank on which it would be so delightful not to be able to stop running. It made me feel terribly old to find that I was not even tempted to begin. There are indeed a great many steep banks in Greenwich Park, which tumbles up and down in the most adventurous fashion. It is a charming place, rather shabby and foot-worn, as befits a strictly popular resort, but with a character all its own. It is filled with magnificent foreign-looking trees, of which I know nothing but that they have a vain appearance of being chest-nuts, planted in long, convergent avenues, with trunks of extra-ordinary girth and limbs that fling a dusky shadow far over the grass; there are plenty of benches, and there are deer as tame as sleepy children; and from the tops of the bosky hillocks there are views of the widening Thames and the moving ships and the two classic inns by the waterside and the great pompous buildings, de-signed by Inigo Jones, of the old Hospital, which have been de-spoiled of their ancient pensioners and converted into a naval academy.

Taking note of all this, I arrived at a far-away angle in the wall of the park, where a little postern door stood ajar. I pushed the door open and found myself, by a thrilling transition, upon Blackheath Common. One had often heard, in vague, irrecoverable, anecdotic connections, of Blackheath: well, here it was—a great green, breezy place where lads in corduroys were playing cricket. I am, as a rule, moved to disproportionate ecstasy by an English common; it may be curtailed and cockneyfied, as this one was—which had lamp-posts stuck about on its turf and a fresh-painted banister all around —but it generally abounds in the note of English breeziness, and you always seem to have seen it water-coloured or engraved. Even if the turf be too much trodden there is to foreign eyes an intimate insular reference in it and in the day the high-piled, weather-bearing clouds hang over it and drizzle down their gray light. Still further to identify this spot, here was the British soldier emerging from two or three of the roads, with his cap upon his ear, his white gloves in one hand and his foppish little cane in the other. He wore the uniform of the artillery, and I asked him where he had come from. I learned that he had walked over from Woolwich and that this feat might be accomplished in half an hour. Inspired again by vague associations I proceeded to accomplish its equivalent. I bent my steps to Woolwich, a place which I knew, in a general way, to be a nursery of British valour. At the end of my half-hour I emerged upon another common, where the water-colour bravery had even a higher pitch. The scene was like a chapter of some forgotten record. The open grassy expanse was immense, and, the evening being beautiful, it was dotted with strolling soldiers and townsfolk. There were half a dozen cricket matches, both civil and military. At one end of this peaceful *campus martius*, which stretches over a hilltop, rises an interminable façade—one of the fronts of the Royal Artillery barracks. It has a very honourable air, and more windows and doors, I imagine, than any building in Britain. There is a great clean parade before it, and there are many sentinels pacing in front of neatly kept places of ingress to officers' quarters. Everything it looks out upon is in the smartest military trim—the distinguished college (where the poor young man whom it would perhaps be premature to call the last of the Bonapartes lately studied the art of war) on one side; a sort of model camp, a collection of the tidiest plank huts, on the other: a hospital, on a well-ventilated site, at the remoter end. And then in the town below there are a great many more military matters; barracks on an immense scale; a dockyard that presents an interminable dead wall to the street; an arsenal which the gatekeeper (who refused to admit me) declared to be 'five miles' in circumference; and, lastly, grogshops enough to inflame the most craven spirit. These latter institutions I glanced at on my way to the railway station at the bottom of the hill; but before departing I had spent half an hour in strolling about the common in vague consciousness of certain emotions that are called into play (I speak but for myself) by almost any glimpse of the imperial machinery of this great country. The glimpse may be of the slightest; it stirs a peculiar sentiment. I know not what to call this sentiment unless it be simply an admiration for the greatness of England. The greatness of England; that is a very off-hand phrase, and of course I don't pretend to use it analytically. I use it romantically, as it sounds in the ears of any American who remounts the stream of time to the head-waters of his own loyalties. I think of the great part that England has played in human affairs, the great space she has occupied, her tremendous might, her far-stretching rule. That these clumsily general ideas should be suggested by the sight of some infinitesimal fraction of the English administrative system may seem to indicate a cast of fancy too hysterical; but if so I must plead guilty to the weakness. Why should a sentry-box more or less set one thinking of the glory of this little island, which has found in her mere genius the means of such a sway? This is more than I can tell; and all I shall attempt to say is that in the difficult days that are now elapsing a sympathetic stranger finds his meditations singularly quickened. It is the imperial element in English history that he has chiefly cared for, and he finds himself wondering whether the imperial epoch is completely closed. It is a moment when all the nations of Europe seem to be doing something, and he waits to see what England, who has done so much, will do. He has been meeting of late a good many of his country-people—Americans who live on the Continent and pretend to speak with assurance of continental ways of feeling. These people have been passing through London, and many of them are in that irritated condition of mind which appears to be the portion of the American sojourner in the British metropolis when he is not given up to the delights of the historic sentiment. They have declared with assurance that the continental nations have ceased to care a straw for what England thinks, that her traditional prestige is completely extinct and that the affairs of Europe will be settled quite independently of her action and still more of her inaction. England will do nothing, will risk nothing; there is no cause bad enough for her not to find a selfish interest in it—there is no cause good enough for her to fight about it. Poor old England is defunct; it is about time she should seek the most decent burial possible. To all this the sympathetic stranger replies that in the first place he doesn't believe a word of it, and in the second doesn't care a fig for it—care, that is, what the continental nations think. If the greatness of England were really waning it would be to him as a personal grief; and as he strolls about the breezy common of Woolwich, with all those mementoes of British dominion around him, he vibrates quite too richly to be distracted by such vapours.

He wishes nevertheless, as I said before, that England would *do* something—something striking and powerful, which should be at once characteristic and unexpected. He asks himself what she can do, and he remembers that this greatness of England which he so much admires was formerly much exemplified in her 'taking' something. Can't she 'take' something now? There is the *Spectator*, who wants her to occupy Egypt: can't she occupy Egypt? The *Spectator* considers this her moral duty—inquires even whether she has a right *not* to bestow the blessings of her beneficent rule upon the down-trodden Fellaheen. I found myself in company with an acute young Frenchman a day or two after this eloquent plea for a partial annexation of the Nile had appeared in the supersubtle sheet. Some allusion was made to it, and my companion of course pronounced it the most finished example conceivable of insular hypocrisy. I don't know how powerful a defence I made of it, but while I read it I had found the hypocrisy contagious. I recalled it while I pursued my contemplations, but I recalled at the same time that sadly prosaic speech of Mr Gladstone's to which it had been a reply. Mr Gladstone had said that England had much more urgent duties than the occupation of Egypt: she had to attend to the great questions of —— What were the great questions? Those of local taxation and the liquor-laws! Local taxation and the liquor-laws! The phrase, to my ears, just then, sounded almost squalid. These were not the things I had been thinking of; it was not as she should bend anxiously over these doubtless interesting subjects that the sympathising stranger would seem to see England in his favourite posture—that, as Macaulay says, of hurling defiance at her foes. Mr Gladstone may perhaps have been right, but Mr Gladstone was far from being a sympathising stranger.

Two Excursions

I

THEY differed greatly from each other, but there was something to be said for each. There seemed in respect to the first a high consensus as to its being a pity that any stranger should ever miss the Derby day. Every one assured me that this was the great festival of the English people and that one didn't really know them unless one had seen them at it. So much, since it had to do with horse-flesh, I could readily believe. Had not the newspapers been filled for weeks with recurrent dissertations upon the animals concerned in the ceremony? and was not the event, to the nation at large, only imperceptibly less momentous than the other great question of the day—the fate of empires and the reapportionment of the East? The space allotted to sporting intelligence in a compact, eclectic, 'intellectual' journal like the *Pall Mall Gazette*, had seemed for some time past a measure of the hold of such questions upon the native mind. These things, however, are very natural in a country in which in 'society' you are liable to make the acquaintance of some such syllogism as the following. You are seated at dinner next a foreign lady who has on her other hand a communicative gentleman through whom she is under instruction in the art of the right point-of-view for English life. I profit by their conversation and I learn that this point-of-view is apparently the saddle. 'You see, English life,' says the gentleman, 'is really English country life. It's the country that is the basis of English society. And you see, country life is—well, it's the *hunting*. It's the hunting that is at the bottom of it all.' In other words 'the hunting' is the basis of English society. Duly impressed with this explanation, the American observer is prepared for the huge proportions of the annual pilgrimage to Epsom. This pilgrimage, however, I was assured, though still well worth taking part in, is by no means so

characteristic as in former days. It is now performed in a large
measure by rail, and the spectacle on the road has lost many of its
earlier and most of its finer features. The road has been given up
more and more to the populace and the strangers and has ceased
to be graced by the presence of ladies. Nevertheless, as a man and a
stranger, I was strongly recommended to take it, for the return from
the Derby is still, with all its abatements, a classic show.

I mounted upon a four-horse coach, a charming coach with a
yellow body and handsome, clean-flanked leaders; placing myself
beside the coachman, as I had been told this was the point of vantage. The coach was one of the vehicles of the new fashion—the
fashion of public conveyances driven, for the entertainment of
themselves and of the public, by gentlemen of leisure. On the
Derby day all the coaches that start from the classic headquarters—
'The White Horse' in Piccadilly—and stretch away from London
toward a dozen different and well-selected goals, had been dedicated
to the Epsom road. The body of the vehicle is empty, as no one
thinks of occupying any but one of the thirteen places on the top.
On the Derby day, however, a properly laden coach carries a company of hampers and champagne-baskets in its inside places. I must
add that on this occasion my companion was by exception a professional whip, who proved a friendly and amusing cicerone. Other
companions there were, perched in the twelve places behind me,
whose social quality I made less of a point of testing—though in
the course of the expedition their various characteristics, under the
influence of champagne, expanded so freely as greatly to facilitate
the process. We were a society of exotics—Spaniards, Frenchmen,
Germans. There were only two Britons, and these, according to my
theory, were Australians—an antipodal bride and groom on a cen-
tripetal wedding-tour.

The drive to Epsom, when you get well out of London, is sufficiently pretty; but the part of it which most took my fancy was a
district pre-eminently surburban—the classic community of Clapham. The vision of Clapham had been a part of the furniture of
one's milder historic consciousness—the vision of its respectable
common, its evangelical society, its rich drab humanity, its goodly
brick mansions of the Georgian era. I now seemed really to focus

these elements for the first time, and I thought them very charming. This epithet indeed scarcely applies to the evangelical society, which naturally, on the morning of the Derby day and during the desecrating progress of the Epsom revellers, was not much in the foreground. But all around the verdant if cockneyfied common are ranged commodious houses of a sober red complexion, from under whose neo-classic pediments you expect to see a mild-faced lady emerge—a lady in a cottage-bonnet and mittens, distributing tracts from a green silk satchel. It would take, however, the very ardour of the missionary among cannibals to stem the current of heterogeneous vehicles which at about this point takes up its metropolitan affluents and bears them in its rumbling, rattling tide. The concourse of wheeled conveyances of every possible order here becomes dense, and the spectacle from the top of the coach proportionately absorbing. You begin to perceive that the brilliancy of the road has in truth departed, and that a sustained high tone of appearance is not the note of the conditions. But when once you have grasped this fact your entertainment is continuous. You perceive that you are 'in' for the vulgar on an unsurpassable scale, something blatantly, unimaginably, heroically shocking to timid 'taste'; all that is necessary is to accept this situation and look out for illustrations. Beside you, before you, behind you, is the mighty London populace taking its *ébats*. You get for the first time a notion of the London population at large. It has piled itself into carts, into omnibuses, into every possible and impossible species of 'trap'. A large proportion of it is of course on foot, trudging along the perilous margin of the middle way in such comfort as may be gathered from fifteen miles' dodging of broken shins. The smaller the vehicle, the more rat-like the animal that drags it, the more numerous and ponderous its human freight; and as every one is nursing in his lap a parcel of provender as big as himself, wrapped in ragged newspaper, it is not surprising that roadside halts are frequent and that the taverns all the way to Epsom (it is wonderful how many there are) are encompassed by dense groups of dusty pilgrims, indulging liberally in refreshment for man and beast. And when I say man I must by no means be understood to exclude woman. The female contingent on the Derby day is not the least remarkable part of the

London outpouring. Every one is prepared for 'larks', but the women are even more brilliantly and resolutely prepared than the men; there is no better chance to follow the range of type—not that it is to be called large—of the British female of the lower orders. The lady in question is usually not ornamental. She is useful, robust, prolific, excellently fitted to play the somewhat arduous part allotted to her in the great scheme of English civilisation, but she has not those graces which enable her to lend herself easily to the decoration of life. On smaller holidays—or on simple working-days—in London crowds, I have often thought she had points to contribute to the primary fine drawing, as to head and shoulders, of the Briton of the two sexes as the race at large sketches them. But at Epsom she is too stout, too hot, too red, too thirsty, too boisterous, too strangely accoutred. And yet I wish to do her justice; so I must add that if there is something to which an American cannot refuse a tribute of admiration in the gross plebeian jollity of the Derby day, it is not evident why these dowdy Bacchantes should not get part of the credit of it. The striking thing, the interesting thing, both on the outward drive and on the return, was that the holiday was so frankly, heartily, good-humouredly taken. The people that of all peoples is habitually the most governed by decencies, proprieties, rigidities of conduct, was for one happy day unbuttoning its respectable straight-jacket and affirming its large and simple sense of the joy of life. In such a spectacle there was inevitably much that was unlucky and unprofitable; these things came uppermost chiefly on the return, when demoralisation was supreme, when the temperament of the people had begun really to take the air. For the rest, to be dressed with a kind of brutal gaudiness, to be very thirsty and violently flushed, to laugh perpetually at everything and at nothing, thoroughly to enjoy, in short, a momentous occasion—all this is not, in simple persons of the more susceptible sex, an unpardonable crime.

The course at Epsom is in itself very pretty, and disposed by nature herself in sympathetic prevision of the sporting passion. It is something like the crater of a volcano without the mountain. The outer rim is the course proper; the space within it is a vast, shallow, grassy concavity in which vehicles are drawn up and beasts tethered and in which the greater part of the multitude—the mountebanks, the betting-men and the myriad hangers-on of the scene—are congregated. The outer margin of the uplifted rim in question is occupied by the grand stand, the small stands, the paddock. The day was exceptionally beautiful; the charming sky was spotted over with little idle-looking, loafing, irresponsible clouds; the Epsom Downs went swelling away as greenly as in a coloured sporting-print, and the wooded uplands, in the middle distance, looked as innocent and pastoral as if they had never seen a policeman or a rowdy. The crowd that spread itself over this immense expanse was as rich representation of human life off its guard as one need see. One's first fate after arriving, if one is perched upon a coach, is to see the coach guided, by means best known to the coachman himself, through the tremendous press of vehicles and pedestrians, introduced into a precinct roped off and guarded from intrusion save under payment of a fee, and then drawn up alongside of the course, as nearly as possible opposite the grand stand and the winning-post. Here you have only to stand up in your place—on tiptoe, it is true, and with a good deal of stretching—to see the race fairly well. But I hasten to add that seeing the race is indifferent entertainment. In the first place you *don't* see it, and in the second —to be Irish on the occasion of a frolic—you perceive it to be not much worth the seeing. It may be fine in quality, but in quantity it is inappreciable. The horses and their jockeys first go dandling and cantering along the course to the starting-point, looking as insubstantial as sifted sunbeams. Then there is a long wait, during which, of the sixty thousand people present (my figures are imaginary), thirty thousand declare positively that they have started, and thirty thousand as positively deny it. Then the whole sixty thousand are suddenly resolved into unanimity by the sight of a dozen small jockey-heads whizzing along a very distant sky-line. In a shorter space of time than it takes me to write it, the whole thing is before you, and for the instant it is anything but beautiful. A dozen furiously revolving arms—pink, green, orange, scarlet, white—whacking the flanks of as many straining steeds; a glimpse of this, and the spectacle is over. The spectacle, however, is of course an infinitesimally small part of the purpose of Epsom and the interest of the Derby.

The finer vibration resides presumably in having money on the affair.

When the Derby Stakes had been carried off by a horse of which I confess I am barbarous enough to have forgotten the name, I turned my back to the running, for all the world as if I too were largely 'interested', and sought entertainment in looking at the crowd. The crowd was very animated; that is the most succinct description I can give of it. The horses of course had been removed from the vehicles, so that the pedestrians were free to surge against the wheels and even to a certain extent to scale and overrun the carriages. This tendency became most pronounced when, as the mid-period of the day was reached, the process of lunching began to unfold itself and every coach-top to become the scene of a picnic. From this moment, at the Derby, demoralisation begins. I was in a position to observe it, all around me, in the most characteristic forms. The whole affair, as regards the conventional rigidities I spoke of a while since, becomes a real *dégringolade*. The shabbier pedestrians bustle about the vehicles, staring up at the lucky mortals who are perched in a kind of tormentingly near empyrean—a region in which dishes of lobster-salad are passed about and champagne-corks cleave the air like celestial meteors. There are nigger-minstrels and beggars and mountebanks and spangled persons on stilts and gipsy matrons, as genuine as possible, with glowing Oriental eyes and dropping their *h*'s; these last offer you for sixpence the promise of everything genteel in life except the aspirate. On a coach drawn up beside the one on which I had a place, a party of opulent young men were passing from stage to stage of the higher beatitude with a zeal which excited my admiration. They were accompanied by two or three young ladies of the kind that usually shares the choicest pleasures of youthful British opulence— young ladies in whom nothing has been neglected that can make a complexion superlative. The whole party had been drinking deep, and one of the young men, a pretty lad of twenty, had in an indiscreet moment staggered down as best he could to the ground. Here his cups proved too many for him, and he collapsed and rolled over. In plain English he was beastly drunk. It was the scene that followed that arrested my observation. His companions on the top of the coach called down to the people herding under the wheels to pick him up and put him away inside. These people were the grimiest of the rabble, and a couple of men who looked like coal-heavers out of work undertook to handle this hapless youth. But their task was difficult; it was impossible to imagine a young man more drunk. He was a mere bag of liquor—at once too ponderous and too flaccid to be lifted. He lay in a helpless heap under the feet of the crowd— the best intoxicated young man in England. His extemporised chamberlains took him first in one way and then in another; but he was like water in a sieve. The crowd hustled over him; every one wanted to see; he was pulled and shoved and fumbled. The spectacle had a grotesque side, and this it was that seemed to strike the fancy of the young man's comrades. They had not done lunching, so they were unable to bestow upon the incident the whole of that consideration which its high comicality deserved. But they did what they could. They looked down very often, glass in hand, during the half-hour that it went on, and they stinted neither their generous, joyous laughter nor their appreciative comments. Women are said to have no sense of humour; but the young ladies with the complexions did liberal justice to the pleasantry of the scene. Toward the last indeed their attention rather flagged; for even the best joke suffers by reiteration, and when you have seen a stupefied young man, infinitely bedusted, slip out of the embrace of a couple of clumsy roughs for the twentieth time, you may very properly suppose that you have arrived at the furthest limits of the ludicrous.

After the great race had been run I quitted my perch and spent the rest of the afternoon in wandering about the grassy concave I have mentioned. It was amusing and picturesque; it was just a huge Bohemian encampment. Here also a great number of carriages were stationed, freighted in like manner with free-handed youths and young ladies with gilded hair. These young ladies were almost the only representatives of their sex with pretensions to elegance; they were often pretty and always exhilarated. Gentlemen in pairs, mounted on stools, habited in fantastic sporting garments and offering bets to whomsoever listed, were a conspicuous feature of the scene. It was equally striking that they were not preaching in the desert and that they found plenty of patrons among the baser sort.

I returned to my place in time to assist at the rather complicated operation of starting for the drive back to London. Putting in horses and getting vehicles into line seemed in the midst of the general crush and entanglement a process not to be facilitated even by the most liberal swearing on the part of those engaged in it. But little by little we came to the end of it; and as by this time a kind of mellow cheerfulness pervaded the upper atmosphere—the region of the perpendicular whip—even those interruptions most trying to patience were somehow made to minister to jollity. It was for people below not to get trampled to death or crunched between opposing wheel-hubs, but it was all for *them* to manage it. Above, the carnival of 'chaff' had set in, and it deepened as the lock of vehicles grew denser. As they were all locked together (with a comfortable padding of pedestrians at points of acutest contact), they contrived somehow to move together; so that we gradually got away and into the road. The four or five hours consumed on the road were simply an exchange of repartee, the profusely good-humoured savour of which, on the whole, was certainly striking. The chaff was not brilliant nor subtle nor especially graceful; and here and there it was quite too tipsy to be even articulate. But as an expression of that unbuttoning of the popular straight-jacket of which I spoke a while since, it had its wholesome and even innocent side. It took indeed frequently an importunate physical form; it sought emphasis in the use of pea-shooters and water-squirts. At its best, too, it was extremely low and rowdyish. But a stranger even of the most refined tastes might be glad to have a glimpse of this popular revel, for it would make him feel that he was learning something more about the English people. It would give a meaning to the old description of England as merry. It would remind him that the natives of that country are subject to some of the lighter of the human impulses, and that the decent, dusky vistas of the London residential streets—those discreet creations of which Thackeray's Baker Street is the type—are not a complete symbol of the complicated race that erected them.

II

It seemed to me such a piece of good fortune to have been asked down to Oxford at Commemoration by a gentleman implicated in the remarkable ceremony which goes on under that name, who kindly offered me the hospitality of his college, that I scarcely stayed even to thank him—I simply went and awaited him. I had had a glimpse of Oxford in former years, but I had never slept in a low-browed room looking out on a grassy quadrangle and opposite a mediaeval clock-tower. This satisfaction was vouchsafed me on the night of my arrival; I was made free of the rooms of an absent undergraduate. I sat in his deep armchairs; I burned his candles and read his books, and I hereby thank him as effusively as possible. Before going to bed I took a turn through the streets and renewed in the silent darkness that impression of the charm imparted to them by the quiet college-fronts which I had gathered in former years. The college-fronts were now quieter than ever, the streets were empty, and the old scholastic city was sleeping in the warm starlight. The undergraduates had retired in large numbers, encouraged in this impulse by the collegiate authorities, who deprecate their presence at Commemoration. However many young gownsmen may be sent away, there yet always remain a collection sufficient to represent the sound of many voices. There can be no better indication of the resources of Oxford in a spectacular way than this fact that the first step toward preparing an impressive ceremony is to get rid of as many as possible of the actors.

In the morning I breakfasted with a young American who, in common with a number of his countrymen, had come hither to seek stimulus for a finer strain of study. I know not whether he would have reckoned as such stimulus the conversation of a couple of those ingenuous youths, sons of the soil, whose society I always find charming; but it added, from my own point of view, in respect to the place, to the element of intensity of character. After the entertainment was over I repaired, in company with a crowd of ladies and elderly people, interspersed with gownsmen, to the hoary rotunda of the Sheldonian theatre, which every visitor to Oxford will remember from its curious cincture of clumsily carven heads of warriors and sages perched upon stone posts. The interior of this edifice is the scene of the classic hooting, stamping, and cat-calling by which the undergraduates confer the last consecration upon the distinguished gentlemen who come up for the honorary degree of D.C.L. It is with the design of attenuating as much as possible this volume of sound that the heads of colleges, on the close of the term, a few days before Commemoration, speed their too demonstrative disciples upon the homeward way. As I have already hinted, however, the contingent of irreverence was on this occasion quite large enough to preserve the type of the racket. This made the scene a very singular one. An American of course, with his fondness for antiquity, his relish for picturesqueness, his 'emotional' attitude at historic shrines, takes Oxford much more seriously than its sometimes unwilling familiars can be expected to do. These people are not always upon the high horse; they are not always in a state of fine vibration. Nevertheless, there is a certain maximum of disaccord with their beautiful circumstances which the ecstatic outsider vaguely expects them not to transcend. No effort of the intellect beforehand would enable him to imagine one of those silvergray temples of learning converted into a semblance of the Bowery Theatre when the Bowery Theatre is being trifled with.

The Sheldonian edifice, like everything at Oxford, is more or less monumental. There is a double tier of galleries, with sculptured pulpits protruding from them; there are full-length portraits of kings and worthies; there is a general air of antiquity and dignity, which, on the occasion of which I speak, was enhanced by the presence of certain ancient scholars seated in crimson robes in highbacked chairs. Formerly, I believe, the undergraduates were placed apart—packed together in a corner of one of the galleries. But now they are scattered among the general spectators, a large number of whom are ladies. They muster in especial force, however, on the floor of the theatre, which has been cleared of its benches. Here the dense mass is at last severed in twain by the entrance of the prospective D.C.L.'s walking in single file, clad in crimson gowns, preceded by mace-bearers and accompanied by the Regius Professor of Civil Law, who presents them individually to the Vice-Chancellor of the University, in a Latin speech which is of course a glowing eulogy. The five gentlemen to whom this distinction had been offered in 1877 were not among those whom fame has trumpeted most loudly; but there was something 'as pretty as a picture' in their standing in their honourable robes, with heads modestly bent, while the orator, as effectively draped, recited their titles sonorously to the venerable dignitary in the high-backed chair. Each of them, when the little speech is ended, ascends the steps leading to the chair; the Vice-Chancellor bends forward and shakes his hand, and the new D.C.L. goes and sits in the blushing row of his fellow doctors. The impressiveness of all this is much diminished by the boisterous conduct of the 'students', who superabound in extravagant applause, in impertinent interrogation and in lively disparagement of the orator's Latinity. Of the scene that precedes the episode I have just described I have given no account; vivid portrayal of it it not easy. Like the return from the Derby it is a carnival of 'chaff'; and it is a singular fact that the scholastic festival should have forcibly reminded me of the great popular 'lark'. In each case it is the same race enjoying a certain definitely chartered licence; in the young votaries of a liberal education and the London rabble on the Epsom road it is the same perfect good-humour, the same muscular jocosity.

After the presentation of the doctors came a series of those collegiate exercises which have a generic resemblance all the world over: a reading of Latin verses and English essays, a spouting of prize poems and Greek paraphrases. The prize poem alone was somewhat attentively listened to; the other things were received with an infinite variety of critical ejaculation. But after all, I reflected as the ceremony drew to a close, the romping element is more characteristic than it seems; it is at bottom only another expression of the venerable and historic side of Oxford. It is tolerated because it is traditional; it is possible because it is classical. Looked at in this light it became romantically continuous with the human past that everything else referred to.

I was not obliged to find ingenious pretexts for thinking well of another ceremony of which I was witness after we adjourned from the Sheldonian theatre. This was a lunch-party at the particular college in which I should find it the highest privilege to reside and which I may not further specify. Perhaps indeed I may go so far as to say that the reason for my dreaming of this privilege is that it is deemed by persons of a reforming turn the best-appointed abuse in a nest of abuses. A commission for the expurgation of the universities has lately been appointed by Parliament to look into it—a commission armed with a gigantic broom, which is to sweep away all the fine old ivied and cobwebbed improprieties. Pending these righteous changes, one would like while one is about it—about, that is, this business of admiring Oxford—to attach one's self to the abuse, to bury one's nostrils in the rose before it is plucked. At the college in question there are no undergraduates. I found it agreeable to reflect that those gray-green cloisters had sent no delegates to the slangy congregation I had just quitted. This delightful spot exists for the satisfaction of a small society of Fellows who, having no dreary instruction to administer, no noisy hobbledehoys to govern, no obligations but toward their own culture, no care save for learning as learning and truth as truth, are presumably the happiest and most charming people in the world. The party invited to lunch assembled first in the library of the college, a cool, gray hall, of very great length and height, with vast wall-spaces of rich-looking book-titles and statues of noble scholars set in the midst. Had the charming Fellows ever anything more disagreeable to do than to finger these precious volumes and then to stroll about together in the grassy courts, in learned comradeship, discussing their precious contents? Nothing, apparently, unless it were to give a lunch at Commemoration in the dining-hall of the college. When lunch was ready there was a very pretty procession to go to it. Learned gentlemen in crimson gowns, ladies in bright finery, paired slowly off and marched in a stately diagonal across the fine, smooth lawn of the quadrangle, in a corner of which they passed through a hospitable door. But here we cross the threshold of privacy; I remained on the further side of it during the rest of the day. But I brought back with me certain memories of which, if I were not at the end of my space, I should attempt a discreet adumbration: memories of a *fête champêtre* in the beautiful gardens of one of the other colleges— charming lawns and spreading trees, music of Grenadier Guards, ices in striped marquees, mild flirtation of youthful gownsmen and bemuslined maidens; memories, too, of quiet dinner in common-room, a decorous, excellent repast; old portraits on the walls and great windows open upon the ancient court, where the afternoon light was fading in the stillness; superior talk upon current topics, and over all the peculiar air of Oxford—the air of liberty to care for the things of the mind assured and secured by machinery which is in itself a satisfaction to sense.

In Warwickshire

THERE is no better way to plunge *in medias res*, for the stranger who wishes to know something of England, than to spend a fortnight in Warwickshire. It is the core and centre of the English world; midmost England, unmitigated England. The place has taught me a great many English secrets; I have been interviewing the genius of pastoral Britain. From a charming lawn—a lawn delicious to one's sentient boot-sole—I looked without obstruction at a sombre, soft, romantic mass whose outline was blurred by mantling ivy. It made a perfect picture, and in the foreground the great trees overarched their boughs, from right and left, so as to give it a majestic frame. This interesting object was the castle of Kenilworth. It was within distance of an easy walk, but one hardly thought of walking to it, any more than one would have thought of walking to a purple-shadowed tower in the background of a Berghem or a Claude. Here were purple shadows and slowly shifting lights, with a soft-hued, bosky country for the middle distance.

Of course, however, I did walk over to the castle; and of course the walk led me through leafy lanes and beside the hedgerows that make a tangled screen for large lawn-like meadows. Of course too, I am bound to add, there was a row of ancient pedlars outside the castle-wall, hawking twopenny pamphlets and photographs. Of course, equally, at the foot of the grassy mound on which the ruin stands were half a dozen public-houses and, always of course, half a dozen beery vagrants sprawling on the grass in the moist sunshine. There was the usual respectable young woman to open the castle-gate and to receive the usual sixpenny fee. There were the usual squares of printed cardboard, suspended upon venerable surfaces, with further enumeration of twopence, threepence, fourpence. I do not allude to these things querulously, for Kenilworth is a very tame lion—a lion that, in former years, I had stroked more than once. I remember perfectly my first visit to this romantic spot; how

I chanced upon a picnic; how I stumbled over beer-bottles; how the very echoes of the beautiful ruin seemed to have dropped all their *h*'s. That was a sultry afternoon; I allowed my spirits to sink and I came away hanging my head. This was a beautiful fresh morning, and in the interval I had grown philosophic. I had learned that, with regard to most romantic sites in England, there is a constant cockneyfication with which you must make your account. There are always people on the field before you, and there is generally something being drunk on the premises.

I hoped, on the occasion of which I am now speaking, that the attack would not be acute, and indeed for the first five minutes I flattered myself that this was the case. In the beautiful grassy court of the castle, on my entrance, there were not more than eight or ten fellow intruders. There were a couple of old ladies on a bench, eating something out of a newspaper; there was a dissenting minister, also on a bench, reading the guide-book aloud to his wife and sister-in-law; there were three or four children pushing each other up and down the turfy hillocks. This was sweet seclusion indeed; and I got a capital start with the various noble square-windowed fragments of the stately pile. They are extremely majestic, with their even, pale-red colour, their deep-green drapery, their princely vastness of scale. But presently the tranquil ruin began to swarm like a startled hive. There were plenty of people, if they chose to show themselves. They emerged from crumbling doorways and gaping chambers with the best conscience in the world; but I know not, after all, why I should bear them a grudge, for they gave me a pretext for wandering about in search of a quiet point of view. I cannot say that I found my point of view, but in looking for it I saw the castle, which is certainly an admirable ruin. And when the respectable young woman had let me out of the gate again, and I had shaken my head at the civil-spoken pedlars who form a little avenue for the arriving and departing visitor, I found it in my good-nature to linger a moment on the trodden, grassy slope, and to think that in spite of the hawkers, the paupers and the beer-shops, there was still a good deal of old England in the scene. I say in spite of these things, but it may have been, in some degree, because of them. Who shall resolve into its component parts any impression of this richly complex English world, where the present is always seen, as it were, in profile, and the past presents a full face? At all events the solid red castle rose behind me, towering above its small old ladies and its investigating parsons; before me, across the patch of common, was a row of ancient cottages, black-timbered, red-gabled, pictorial, which evidently had a memory of the castle in its better days. A quaintish village straggled away on the right, and on the left the dark, fat meadows were lighted up with misty sun-spots and browsing sheep. I looked about for the village stocks; I was ready to take the modern vagrants for Shakespearean clowns; and I was on the point of going into one of the ale-houses to ask Mrs Quickly for a cup of sack.

I began these remarks, however, with no intention of talking about the celebrated curiosities in which this region abounds, but with a design rather of noting a few impressions of some of the shyer and more elusive ornaments of the show. Stratford of course is a very sacred place, but I prefer to say a word, for instance, about a charming old rectory a good many miles distant, and to mention the pleasant picture it made, of a summer afternoon, during a domestic festival. These are the happiest of a stranger's memories of English life, and he feels that he need make no apology for lifting the corner of the curtain. I drove through the leafy lanes I spoke of just now, and peeped over the hedges into fields where the yellow harvest stood waiting. In some places they were already shorn, and, while the light began to redden in the west and to make a horizontal glow behind the dense wayside foliage, the gleaners here and there came brushing through gaps in the hedges with enormous sheaves upon their shoulders. The rectory was an ancient, gabled building, of pale red brick, with facings of white stone and creepers that wrapped it up. It dates, I imagine from the early Hanoverian time; and as it stood there upon its cushiony lawn and among its ordered gardens, cheek to cheek with its little Norman church, it seemed to me the model of a quiet, spacious, easy English home. The cushiony lawn, as I have called it, stretched away to the edge of a brook, and afforded to a number of very amiable people an opportunity of playing lawn-tennis. There were half a dozen games going forward at once, and at each of them a great many 'nice girls', as they say in England, were distinguishing themselves. These young ladies kept the ball going with an agility worthy of the sisters and sweethearts of a race of cricketers, and gave me a chance to admire their flexibility of figure and their freedom of action. When they came back to the house, after the games, flushed a little and a little dishevelled, they might have passed for the attendant nymphs of Diana flocking in from the chase. There had, indeed, been a chance for them to wear the quiver, a target for archery being erected on the lawn. I remembered George Eliot's Gwendolen, and waited to see her step out of the muslin group; but she was not forthcoming, and it was plain that if lawn-tennis had been invented in Gwendolen's day this young lady would have captivated Mr Grandcourt by her exploits with the racket. She certainly would have been a mistress of the game; and, if the suggestion be not too gross, the alertness she would have learned from it might have proved an inducement to her boxing the ears of the insupportable Deronda.

After a while it grew too dark for lawn-tennis; but while the twilight was still mildly brilliant I wandered away, out of the grounds of the charming parsonage, and turned into the little churchyard beside it. The small weather-worn, rust-coloured church had an appearance of high antiquity; there were some curious Norman windows in the apse. Unfortunately I could not get inside; I could only glance into the open door across the interval of an old-timbered heavy-hooded, padlocked porch. But the sweetest evening stillness hung over the place, and the sunset was red behind a dark row of rook-haunted elms. The stillness seemed the greater because three or four rustic children were playing, with little soft cries, among the crooked, deep-buried grave-stones. One poor little girl, who seemed deformed, had climbed some steps that served as a pedestal for a tall, mediaeval-looking cross. She sat perched there and stared at me through the gloaming. This was the heart of England, unmistakably; it might have been the very pivot of the wheel on which her fortune revolves. One need not be a rabid Anglican to be extremely sensible of the charm of an English country church—and indeed of some of the features of an English rural Sunday. In London there is a certain flatness in the observance of this festival; but in the country some of the ceremonies that accompany it have

an indefinable harmony with an ancient, pastoral landscape. I made
this reflection on an occasion that is still very fresh in my memory.
I said to myself that the walk to church from a beautiful country-
house, of a lovely summer afternoon, may be the prettiest possible
adventure. The house stands perched upon a pedestal of rock and
looks down from its windows and terraces upon a shadier spot in
the wooded meadows, of which the blunted tip of a spire explains
the character. A little company of people, whose costume denotes
the highest pitch of civilisation, winds down through the blooming
gardens, passes out of a couple of small gates and reaches the footpath in the fields. This is especially what takes the fancy of the sympathetic stranger; the level, deep-green meadows, studded here and
there with a sturdy oak; the denser grassiness of the footpath, the
lily-sheeted pool beside which it passes, the rustic stiles, where he
stops and looks back at the great house and its wooded background.
It is in the highest degree probable that he has the privilege of
walking with a pretty girl, and it is morally certain that he thinks a
pretty English girl the very type of the maddening magic of youth.
He knows that she doesn't know how lovely is this walk of theirs;
she has been taking it—or taking another quite as good—any time
these twenty years. But her want of immediate intelligence only
makes her the more a part of his delicate entertainment. The latter
continues unbroken while they reach the little churchyard and pass
up to the ancient porch, round which the rosy rustics are standing,
decently and deferentially, to watch the arrival of the smarter contingent. This party takes its place in a great square pew, as large as
a small room, and with seats all round, and while he listens to the
respectable intonings the sympathetic stranger reads over the inscriptions on the mural tablets before him, all to the honour of the
earlier bearers of a name which is, for himself, a symbol of hospitality.

When I came back to the parsonage the entertainment had been
transferred to the interior, and I had occasion to admire the maidenly
vigour of all the nice girls who, after playing lawn-tennis all the
afternoon, were modestly expecting to dance all the evening. And
in regard to this it is not impertinent to say that from almost any
group of young English creatures of this order—though preferably

from such as have passed their lives in quiet country homes—an American receives a delightful impression of something that he may describe as an intimate salubrity. He notices face after face in which this rosy absence of a morbid strain—this simple, natural, affectionate development—amounts to positive beauty. If the young lady have no other beauty the air I speak of is a charm in itself; but when it is united, as it so often is, to real perfection of feature and colour the result is the most delightful thing in nature. It makes the highest type of English beauty, and to my sense there is nothing so satisfyingly high as that. Not long since I heard a clever foreigner indulge, in conversation with an English lady—a very wise and liberal woman—in a little lightly restrictive criticism of her country-women. 'It is possible,' she answered, in regard to one of his objections; 'but such as they are, they are inexpressibly dear to their husbands.' This is doubtless true of good wives all over the world; but I felt, as I listened to these words of my friend, that there is often something in an English girl-face which gives it an extra touch of *justesse*. Such as the woman is, she has here, more than else-where, the look of being completely and profoundly, without reser-vations for other uses, at the service of the man she loves. This look, after one has been a while in England, comes to seem so much a proper and indispensable part of a 'nice' face, that the absence of it appears a sign of irritability or of shallowness. Latent responsive-ness to the manly appeal—that is what it means; which one must take as a very comfortable meaning.

As for the prettiness, I cannot forbear, in the face of a fresh reminiscence, to give it another word. And yet in regard to pretti-ness what do words avail? This was what I asked myself the other day as I looked at a young girl who stood in an old oaken parlour, the rugged panels of which made a background for her lovely head, in simple conversation with a handsome lad. I said to myself that the faces of the English young have often a perfect charm, but that this same charm is too soft and shy a thing to talk about. The face of this fair creature had a pure oval, and her clear brown eyes a quiet warmth. Her complexion was as bright as a sunbeam after rain, and she smiled in a way that made any other way of smiling than that seem a shallow grimace—a mere creaking of the facial muscles. The young man stood facing her, slowly scratching his thigh and shifting from one foot to the other. He was tall and straight, and so sun-burned that his fair hair was lighter than his complexion. He had honest, stupid blue eyes, and a simple smile that showed handsome teeth. He had the look of a gentleman. Presently I heard what they were saying. 'I suppose it's pretty big,' said the beautiful young girl. 'Yes; it's pretty big,' said the handsome young man. 'It's nicer when they are big,' said his interlocutress. The young man looked at her, and at everything in general, with his slowly apprehending blue eye, and for some time no further remark was made. 'It draws ten feet of water,' he at last went on. 'How much water is there?' said the young girl. She spoke in a charming voice. 'There are thirty feet of water,' said the young man. 'Oh, that's enough,' rejoined the damsel. I had had an idea they were flirting, and perhaps indeed that is the way it is done. It was an ancient room and extremely delightful; everything was polished over with the brownness of centuries. The chimney-piece was carved a foot thick, and the windows bore, in coloured glass, the quarterings of ancestral couples. These had stopped two hundred years before; there was nothing newer than that date. Outside the windows was a deep, broad moat, which washed the base of gray walls—gray walls spotted over with the most delicate yellow lichens.

In such a region as this mellow conservative Warwickshire an appreciative American finds the small things quite as suggestive as the great. Everything indeed is suggestive, and impressions are constantly melting into each other and doing their work before he has had time to ask them whence they came. He can scarce go into a cottage muffled in plants, to see a genial gentlewoman and a 'nice girl', without being reminded forsooth of 'The Small House at Allington'. Why of 'The Small House at Allington'? There is a larger house to which the ladies come up to dine; but that is surely an insufficient reason. That the ladies are charming—even that is not reason enough; for there have been other nice girls in the world than Lily Dale and other mild matrons than her mamma. Reminded, however, he is—especially when he goes out upon the lawn. Of course there is lawn-tennis, and it seems all ready for Mr Crosbie to come and take a racket. This is a small example of the way in which in the presence of English life the imagination must be constantly at play on the part of members of a race in whom it has necessarily been trained to do extra service. In driving and walking, in looking and listening, everything affected one as in some degree or other characteristic of a rich, powerful, old-fashioned society. One had no need of being told that this is a conservative county; the fact seemed written in the hedgerows and in the verdant acres behind them. Of course the owners of these things were conservative; of course they were stubbornly unwilling to see the harmonious edifice of their constituted, convenient world the least bit shaken. I had a feeling, as I went about, that I should find some very ancient and curious opinions still comfortably domiciled in the fine old houses whose clustered gables and chimneys appeared here and there, at a distance, above their ornamental woods. Imperturbable British Toryism, viewed in this vague and conjectural fashion —across the fields and behind the oaks and beeches—is by no means a thing the irresponsible stranger would wish away; it deepens the very colour of the air; it may be said to be the style of the landscape. I got a sort of constructive sense of its presence in the picturesque old towns of Coventry and Warwick, which appear to be filled with those institutions—chiefly of an eleemosynary order—that make the undoubting more undoubting still. There are ancient charities in these places—hospitals, alms-houses, asylums, infant-schools—so quaint and venerable that they almost make the existence of respectful dependence a delectable and satisfying thought. In Coventry in especial, I believe, these pious foundations are so numerous as fairly to place a premium upon personal woe. Invidious reflections apart, however, there are few things that speak more quaintly and suggestively of the old England that an American loves than these clumsy little monuments of ancient benevolence. Such an institution as Leicester's Hospital at Warwick seems indeed to exist primarily for the sake of its spectacular effect upon the American tourists, who, with the dozen rheumatic old soldiers maintained in affluence there, constitute its principal *clientèle*.

The American tourist usually comes straight to this quarter of England—chiefly for the purpose of paying his respects to the birthplace of Shakespeare. Being here, he comes to Warwick to see the castle; and being at Warwick, he comes to see the odd little theatrical-looking refuge for superannuated warriors which lurks in the shadow of one of the old gate-towers. Every one will remember Hawthorne's account of the place, which has left no touch of charming taste to be added to any reference to it. The hospital struck me as a little museum kept up for the amusement and confusion of those inquiring Occidentals who are used to seeing charity more dryly and practically administered. The old hospitallers—I am not sure, after all, whether they are necessarily soldiers, but some of them happen to be—are at once the curiosities and the keepers. They sit on benches outside of their door, at the receipt of custom, all neatly brushed and darned and ready to do you the honours. They are only twelve in number, but their picturesque dwelling, perched upon the old city rampart and full of dusky little courts, cross-timbered gable-ends and deeply sunken lattices, seems a wonderfully elaborate piece of machinery for its humble purpose. Each of the old gentlemen must be provided with a wife or 'housekeeper'; each of them has a dusky parlour of his own; and they pass their latter days in their scoured and polished little refuge as softly and honourably as a company of retired lawgivers or pensioned soothsayers.

At Coventry I went to see a couple of old charities of a similar pattern—places with black-timbered fronts, little clean-swept courts and Elizabethan windows. One of them was a romantic residence for a handful of old women, who sat, each of them, in a cosy little bower, in a sort of mediaeval darkness; the other was a school for little boys of humble origin, and this last establishment was charming. I found the little boys playing at 'top' in a gravelled court, in front of the prettiest old building of tender-coloured stucco and painted timber, ornamented with two delicate little galleries and a fantastic porch. They were dressed in small blue tunics and odd caps, like those worn by sailors. but, if I remember rightly, with little yellow tags affixed. I was able to wander at my pleasure all over the establishment; there was no sign of pastor or master anywhere; nothing but the little yellow-headed boys playing before the ancient house and practising most correctly the Warwickshire accent. I went indoors and looked at a fine old oaken staircase; I even ascended it and walked along a gallery and peeped into a dormitory at a row of very short beds; and then I came down and sat for five minutes on a bench hardly wider than the top rail of a fence, in a little, cold, dim refectory where there was not a crumb to be seen, nor any lingering odour of bygone repasts to be perceived. And yet I wondered how it was that the sense of many generations of boyish feeders seemed to abide there. It came, I suppose, from the very bareness and, if I may be allowed the expression, the clean-licked aspect of the place, which wore the appearance of the famous platter of Jack Sprat and his wife.

Inevitably, of course, the sentimental tourist has a great deal to say to himself about this being Shakespeare's county—about these densely grassed meadows and parks having been, to his musing eyes, the normal landscape, the green picture of the world. In Shakespeare's day, doubtless, the coat of nature was far from being so prettily trimmed as it is now; but there is one place, nevertheless, which, as he passes it in the summer twilight, the traveller does his best to believe unaltered. I allude, of course, to Charlecote Park, whose venerable verdure seems a survival from an earlier England and whose innumerable acres, stretching away, in the early evening, to vaguely seen Tudor walls, lie there like the backward years receding to the age of Elizabeth. It was, however, no part of my design in these remarks to pause before so thickly besieged a shrine as this; and if I were to allude to Stratford it would not be in connection with the fact that Shakespeare planted there, to grow for ever, the torment of his unguessed riddle. It would be rather to speak of a delightful old house, near the Avon, which struck me as the ideal home for a Shakespearean scholar, or indeed for any passionate lover of the poet. Here, with books and memories and the recurring reflection that he had taken his daily walk across the bridge at which you look from your windows straight down an avenue of fine old trees, with an ever-closed gate at the end of them and a carpet of turf stretched over the decent drive—here, I say, with old brown wainscotted chambers to live in, old polished doorsteps to lead you from one to the other, deep window-seats to sit in, with a play in your lap, here a person for whom the cares of life should have resolved themselves into a care for the greatest genius who has represented and ornamented life might find a very congruous asylum. Or, speaking a little wider of the mark, the charming, rambling, low-gabled, many-staired, much-panelled mansion would be a very agreeable home for any person of taste who should prefer an old house to a new. I find I am talking about it quite like an auctioneer; but what I chiefly had at heart was to commemorate the fact that I had lunched there and, while I lunched, kept saying to myself that there is nothing in the world so delightful as the happy accidents of old English houses.

And yet that same day, on the edge of the Avon, I found it in me to say that a new house too may be a very charming affair. But I must add that the new house I speak of had really such exceptional advantages that it could not fairly be placed in the scale. Besides, was it new after all? It must have been, and yet one's impression there was all of a kind of silvered antiquity. The place stood upon a decent Stratford road, from which it looked usual enough; but when, after sitting a while in a charming modern drawing-room, one stepped thoughtlessly through an open window upon a verandah, one found that the horizon of the morning call had been wonderfully widened. I will not pretend to detail all I saw after I stepped off the verandah; suffice it that the spire and chancel of the beautiful old church in which Shakespeare is buried, with the Avon sweeping its base, were one of the elements of the vision. Then there were the smoothest lawns in the world stretching down to the edge of this liquid slowness and making, where the water touched them, a line as even as the rim of a champagne-glass—a verge near which you inevitably lingered to see the spire and the chancel (the church was close at hand) among the well-grouped trees, and look for their reflection in the river. The place was a garden of delight; it was a stage set for one of Shakespeare's comedies—for *Twelfth Night* or *Much Ado*. Just across the river was a level meadow, which rivalled the lawn on which I stood, and this meadow seemed only the more essentially a part of the scene by reason of the voluminous sheep that were grazing on it. These sheep were by no means mere edible mutton; they were poetic, historic, romantic sheep; they were not there for their weight or their wool, they were there for their presence and their compositional value, and they visibly knew it.

And yet, knowing as they were, I doubt whether the wisest old ram of the flock could have told me how to explain why it was that this happy mixture of lawn and river and mirrored spire and blooming garden seemed to me for a quarter of an hour the richest corner of England.

If Warwickshire is Shakespeare's country, I found myself not dodging the consciousness that it is also George Eliot's. The author of 'Adam Bede' and 'Middlemarch' has called the rural background of those admirable fictions by another name, but I believe it long ago ceased to be a secret that her native Warwickshire had been in her intention. The stranger who treads its eternal stretched velvet recognises at every turn the elements of George Eliot's novels—especially when he carries himself back in imagination to the Warwickshire of forty years ago. He says to himself that it would be impossible to conceive anything—anything equally rural—more sturdily central, more densely definite. It was in one of the old nestling farmhouses, beyond a hundred hedgerows, that Hetty Sorrel smiled into her milk-pans as if she were looking for a reflection of her pretty face; it was at the end of one of the leafy-pillared avenues that poor Mrs Casaubon paced up and down with her many questions. The country suggests in especial both the social and the natural scenery of 'Middlemarch'. There must be many a genially perverse old Mr Brooke there yet, and whether there are many Dorotheas or not, there must be many a well-featured and well-acred young country gentleman, of the pattern of Sir James Chettam, who, as he rides along the leafy lanes, softly cudgels his brain to know why a clever girl shouldn't wish to marry him. But I doubt whether there be many Dorotheas, and I suspect that the Sir James Chettams of the county are not often pushed to that intensity of meditation. You feel, however, that George Eliot could not have placed her heroine in a local medium better fitted to throw her fine impatience into relief—a community more likely to be startled and perplexed by a questioning attitude on the part of a well-housed and well-fed young gentlewoman.

Among the edifying days that I spent in these neighbourhoods there is one in especial of which I should like to give a detailed account. But I find on consulting my memory that the details have melted away into the single deep impression of a perfect ripeness of civilisation. It was a long excursion, by rail and by carriage, for the purpose of seeing three extremely interesting old country-houses. Our errand led us, in the first place, into Oxfordshire, through the ancient market-town of Banbury, where of course we made a point of looking out for the Cross referred to in the famous nursery-rhyme. It stood there in the most natural manner—though I am afraid it has been 'done up'—with various antique gables around it, from one of whose exiguous windows the young person appealed to in the rhyme may have looked at the old woman as she rode and heard the music of her bells. The houses we went to see have not a national reputation; they are simply interwoven figures in the rich pattern of the Midlands. They have indeed a local renown but they are not thought of as unexampled, still less as abnormal, and the stranger has a feeling that his surprises and ecstasies are held to betray the existence, on his part, of a blank background. Such places, to a Warwickshire mind of good habits, must appear the pillars and props of a heaven-appointed order of things; and accordingly, in a land on which heaven smiles, they are as natural as the geology of the county or the supply of mutton. But nothing could well give a stranger a stronger impression of the wealth of England in such matters—of the interminable list of her territorial homes—than this fact that the so eminent specimens I speak of should have but a limited fame, should not be lions of the first magnitude. Of one of them, the finest in the group, one of my companions, who lived but twenty miles away, had never even heard. Such a place was not thought a subject for local swagger. Its peers and mates are scattered all over the country; half of them are not even mentioned in the county guide-books. You stumble upon them in a drive or a walk. You catch a glimpse of an ivied front at some midmost point of wide acres, and taking your way, by leave of a serious old woman at a lodge-gate, along an overarching avenue, you find yourself introduced to an edifice so human-looking in its beauty that it seems for the occasion fairly to reconcile art and morality.

To Broughton Castle, the first seen in this beautiful group, I must do no more than allude; but this is not because I failed to think it, as I think every house I see, the most delightful habitation in England. It lies rather low, and its woods and pastures slope down to it; it has a deep, clear moat all round it, spanned by a bridge that passes under a charming old gate-tower, and nothing can be sweeter than to see its clustered walls of yellow-brown stone so sharply islanded while its gardens bloom on the other side of the water. Like several other houses in this part of the country, Broughton Castle played a part (on the Parliamentary side) in the civil wars, and not the least interesting features of its beautiful interior are the several mementoes of Cromwell's station there. It was within a moderate drive of this place that in 1642 the battle of Edgehill was fought—the first great battle of the war—and gained by neither party. We went to see the battlefield, where an ancient tower and an artificial ruin (of all things in the world) have been erected for the entertainment of convivial visitors. These ornaments are perched upon the edge of a slope which commands a view of the exact scene of the contest, upwards of a mile away. I looked in the direction indicated and saw misty meadows a little greener perhaps than usual and colonnades of elms a trifle denser. After this we paid our respects to another old house which is full of memories and suggestions of that most dramatic period of English history. But of Compton Wyniates (the name of this seat of enchantment) I despair of giving any coherent or adequate account. It belongs to the Marquis of Northampton, and it stands empty all the year round. It sits on the grass at the bottom of a wooden hollow, and the glades of a superb old park go wandering upward away from it. When I came out in front of the house from a short and steep but stately avenue I said to myself that here surely we had arrived at the farthest limits of what ivy-smothered brick-work and weather-beaten gables, conscious old windows and clustered mossy roofs can accomplish for the eye. It is impossible to imagine a more finished picture. And its air of solitude and delicate decay—of having been dropped into its grassy hollow as an ancient jewel is deposited upon a cushion, and being shut in from the world and back into the past by its circling woods—all this drives the impression well home. The house is not large, as great houses go, and it sits, as I have said, upon the grass, without even a flagging or a footpath to conduct you from the point where the avenue stops to the beautiful sculptured doorway which admits you into the small, quaint inner court. From this court you are at liberty to pass through the crookedest series of oaken halls and chambers, adorned with treasures of old wainscotting and elaborate doors and chimneypieces. Outside, you may walk all round the house on a grassy bank, which is raised above the level on which it stands, and find it from every point of view a more charming composition. I should not omit to mention that Compton Wyniates is supposed to have been in Scott's eye when he described the dwelling of the old royalist knight in 'Woodstock'. In this case he simply transferred the house to the other side of the county. He has indeed given several of the features of the place, but he has not given what one may call its colour. I must add that if Sir Walter could not give the colour of Compton Wyniates, it is useless for any other writer to try. It is a matter for the brush and not for the pen.

And what shall I say of the colour of Wroxton Abbey, which we visited last in order and which in the thickening twilight, as we approached its great ivy-muffled face, laid on the mind the burden of its felicity? Wroxton Abbey, as it stands, is a house of about the same period as Compton Wyniates—the latter years, I suppose, of the sixteenth century. But it is quite another affair. The place is inhabited, 'kept up', full of the most interesting and most splendid detail. Its happy occupants, however, were fortunately not in the act of staying there (happy occupants, in England, are almost always absent), and the house was exhibited with a civility worthy of its merit. Everything that in the material line can render life noble and charming has been gathered into it with a profusion which makes the whole place a monument to past opportunity. As I wandered from one rich room to another and looked at these things that intimate appeal to the romantic sense which I just mentioned was mercilessly emphasised. But who can tell the story of the romantic sense when that adventurer really rises to the occasion— takes its ease in an old English country-house while the twilight darkens the corners of expressive rooms and the victim of the scene, pausing at the window, turns his glance from the observing portrait of a handsome ancestral face and sees the great soft billows of the lawn melt away into the park?

Abbeys and Castles

IT is a frequent perception with the stranger in England that the beauty and interest of the country are private property and that to get access to them a key is always needed. The key may be large or it may be small, but it must be something that will turn a lock. Of the things that contribute to the happiness of an American observer in these tantalising conditions, I can think of very few that do not come under this definition of private property. When I have mentioned the hedgerows and the churches I have almost exhausted the list. You can enjoy a hedgerow from the public road, and I suppose that even if you are a Dissenter you may enjoy a Norman abbey from the street. If therefore you talk of anything beautiful in England, the presumption will be that it is private; and indeed such is my admiration of this delightful country that I feel inclined to say that if you talk of anything private the presumption will be that it is beautiful. This is something of a dilemma. When the observer permits himself to commemorate charming impressions he is in danger of giving to the world the fruits of friendship and hospitality. When on the other hand he withholds his impression he lets something admirable slip away without having marked its passage, without having done it proper honour. He ends by mingling discretion with enthusiasm, and he says to himself that it is not treating a country ill to talk of its treasures when the mention of each has tacit reference to some kindness conferred.

The impressions I have in mind in writing these lines were gathered in a part of England of which I had not before had even a traveller's glimpse; but as to which, after a day or two, I found myself quite ready to agree with a friend who lived there and who knew and loved it well, when he said very frankly 'I do believe it is the loveliest corner of the world!' This was not a dictum to quarrel about, and while I was in the neighbourhood I was quite of his opinion. I felt I might easily come to care for it very much as he cared for it; I had a glimpse of the kind of romantic passion such a country may inspire. It is a capital example of that density of feature which is the great characteristic of English scenery. There are no waste details; everything in the landscape is something particular— has a history, has played a part, has a value to the imagination. It is a region of hills and blue undulations, and, though none of the hills are high, all of them are interesting—interesting as such things are interesting in an old, small country, by a kind of exquisite modulation, something suggesting that outline and colouring have been retouched and refined by the hand of time. Independently of its castles and abbeys, the definite relics of the ages, such a landscape seems charged and interfused. It has, has always had, human relations and is intimately conscious of them. That little speech about the loveliness of his county, or of his own part of his county, was made to me by my companion as we walked up the grassy slope of a hill, or 'edge', as it is called there, from the crest of which we seemed in an instant to look away over most of the remainder of England. Certainly one would have grown to love such a view as that quite in the same way as to love some magnificent yet sensitive friend. The 'edge' plunged down suddenly, as if the corresponding slope on the other side had been excavated, and you might follow the long ridge for the space of an afternoon's walk with this vast, charming prospect before your eyes. Looking across an English county into the next but one is a very pretty entertainment, the county seeming by no means so small as might be supposed. How can a county seem small in which, from such a vantage-point as the one I speak of, you see, as a darker patch across the lighter green, the great territory of one of the greatest representatives of territorial greatness? These things constitute immensities, and beyond them are blue undulations of varying tone, and then another bosky province which furnishes forth, as you are told. the residential and other umbrage of another magnate. And to right and left of these, in wooded expanses, lie other domains of equal consequence. It was therefore not the smallness but the vastness of the country that struck me, and I was not at all in the mood of a certain American who once, in my hearing, burst out laughing at an English answer to my inquiry as to whether my interlocutor often saw Mr B——.

'Oh no,' the answer had been, 'we never see him: he lives away off in the West.' It was the western part of his county our friend meant, and my American humorist found matter for infinite jest in his meaning. 'I should as soon think', he remarked, 'of talking of my own west or east foot.'

I do not think, even, that my sensibility to the charm of this delightful region—for its hillside prospect of old red farmhouses lighting up the dark-green bottoms of gables, and chimney-tops of great houses peeping above miles of woodland, and, in the vague places of the horizon, of far away towns and sites that one had always heard of—was conditioned upon having 'property' in the neighbourhood, so that the little girls in the town should suddenly drop curtsies to me in the street; though that too would certainly have been pleasant. At the same time having a little property would without doubt have made the attachment stronger. People who wander about the world without money in their pockets indulge in dreams—dreams of the things they would buy if their pockets were workable. These dreams are very apt to have relation to a good estate in any neighbourhood in which the wanderer may happen to find himself. For myself, I have never been in a country so unattractive that I didn't find myself 'drawn' to its most exemplary mansion. In New England and other portions of the United States I have felt my heart go out to the Greek temple, the small Parthenon, in white-painted wood; in Italy I have made imaginary proposals for the yellow-walled villa with statues on the roof. My fancy, in England, has seldom fluttered so high as the very best house, but it has again and again hovered about one of the quiet places, unknown to fame, which are locally spoken of as merely 'good'. There was one in especial, in the neighbourhood I allude to, as to which the dream of having impossibly acquired it from an embarrassed owner kept melting into the vision of 'moving in' on the morrow. I saw this place unfortunately, to small advantage; I saw it in the rain, but I am glad fine weather didn't meddle with the affair, for the irritation of envy might in this case have poisoned the impression. It was a long, wet Sunday, and the waters were deep. I had been in the house all day, for the weather can best be described by my saying that it had been deemed to exonerate us from church. But in the afternoon, the prospective interval between lunch and tea assuming formidable proportions, my host took me a walk, and in the course of our walk he led me into a park which he described as 'the paradise of a small English country-gentleman'. It was indeed a modern Eden, and the trees might have been trees of knowledge. They were of high antiquity and magnificent girth and stature; they were strewn over the grassy levels in extraordinary profusion, and scattered upon and down the slopes in a fashion than which I have seen nothing more felicitous since I last looked at the chestnuts above the Lake of Como. The point was that the property was small, but that one could perceive nowhere any limit. Shortly before we turned into the park the rain had renewed itself, so that we were awkwardly wet and muddy; but, being near the house, my companion proposed to leave his card in a neighbourly way. The house was most agreeable: it stood on a kind of terrace, in the middle of a lawn and garden, and the terrace overhung one of the most copious rivers in England, as well as looking across to those blue undulations of which I have already spoken. On the terrace also was a piece of ornamental water, and there was a small iron paling to divide the lawn from the park. All this I beheld in the rain. My companion gave his card to the butler with the remark that we were too much bespattered to come in, and we turned away to complete our circuit. As we turned away I became acutely conscious of what I should have been tempted to call the cruelty of this proceeding. My imagination gauged the whole position. It was a blank, a blighted Sunday afternoon—no one could come. The house was charming, the terrace delightful, the oaks magnificent, the view most interesting. But the whole thing confessed to the blankness if not to the dulness. In the house was a drawing-room, and in the drawing-room was—by which I meant *must be*—an English lady, a perfectly harmonious figure. There was nothing fatuous in believing that on this rainy Sunday afternoon it would not please her to be told that two gentlemen had walked across the country to her door only to go through the ceremony of leaving a card. Therefore, when, before we had gone many yards, I heard the butler hurrying after us, I felt how just my sentiment of the situation had been. Of course we went back, and I carried my muddy boots into the draw-

ing-room—just the drawing-room I had imagined—where I found
—I will not say just the lady I had imagined, but a lady even more
in keeping. Indeed there were two ladies, one of whom was staying
in the house. In whatever company you find yourself in England,
you may always be sure that some one present is 'staying', and you
come in due time to feel the abysses within the word. The large
windows of the drawing-room I speak of looked away over the
river to the blurred and blotted hills, where the rain was drizzling
and drifting. It was very quiet, as I say; there was an air of large
leisure. If one wanted to do anything here, there was evidently
plenty of time—and indeed of every other appliance—to do it. The
two ladies talked about 'town': that is what people talk about in the
country. If I were disposed I might represent them as talking with
a positive pathos of yearning. At all events I asked myself how it
could be that one should live in this charming place and trouble
one's head about what was going on in London in July. Then we
had fine strong tea and bread and butter.

I returned to the habitation of my friend—for I too was guilty of
'staying'—through an old Norman portal, massively arched and
quaintly sculptured, across whose hollow threshold the eye of fancy
might see the ghosts of monks and the shadows of abbots pass
noiselessly to and fro. This aperture admits you to a beautiful ambu-
latory of the thirteenth century—a long stone gallery or cloister,
repeated in two stories, with the interstices of its traceries now
glazed, but with its long, low, narrow, charming vista still perfect
and picturesque, with its flags worn away by monkish sandals and
with huge round-arched doorways opening from its inner side into
great rooms roofed like cathedrals. These rooms are furnished with
narrow windows, of almost defensive aspect, set in embrasures three
feet deep and ornamented with little grotesque mediaeval faces. To
see one of the small monkish masks grinning at you while you dress
and undress, or while you look up in the intervals of inspiration
from your letter-writing, is a mere detail in the entertainment of
living in a *ci-devant* priory. This entertainment is inexhaustible; for
every step you take in such a house confronts you in one way or
another with the remote past. You devour the documentary, you
inhale the historic. Adjoining the house is a beautiful ruin, part of

the walls and windows and bases of the piers of the magnificent church administered by the predecessor of your host, the mitred abbot. These relics are very desultory, but they are still abundant, and they testify to the great scale and the stately beauty of the abbey. You may lie upon the grass at the base of an ivied fragment, measure the girth of the great stumps of the central columns, half smothered in soft creepers, and think how strange it is that in this quiet hollow, in the midst of lonely hills, so exquisite and elaborate a work of art should have risen. It is but an hour's walk to another great ruin, which has held together more completely. There the central tower stands erect to half its altitude and the round arches and massive pillars of the nave make a perfect vista on the unencumbered turf. You get an impression that when catholic England was in her prime great abbeys were as thick as milestones. By native amateurs even now the region is called 'wild', though to American eyes it seem almost suburban in its smoothness and finish. There is a noiseless little railway running through the valley, and there is an ancient little town at the abbey-gates—a town indeed with no great din of vehicles, but with goodly brick houses, with a dozen 'publics', with tidy, whitewashed cottages, and with little girls, as I have said, bobbing curtsies in the street. Yet even now, if one had wound one's way into the valley by the railroad, it would be rather a surprise to find a great architectural display in a setting so peaceful and pastoral. How impressive then must the beautiful church have been in the days of its prosperity, when the pilgrim came down to it from the grassy hillside and its bells made the stillness sensible! The abbey was in those days a great affair; it sprawled, as my companion said, all over the place. As you walk away from it you think you have got to the end of its geography, but you encounter it still in the shape of a rugged outhouse enriched with an early-English arch, of an ancient well hidden in a kind of sculptured cavern. It is noticeable that even if you are a traveller from a land where there are no early-English—and indeed few late-English—arches, and where the well-covers are, at their hoariest, of fresh-looking shingles, you grow used with little delay to all this antiquity. Anything very old seems extremely natural; there is nothing we suffer to get so near us as the tokens of the remote. It is not too much to say that after spending twenty-four hours in a house that is six hundred years old you seem yourself to have lived in it six hundred years. You seem yourself to have hollowed the flags with your tread and to have polished the oak with your touch. You walk along the little stone gallery where the monks used to pace, looking out of the Gothic window-places at their beautiful church, and you pause at the big, round, rugged doorway that admits you to what is now the drawing-room. The massive step by which you ascend to the threshold is a trifle crooked, as it should be; the lintels are cracked and worn by the myriad-fingered years. This strikes your casual glance. You look up and down the miniature cloister before you pass in; it seems wonderfully old and queer. Then you turn into the drawing-room, where you find modern conversation and late publications and the prospect of dinner. The new life and the old have melted together; there is no dividing-line. In the drawing-room wall is a queer funnel-shaped hole, with the broad end inward, like a small casemate. You ask what it is, but people have forgotten. It is something of the monks; it is a mere detail. After dinner you are told that there is of course a ghost—a gray friar who is seen in the dusky hours at the end of passages. Sometimes the servants see him; they afterwards go surreptitiously to sleep in the village. Then, when you take your chamber-candle and go wandering bedward by a short cut through empty rooms, you are conscious of an attitude toward the gray friar which you hardly know whether to read as a fond hope or as a great fear.

A friend of mine, an American, who knew this country, had told me not to fail, while I was in the neighbourhood, to go to Stokesay and two or three other places. 'Edward IV and Elizabeth', he said, 'are still hanging about there.' So admonished, I made a point of going at least to Stokesay, and I saw quite what my friend meant. Edward IV and Elizabeth indeed are still to be met almost anywhere in the county; as regards domestic architecture few parts of England are still more vividly old-English. I have rarely had, for a couple of hours, the sensation of dropping back personally into the past so straight as while I lay on the grass beside the well in the little sunny court of this small castle and lazily appreciated the still definite details of mediaeval life. The place is a capital example of a small *gentilhommière* of the thirteenth century. It has a good deep moat, now filled with wild verdure, and a curious gatehouse of a much later period—the period when the defensive attitude had been well-nigh abandoned. This gatehouse, which is not in the least in the style of the habitation, but gabled and heavily timbered, with quaint cross-beams protruding from surfaces of coarse white plaster, is a very effective anomaly in regard to the little gray fortress on the other side of the court. I call this a fortress, but it is a fortress which might easily have been taken, and it must have assumed its present shape at a time when people had ceased to peer through narrow slits at possible besiegers. There are slits in the outer walls for such peering, but they are noticeably broad and not particularly oblique, and might easily have been applied to the uses of a peaceful parley. This is part of the charm of the place; human life there must have lost an earlier grimness; it was lived in by people who were beginning to believe in good intentions. They must have lived very much together; that is one of the most obvious reflections in the court of a mediaeval dwelling. The court was not always grassy and empty, as it is now, with only a couple of gentlemen in search of impressions lying at their length, one of them handling a wine-flask that colours the clear water drawn from the well into a couple of tumblers by a decent, rosy, smiling, talking old woman who has come bustling out of the gatehouse and who has a large, dropsical, innocent husband standing about on crutches in the sun and making no sign when you ask after his health. This poor man has reached that ultimate depth of human simplicity at which even a chance to talk about one's ailments is not appreciated. But the civil old woman talks for every one, even for an artist who has come out of one of the rooms, where I see him afterward reproducing its mouldering repose. The rooms are all unoccupied and in a state of extreme decay, though the castle is, as yet, far from being a ruin. From one of the windows I see a young lady sitting under a tree, across a meadow, with her knees up, dipping something into her mouth. It is indubitably a camel's hair paint-brush; the young lady is inevitably sketching. These are the only besiegers to which the place is exposed now, and they can do no great harm, as I doubt whether the young lady's aim is very good. We wandered about the empty interior, thinking it a pity such things should fall to pieces. There is a beautiful great hall—great, that is, for a small castle (it would be extremely handsome in a modern house)—with tall, ecclesiastical-looking windows and a long staircase at one end, which climbs against the wall into a spacious bedroom. You may still apprehend very well the main lines of that simpler life; and it must be said that, simpler though it was, it was apparently by no means destitute of many of our own conveniences. The chamber at the top of the staircase ascending from the hall is charming still, with its irregular shape, its low-browed ceiling, its cupboards in the walls, its deep bay window formed of a series of small lattices. You can fancy people stepping out from it upon the platform of the staircase, whose rugged wooden logs, by way of steps, and solid, deeply guttered hand-rail, still remain. They looked down into the hall, where, I take it, there was always a congregation of retainers, much lounging and waiting and passing to and fro, with a door open into the court. The court, as I said just now, was not the grassy, aesthetic spot which you may find it at present of a summer's day; there were beasts tethered in it, and hustling men at arms, and the earth was trampled into puddles. But my lord or my lady, looking down from the chamber-door, commanded the position and, no doubt, issued their orders accordingly. The sight of the groups on the floor beneath, the calling up and down, the oaken tables spread and the brazier in the middle—all this seemed present again; and it was not difficult to pursue the historic vision through the rest of the building —through the portion which connected the great hall with the tower (where the confederate of the sketching young lady without had set up the peaceful three-legged engine of his craft); through the dusky, roughly circular rooms of the tower itself, and up the corkscrew staircase of the same to that most charming part of every old castle, where visions must leap away off the battlements to elude you—the bright, dizzy platform at the tower-top, the place where the castle-standard hung and the vigilant inmates surveyed the approaches. Here, always, you really overtake the impression of the place—here, in the sunny stillness, it seems to pause, panting a little, and give itself up.

It was not only at Stokesay that I lingered a while on the summit of the keep to enjoy the complete impression so overtaken. I spent such another half-hour at Ludlow, which is a much grander and more famous monument. Ludlow, however, is a ruin—the most impressive and magnificent of ruins. The charming old town and the admirable castle form a capital object of pilgrimage. Ludlow is an excellent example of a small English provincial town that has not been soiled and disfigured by industry; it exhibits no tall chimneys and smoke-streamers, no attendant purlieus and slums. The little city is perched upon a hill near which the goodly Severn wanders, and it has a remarkable air of civic dignity. Its streets are wide and clean, empty and a little grass-grown, and bordered with spacious, mildly ornamental brick houses which look as if there had been more going on in them in the first decade of the century than there is in the present, but which can still nevertheless hold up their heads and keep their window-panes clear, their knockers brilliant and their door-steps whitened. The place seems to say that some hundred years ago it was the centre of a large provincial society and that this society was very 'good' of its kind. It must have transported itself to Ludlow for the season—in rumbling coaches and heavy curricles—and there entertained itself in decent emulation of that more majestic capital which a choice of railway lines had not as yet placed within its immediate reach. It had balls at the assembly rooms; it had Mrs Siddons to play; it had Catalani to sing. Miss Burney's and Miss Austen's heroines might perfectly well have had their first love-affair there; a journey to Ludlow would certainly have been a great event to Fanny Price or Emma Woodhouse, or even to those more romantically connected young ladies Evelina and Cecilia. It is a place on which a provincial aristocracy has left so sensible a stamp as to enable you to measure both the grand manners and the small ways. It is a very interesting array of houses of the period after the poetry of domestic architecture had begun to wane and before the vulgarity had come—a fine familiar classic prose. Such places, such houses, such relics and intimations, carry us back to the near antiquity of that pre-Victorian England which it is still easy for a stranger to picture with a certain vividness, thanks to the partial survival of many of its characteristics. It is still easier for a stranger who has dwelt a time in England to form an idea of the tone, the habits, the aspect of the social life before its classic insularity had begun to wane, as all observers agree that it did about thirty years ago. It is true that the mental operation in this matter reduces itself to our imaging some of the things which form the peculiar national notes as infinitely exaggerated: the rigidly aristocratic constitution of society, the unaesthetic temper of the people, the small public fund of convenience, of elegance. Let an old gentleman of conservative tastes, who can remember the century's youth, talk to you at a club *temporis acti*—tell you wherein it is that from his own point of view London, as a residence for a gentleman, has done nothing but fall off for the last forty years. You will listen, of course, with an air of decent sympathy, but privately you will say to yourself how difficult a place of sojourn London must have been in those days for the traveller from other countries—how little cosmopolitan, how bound, in a thousand ways, with narrowness of custom. What was true of the great city at that time was of course doubly true of the provinces; and a community of the type of Ludlow must have been a kind of focus of insular propriety. Even then, however, the irritated alien would have had the magnificent ruins of the castle to dream himself back into good humour in. They would effectually have transported him beyond all waning or waxing Philistinisms.

English Vignettes

I

Toward the last of April, in Monmouthshire, the primroses were as big as your fist. I say in Monmouthshire, because I believe that a certain grassy mountain which I gave myself the pleasure of climbing and to which I took my way across the charming country, through lanes where the hedges were perched upon blooming banks, lay within the borders of this ancient province. It was the festive Eastertide, and a pretext for leaving London had not been wanting. Of course it rained—it rained a good deal—for man and the weather are usually at cross-purposes. But there were intervals of light and warmth, and in England a couple of hours of brightness islanded in moisture assert their independence and leave an uncompromised memory. These reprieves were even of longer duration; that whole morning for instance on which, with a companion, I scrambled up the little Skirrid. One had a feeling that one was very far from London; as in fact one was, after six or seven hours in a swift, straight train. In England this is a long span; it seemed to justify the half-reluctant confession, which I heard constantly made, that the country was extremely 'wild'. There is wildness and wildness, I thought; and though I had not been a great explorer I compared this rough district with several neighbourhoods in another part of the world that passed for tame. I went even so far as to wish that some of its ruder features might be transplanted to that relatively unregulated landscape and commingled with its suburban savagery. We were close to the Welsh border, and a dozen little mountains in the distance were peeping over each other's shoulders, but nature was open to the charge of no worse disorder than this. This Skirrid (I like to repeat the name) wore, it is true, at a distance, the aspect of a magnified extinguisher; but when, after a bright, breezy walk through lane and meadow, we had scrambled over the last of the thickly flowering hedges which lay around its shoulders like loosened strings of coral and begun to ascend the grassy cone (very much in the attitude of Nebuchadnezzar), it proved as smooth-faced as a garden-mound. Hard by, on the flanks of other hills, were troops of browsing sheep, and the only thing that confessed in the least to a point or an edge was the strong, damp wind. But even the high breeze was good-humoured and only wanted something to play with, blowing about the pearly morning mists that were airing themselves upon neighbouring ridges and shaking the vaporous veil that fluttered down in the valley over the picturesque little town of Abergavenny. A breezy, grassy English hill-top, looking down on a country full of suggestive names and ancient memories and implied stories (especially if you are exhilarated by a beautiful walk and have a flask in your pocket), shows you the world as a very smooth place, fairly rubbed so by human use.

I was warned away from church, on Sunday, by my mistrust of its mediaeval chill—lumbago there was so clearly catching. In the still hours, when the roads and lanes were empty, I simply walked to the churchyard and sat upon one of the sun-warmed gravestones. I say the roads were empty, but they were peopled with the big primroses I just now spoke of—primroses of the size of ripe apples and yet, in spite of their rank growth, of as pale, and tender a yellow as if their gold had been diluted with silver. It was indeed a mixture of gold and silver, for there was a wealth of the white wood-anemone as well, and these delicate flowers, each of so perfect a coinage, were tumbled along the green wayside as if a prince had been scattering largess. The outside of an old English country church in service-time is a very pleasant place; and this is as near as I often dare approach the celebration of the Anglican mysteries. A just sufficient sense of their august character may be gathered from that vague sound of village-music which makes its way out into the stillness and from the perusal of those portions of the Prayer-Book which are inscribed upon mouldering slabs and dislocated headstones. The church I speak of was a beautiful specimen of its kind—intensely aged, variously patched, but still solid and useful and with no touch of restoration. It was very big and

massive and, hidden away in the fields, had a kind of lonely grandeur; there was nothing in particular near it but its out-of-the-
world little parsonage. It was only one of ten thousand; I had seen
a hundred such before. But I watched the watery sunshine upon the
rugosities of its ancient masonry; I stood a while in the shade of
two or three spreading yews which stretched their black arms over
graves decorated for Easter, according to the custom of that country, with garlands of primrose and dog-violet; and I reflected that
in a 'wild' region it was a blessing to have so quiet a place of refuge
as that.

Later I chanced upon a couple of other asylums which were more
spacious and no less tranquil. Both of them were old country-houses,
and each in its way was charming. One was a half-modernised feudal
dwelling, lying in a wooded hollow—a large concavity filled with a
delightful old park. The house had a long gray façade and half a
dozen towers, and the usual supply of ivy and of clustered chimneys
relieved against a background of rook-haunted elms. But the windows were all closed and the avenue was untrodden; the house was
the property of a lady who could not afford to live in it in becoming
state and who had let it, furnished, to a rich young man, 'for the
shooting'. The rich young man occupied it but for three weeks in
the year and for the rest of the time left it a prey to the hungry
gaze of the passing stranger, the would-be redresser of aesthetic
wrongs. It seemed a great aesthetic wrong that so charming a place
should not be a conscious, sentient home. In England all this is
very common. It takes a great many plain people to keep a 'perfect'
gentleman going; it takes a great deal of wasted sweetness to make
up a saved property. It is true that, in the other case I speak of, the
sweetness, which here was even greater, was less sensibly squan-
dered. If there was no one else in the house at least there were
ghosts. It had a dark red front and grim-looking gables; it was
perched upon a vague terrace, quite high in the air, which was
reached by steep, crooked, mossy steps. Beneath these steps was an
ancient bit of garden, and from the hither side of the garden
stretched a great expanse of turf. Out of the midst of the turf sprang
a magnificent avenue of Scotch firs—a perfect imitation of the
Italian stone-pine. It looked like the Villa Borghese transplanted to

the Welsh hills. The huge, smooth stems, in their double row, were crowned with dark parasols. In the Scotch fir or the Italian pine there is always an element of oddity; the open umbrella in a rainy country is not a poetical analogy, and the case is not better if you compare the tree to a colossal mushroom. But, without analogies, there was something very striking in the effect of this enormous, rigid vista, and in the grassy carpet of the avenue, with the dusky, lonely, high-featured house looking down upon it. There was something solemn and tragical; the place was made to the hand of a story-seeker, who might have found his characters within, as, the leaden lattices being open, the actors seemed ready for the stage.

II

The Isle of Wight is at first disappointing. I wondered why it should be, and then I found the reason in the influence of the detestable little railway. There can be no doubt that a railway in the Isle of Wight is a gross impertinence, is in evident contravention to the natural style of the place. The place is pure picture or is nothing at all. It is ornamental only—it exists for exclamation and the watercolour brush. It is separated by nature from the dense railway-system of the less dimunitive island, and is the corner of the world where a good carriage-road is most in keeping. Never was a clearer opportunity for sacrificing to prettiness; never was a better chance for not making a railway. But now there are twenty trains a day, so that the prettiness is twenty times less. The island is so small that the hideous embankments and tunnels are obtrusive; the sight of them is as painful as it would be to see a pedlar's pack on the shoulders of a lovely woman. This is your first impression as you travel (naturally by the objectionable conveyance) from Ryde to Ventnor; and the fact that the train rumbles along very smoothly and stops at half a dozen little stations, where the groups on the platform enable you to perceive that the population consists almost exclusively of gentlemen in costumes suggestive of unlimited leisure for attention to cravats and trousers (an immensely large class in England), of old ladies of the species denominated in France *rentières*, of young ladies of the highly educated and sketching variety, this circumstance fails to reconcile you to the chartered cicatrix which forms your course. At Ventnor, however, face to face with the sea, and with the blooming shoulder of the Undercliff close behind you, you lose sight to a certain extent of the super-fluities of civilisation. Not indeed that Ventnor has not been diligently civilised. It is a formed and finished watering-place, it has been reduced to a due degree of cockneyfication. But the glittering ocean remains, shimmering at moments with blue and silver, and the large gorse-covered downs rise superbly above it. Ventnor hangs upon the side of a steep hill, and here and there it clings and scrambles, is propped up and terraced, like one of the bright-faced little towns that look down upon the Mediterranean. To add to the Italian effect the houses are all denominated villas, though it must be added that nothing is less like an Italian villa than an English. Those which ornament the successive ledges at Ventnor are for the most part small semi-detached boxes, predestined, even before they have fairly come into the world, to the entertainment of lodgers. They stand in serried rows all over the place, with the finest names in the Peerage painted upon their gate-posts. Their severe similarity of aspect, however, is such that even the difference between Plantagenet and Percival, between Montgomery and Montmorency, is hardly sufficient to enlighten the puzzled visitor. An English place of recreation is more comfortable than an American; in a Plantagenet villa the art of receiving 'summer guests' has usually been brought to a higher perfection than in an American rural hotel. But what strikes an American, with regard to even so charmingly nestled a little town as Ventnor, is that it is far less natural, less pastoral and bosky than his own fond image of a summer retreat. There is too much brick and mortar; there are too many smoking chimneys and shops and public-houses; there are no woods nor brooks nor lonely headlands; there is none of the virginal stillness of Nature. Instead of these things there is an esplanade mostly paved with asphalt, bordered with benches and little shops and provided with a German band. To be just to Ventnor, however, I must hasten to add that once you get away from the asphalt there is a great deal of vegetation. The little village of Bonchurch, which closely adjoins it, is buried in the most elaborate verdure, muffled in the smoothest lawns and the densest shrubbery. Bonchurch is simply delicious and indeed in a manner quite absurd. It is like a model village in imitative substances, kept in a big glass case; the turf might be of green velvet and the foliage of cut paper. The villagers are all happy gentlefolk, the cottages have plate-glass windows, and the rose-trees on their walls looked as if tied up with ribbon 'to match'. Passing from Ventnor through the elegant umbrage of Bonchurch, and keeping along the coast toward Shanklin, you come to the prettiest part of the Undercliff, or in other words to the prettiest place in the world. The immense grassy cliffs which form the coast of the island make what the French would call a 'false descent' to the sea. At a certain point the descent is broken, so that a wide natural terrace, all over-tangled with wild shrubs and flowers, hangs there in mid-air, half-way above salt water. It is impossible to imagine anything more charming than this long, blooming platform, protected from the north by huge green bluffs and plunging on the other side into the murmuring tides. This delightful arrangement constitutes for a distance of some fifteen miles the south shore of the Isle of Wight; but the best of it, as I have said, is to be found in the four or five that separate Ventnor from Shanklin. Of a lovely afternoon in April these four or five miles are an admirable walk.

Of course you must first catch your lovely afternoon. I caught one; in fact I caught two. On the second I climbed up the downs and perceived that it was possible to put their gorse-covered stretches to still other than pedestrian uses—to devote them to sedentary pleasures. A long lounge in the lee of a stone wall, the lingering, fading afternoon light, the reddening sky, the band of blue sea above the level-topped bunches of gorse—these things, enjoyed as an undertone to the conversation of an amiable com-patriot, seemed indeed a very sufficient substitute for that primitive stillness of the absence of which I ventured just now to complain.

III

It was probably a mistake to stop at Portsmouth. I had done so, however, in obedience to a familiar theory that seaport towns abound in local colour, in curious types, in the quaint and the strange. But these charms, it must be confessed, were signally wanting to Portsmouth, along whose sordid streets I strolled for an hour, vainly glancing about me for an overhanging façade or a group of Maltese sailors. I was distressed to perceive that a famous seaport could be at once untidy and prosaic. Portsmouth is dirty, but it is also dull. It may be roughly divided into the dockyard and the public-houses. The dockyard, into which I was unable to penetrate, is a colossal enclosure, signalised externally by a grim brick wall, as featureless as an empty black-board. The dockyard eats up the town, as it were, and there is nothing left over but the gin-shops, which the town drinks up. There is not even a crooked old quay of any consequence, with brightly patched houses looking out upon a forest of masts. To begin with, there are no masts; and then there are no polyglot sign-boards, no overhanging upper stories, no outlandish parrots and macaws perched in open lattices. I had another hour or so before my train departed, and it would have gone hard with me if I had not bethought myself of hiring a boat and being pulled about in the harbour. Here a certain amount of entertainment was to be found. There were great ironclads and white troopships that looked vague and spectral, like the floating home of the Flying Dutchman, and small, devilish vessels whose mission was to project the infernal torpedo. I coasted about these metallic islets, and then, to eke out my entertainment, I boarded the *Victory*. The *Victory* is an ancient frigate of enormous size, which in the days of her glory carried I know not how many hundred guns, but whose only function now is to stand year after year in Portsmouth waters and exhibit herself to the festive cockney. Bank-holiday is now her great date; once upon a time it was Trafalgar. The *Victory*, in short, was Nelson's ship; it was on her huge deck that he was struck, and in her deep bowels he breathed his last. The venerable shell is provided with a company of ushers, like the Tower of London or Westminster Abbey, and is hardly less solid and spacious than either of the land-vessels. A good man in uniform did me the honours of the ship with a terrible displacement of *h*'s, and there seemed something strange in the way it had lapsed from its heroic part. It had carried two hundred guns and a mighty warrior, and boomed against the enemies of England; it had been the scene of one of the most thrilling and touching events in English history. Now, it was hardly more than a mere source of income to the Portsmouth watermen, an objective point for Whitsuntide excursionists, a thing a pilgrim from afar must allude to very casually, for fear of seeming vulgar or even quite serious.

IV

But I recouped myself, as they say, by stopping afterwards at Chichester. In this dense and various old England two places may be very near together and yet strike a very different note. I knew in a general way that this one had for its main sign a cathedral, and indeed had caught the sign, in the form of a beautiful spire, from the window of the train. I had always regarded an afternoon in a small cathedral-town as a high order of entertainment, and a morning at Portsmouth had left me in the mood for not missing such an exhibition. The spire of Chichester at a little distance greatly resembles that of Salisbury. It is on a smaller scale, but it tapers upward with a delicate slimness which, like that of its famous rival, makes a picture of the level landscape in which it stands. Unlike the spire of Salisbury, however, it has not at present the charm of antiquity. A few years ago the old steeple collapsed and tumbled into the church, and the present structure is but a modern facsimile. The cathedral is not of the highest interest; it is rather inexpressive, and, except for a curious old detached bell-tower which stands beside it, has no particular element of unexpectedness. But an English cathedral of restricted grandeur may yet be a very charming affair; and I spent an hour or so circling round this highly respectable edifice, with the spell of contemplation unbroken by satiety. I approached it, from the station, by the usual quiet red-brick street of the usual cathedral town—a street of small, excellent shops, before which, here and there, one of the vehicles of the neighbouring gentry was drawn up beside the curbstone while the grocer or the bookseller, who had hurried out obsequiously, was waiting upon the comfortable occupant. I went into a bookseller's to buy a Chichester guide, which I perceived in the window; I found the shopkeeper talking to a young curate in a soft hat. The guide seemed very desirable, though it appeared to have been but scantily desired; it had been published in the year 1841, and a very large remnant of the edition, with a muslin back and a little white label and paper-covered boards, was piled up on the counter. It was dedicated, with terrible humility, to the Duke of Richmond, and ornamented with primitive woodcuts and steel plates; the ink had turned brown and the page musty; and the style itself—that of a provincial antiquary of upwards of forty years ago penetrated with the grandeur of the aristocracy—had grown rather sallow and stale. Nothing could have been more mellifluous and urbane than the young curate: he was arranging to have the *Times* newspaper sent him every morning for perusal. 'So it will be a penny if it is fetched away at noon?' he said, smiling very sweetly and with the most gentlemanly voice possible; 'and it will be three halfpence if it is fetched away at four o'clock?' At the top of the street, into which, with my guide-book, I relapsed, was an old market-cross of the fifteenth century—a florid, romantic little structure. It consists of a stone pavilion, with open sides and a number of pinnacles and crockets and buttresses, besides a goodly medallion of the high-nosed visage of Charles I, which was placed above one of the arches, at the Restoration, in compensation for the violent havoc wrought upon the little town by the Parliamentary soldiers, who had wrested the place from the Royalists and who amused themselves, in their grim fashion, with infinite hacking and hewing in the cathedral. Here, to the left, the cathedral discloses itself, lifting its smart gray steeple out of a plea-sant garden. Opposite to the garden was the Dolphin or the Dragon —in fine the most eligible inn. I must confess that for a time it divided my attention with the cathedral, in virtue of an ancient, musty parlour on the second floor, with hunting-pictures hung above haircloth sofas; of a red-faced waiter, in evening dress; of a big round of cold beef and a tankard of ale. The prettiest thing at Chichester is a charming little three-sided cloister, attached to the cathedral, where, as is usual in such places, you may sit upon a gravestone amid the deep grass in the middle and measure the great central mass of the church—the large gray sides, the high founda-tions of the spire, the parting of the nave and transept. From this point the greatness of a cathedral seems more complex and impressive. You watch the big shadows slowly change their relations; you listen to the cawing of rooks and the twittering of swallows; you hear a slow footstep echoing in the cloisters.

V

If Oxford were not the finest thing in England the case would be clearer for Cambridge. It was clear enough there, for that matter, to my imagination, for thirty-six hours. To the barbaric mind, ambitious of culture, Oxford is the usual image of the happy reconciliation between research and acceptance. It typifies to an American the union of science and sense—of aspiration and ease. A German university gives a greater impression of science and an English country-house or an Italian villa a greater impression of idle enjoyment; but in these cases, on one side, knowledge is too rugged, and on the other satisfaction is too trivial. Oxford lends sweetness to labour and dignity to leisure. When I say Oxford I mean Cambridge, for a stray savage is not the least obliged to know the difference, and it suddenly strikes me as being both very pedantic and very good-natured in him to pretend to know it. What institution is more majestic than Trinity College? what can effect more a stray savage than the hospitality of such an institution? The first quadrangle is of immense extent, and the buildings that surround it, with their long, rich fronts of time-deepened gray, are the stateliest in the world. In the centre of the court are two or three acres of close-shaven lawn, out of the midst of which rises a grand Gothic fountain, where the serving men fill up their buckets. There are towers and battlements and statues, and besides these things there are cloisters and gardens and bridges. There are charming rooms in a kind of stately gate-tower, and the rooms, occupying the thickness of the building, have windows looking out on one side over the magnificent quadrangle, with half a mile or so of Decorated architecture, and on the other into deep-bosomed trees. And in the rooms is the best company conceivable—distinguished men who are thoroughly conversible, intimately affable. I spent a beautiful Sunday morning walking about the place with one of these gentlemen and attempting to *débrouiller* its charms. These are a very complicated tangle, and I do not pretend, in memory, to keep the colleges apart. There are none the less half a dozen points that make ineffaceable pictures. Six or eight of the colleges stand in a row, turning their backs to the river; and hereupon ensues the loveliest confusion of Gothic windows and ancient trees, of grassy banks and mossy balustrades, of sun-chequered avenues and groves, of lawns and gardens and terraces, of single-arched bridges spanning the little stream, which is small and shallow and looks as if it had been turned on for ornamental purposes. The thin-flowing Cam appears to exist simply as an occasion for these brave little bridges —the beautiful covered gallery of John's or the slightly collapsing arch of Clare. In the way of college-courts and quiet scholastic porticoes, of gray-walled gardens and ivied nooks of study, in all the pictorial accidents of a great English university, Cambridge is delightfully and inexhaustibly rich. I looked at these one by one and said to myself always that the last was the best. If I were called upon, however, to mention the prettiest corner of the world, I should draw out a thoughtful sigh and point the way to the garden of Trinity Hall. My companion, who was very competent to judge (but who spoke indeed with the partiality of a son of the house), declared, as he ushered me into it, that it was, to his mind, the most beautiful *small* garden in Europe. I freely accepted, and I promptly repeat, an affirmation so magnanimously conditioned. The little garden at Trinity Hall is narrow and crooked; it leans upon the river, from which a low parapet, all muffled in ivy, divides it; it has an ancient wall adorned with a thousand matted creepers on one side, and on the other a group of extraordinary horse-chestnuts. The trees are of prodigious size; they occupy half the garden, and are remarkable for the fact that their giant limbs strike down into the earth, take root again and emulate, as they rise, the majesty of the parent stem. The manner in which this magnificent group of horse-chestnuts sprawls about over the grass, out into the middle of the lawn, is one of the most heart-shaking features of the garden of Trinity Hall. Of course the single object at Cambridge that makes the most abiding impression is the famous chapel of King's College —the most beautiful chapel in England. The effect it attempts to produce within is all in the sphere of the sublime. The attempt succeeds, and the success is attained by a design so light and elegant that at first it almost defeats itself. The sublime usually has more of a frown and straddle, and it is not until after you have looked about you for ten minutes that you perceive the chapel to be saved from being the prettiest church in England by the accident of its being one of the noblest. It is a cathedral without aisles or columns or transepts, but (as a compensation) with such a beautiful slimness of clustered tracery soaring along the walls and spreading, bending and commingling in the roof, that its simplicity seems only a richness the more. I stood there for a quarter of an hour on a Sunday morning; there was no service, but in the choir behind the great screen which divides the chapel in half the young choristers were rehearsing for the afternoon. The beautiful boy-voices rose together and touched the splendid vault; they hung there, expanding and resounding, and then, like a rocket that spends itself, they faded and melted toward the end of the building. It was positively a choir of angels.

VI

Cambridgeshire is one of the so-called ugly counties; which means that it is observably flat. It is for this reason that the absence of terrestrial accent which culminates at Newmarket constitutes so perfect a means to an end. The country is like a board of green cloth; the turf presents itself as a friendly provision of nature. Nature offers her gentle bosom as a gaming-table; card-tables, billiard-tables are but a humble imitation of Newmarket Heath. It was odd to think that amid so much of the appearance of the humility of real virtue, there is more profane betting than anywhere else in the world. The large, neat English meadows roll away to a humid-looking sky, the young partridges jump about in the hedges, and nature looks not in the least as if she were offering you odds. The gentlemen look it, though, the gentlemen whom you meet on the roads and in the railway-carriage; they have that marked air—it pervades a man from the cut of his whisker to the shape of his boot-toe—as of the sublimated stable. It is brought home to you that to an immense number of people in England the events in the *Racing*

Calendar constitute the most important portion of contemporary history. The very breeze has an equine snort, if it doesn't breathe as hard as a hostler; the blue and white of the sky, dappled and spotty, recalls the figure of the necktie of 'spring meetings'; and the landscape is coloured as a sporting-print is coloured—with the same gloss, the same that seems to say a thousand grooms have rubbed it down.

The destruction of partridges is, if an equally classical, a less licentious pursuit, for which, I believe, Cambridgeshire offers peculiar facilities. Among these is a particular shooting-box which is a triumph of the familiar, the accidental style and a temple of clear hospitality. The shooting belongs to the autumn, not to this vernal period; but as I have spoken of echoes I suppose that if I had listened attentively I might have heard the ghostly crack of some of the famous shots that have been discharged there. The air, notedly, had vibrated to several august rifles, but all that I happened to hear by listening was some excellent talk.

In England, at any rate, as I said just now, a couple of places may be very near together and yet have what the philosophers call a connotation strangely different. Only a few miles beyond Newmarket lies Bury St Edmunds, a town whose tranquil antiquity turns its broad gray back straight upon the sporting papers. I confess that I went to Bury simply on the strength of its name, which I had often encountered and which had always seemed to me to have a high value for the picture-seeker. I knew that St Edmund had been an Anglo-Saxon worthy, but my conviction that the little town that bore his name would move me to rapture between trains had nothing definite to rest upon. The event, however, rewarded my faith—rewarded it with the sight of a magnificent old gatehouse of the thirteenth century, the most substantial of many relics of the great abbey which once flourished there. There are many others; they are scattered about the old precinct of the abbey, a large portion of which has been converted into a rambling botanic garden, the resort at Whitsuntide of a thousand very modern merry-makers. The monument I speak of has the proportions of a triumphal arch; it is at once a gateway and a fortress; it is covered with beautiful ornament, and is altogether the lion of Bury.

An English New Year

I￼T will hardly be pretended this year that the English Christmas
has been a merry one, or that the New Year has the promise of
being particularly happy. The winter is proving very cold and
vicious—as if Nature herself were loath to be left out of the general
conspiracy against the comfort and self-complacency of man. The
country at large has a sense of embarrassment and depression, which
is brought home more or less to every class in the closely graduated
social hierarchy, and the light of Christmas firesides has by no means
dispelled the gloom. Not that I mean to overstate the gloom. It is
difficult to imagine any combination of adverse circumstances
powerful enough to infringe very sensibly upon the appearance of
activity and prosperity, social stability and luxury, which English
life must always present to a stranger. Nevertheless the times are
distinctly of the kind synthetically spoken of as hard—there is plenty
of evidence of it—and the spirits of the public are not high. The
depression of business is extreme and universal; I am ignorant
whether it has reached so calamitous a point as that almost hopeless
prostration of every industry which it is assured us you have lately
witnessed in America, and I believe the sound of lamentation is by
no means so loud as it has been on two or three occasions within
the present century. The possibility of distress among the lower
classes has been minimised by the gigantic poor-relief system which
is so characteristic a feature of English civilisation and which, under
especial stress, is supplemented (as is the case at present) by private
charity proportionately huge. I notice too that in some parts of the
country discriminating groups of workpeople have selected these
dismal days as a happy time for striking. When the labouring classes
rise to the recreation of a strike I suppose the situation may be said
to have its cheerful side. There is, however, great distress in the
North, and there is a general feeling of scant money to play with
throughout the country. The *Daily News* has sent a correspondent

to the great industrial regions, and almost every morning for the last three weeks a very cleverly executed picture of the misery of certain parts of Yorkshire and Lancashire has been served up with the matutinal tea and toast. The work is a good one, and, I take it, eminently worth doing, as it appears to have had a visible effect upon the purse-strings of the well-to-do. There is nothing more striking in England than the success with which an 'appeal' is always made. Whatever the season or whatever the cause, there always appears to be enough money and enough benevolence in the country to respond to it in sufficient measure—a remarkable fact when one remembers that there is never a moment of the year when the custom of 'appealing' intermits. Equally striking perhaps is the perfection to which the science of distributing charity has been raised—the way it has been analysed and organised and made one of the exact sciences. You perceive that it has occupied for a long time a foremost place among administrative questions, and has received all the light that experience and practice can throw upon it. Is there in this perception more of a lightened or more of an added weight for the brooding consciousness? Truly there are aspects of England at which one can but darkly stare.

I left town a short time before Christmas and went to spend the festive season in the North, in a part of the country with which I was unacquainted. It was quite possible to absent one's self from London without a sense of sacrifice, for the charms of the capital during the last several weeks have been obscured by peculiarly vile weather. It is of course a very old story that London is foggy, and this simple statement raises no blush on the face of Nature as we see it here. But there are fogs and fogs, and the folds of the black mantle have been during the present winter intolerably thick. The thickness that draws down and absorbs the smoke of the house-tops, causes it to hang about the streets in impenetrable density, forces it into one's eyes and down one's throat, so that one is half blinded and quite sickened—this form of the particular plague has been much more frequent than usual. Just before Christmas, too, there was a heavy snowstorm, and even a tolerably light fall of snow has London quite at its mercy. The emblem of purity is almost immediately converted into a sticky, lead-coloured mush, the cabs skulk out of sight or take up their stations before the lurid windows of a public-house, which glares through the sleety darkness at the desperate wayfarer with an air of vulgar bravado. For recovery of one's nervous balance the only course was flight—flight to the country and the confinement of one's vision to the large area of one of those admirable homes which at this season overflow with hospitality and good cheer. By this means the readjustment is effectually brought about—these are conditions that you cordially appreciate. Of all the great things that the English have invented and made a part of the credit of the national character, the most perfect, the most characteristic, the one they have mastered most completely in all its details, so that it has become a compendious illustration of their social genius and their manners, is the well-appointed, well-administered, well-filled country-house. The grateful stranger makes these reflections—and others besides—as he wanders about in the beautiful library of such a dwelling, of an inclement winter afternoon, just at the hour when six o'clock tea is impending. Such a place and such a time abound in agreeable episodes; but I suspect that the episode from which, a fortnight ago, I received the most ineffaceable impression was but indirectly connected with the charms of a luxurious fireside. The country I speak of was a populous manufacturing region, full of tall chimneys and of an air that is gray and gritty. A lady had made a present of a Christmas-tree to the children of a workhouse, and she invited me to go with her and assist at the distribution of the toys. There was a drive through the early dusk of a very cold Christmas eve, followed by the drawing up of a lamp-lit brougham in the snowy quadrangle of a grim-looking charitable institution. I had never been in an English workhouse before, and this one transported me, with the aid of memory, to the early pages of 'Oliver Twist'. We passed through cold, bleak passages, to which an odour of suet-pudding, the aroma of Christmas cheer, failed to impart an air of hospitality; and then, after waiting a while in a little parlour appertaining to the superintendent, where the remainder of a dinner of by no means eleemosynary simplicity and the attitude of a gentleman asleep with a flushed face on the sofa seemed to effect a tacit exchange of references, we were ushered into a large frigid refectory, chiefly illumined by the twinkling tapers of the Christmas-tree. Here entered to us some hundred and fifty little children of charity, who had been making a copious dinner and who brought with them an atmosphere of hunger memorably satisfied—together with other traces of the occasion upon their pinafores and their small red faces. I have said that the place reminded me of 'Oliver Twist', and I glanced through this little herd for an infant figure that should look as if it were cut out for romantic adventures. But they were all very prosaic little mortals. They were made of very common clay indeed, and a certain number of them were idiotic. They filed up and received their little offerings, and then they compressed themselves into a tight infantine bunch and, lifting up their small hoarse voices, directed a melancholy hymn toward their benefactress. The scene was a picture I shall not forget, with its curious mixture of poetry and sordid prose—the dying wintry light in the big bare, stale room; the beautiful Lady Bountiful, standing in the twinkling glory of the Christmas-tree; the little multitude of staring and wondering, yet perfectly expressionless, faces.

An English Winter Watering-place

I HAVE just been spending a couple of days at a well-known resort upon the Kentish coast, and though such an exploit is by no means unprecedented, yet, as to the truly observing mind no opportunity is altogether void and no impressions are wholly valueless, I have it on my conscience to make a note of my excursion. Superficially speaking, it was wanting in originality; but I am afraid that it afforded me as much entertainment as if the idea of paying a visit to Hastings had been an invention of my own. This is so far from being the case that the most striking feature of the town in question is the immense provision made there for the entertainment of visitors. Hastings and St Leonards, standing side by side, present a united sea-front of more miles in length than I shall venture to compute. It is sufficient that in going from one end of the place to the other I had a greater sense of having taken a long, straight walk through street scenery than I had done since I last measured the populated length of Broadway. This is not an image that evokes any one of the graces, and it must be confessed that the beauty of Hastings does not reside in a soft irregularity or a rural exuberance. Like all the larger English watering-places it is simply a little London *super mare*. The graceful, or at least the pictorial, is always to be found in England if one will take the trouble of looking for it; but it must be conceded that at Hastings this element is less obtrusive than it might be. I had heard it described as a 'dull Brighton', and this description had been intended to dispose of the place. In fact, however—such is the perversity of the inquiring mind—it had rather quickened than quenched my interest. It occurred to me that it might be as entertaining to follow out the variations of Brighton, the possible embroideries of the theme, as it is often found to listen to those with which some expressed musical idea is over-scored by another composer. Four or five miles of lodging-houses and hotels staring at the sea across a 'parade' adorned with iron benches, with hand-organs and German bands, with nursemaids and British babies, with ladies and gentlemen of leisure—looking rather embarrassed with it and trying rather unsuccessfully to get rid of it—this is the great feature which Brighton and Hastings have in common. At Brighton there is a certain variety and gaiety of colour—something suggesting crookedness and yellow paint—which gives the scene a kind of cheerful, easy, more or less vulgar, foreign air. But Hastings is very gray and sober and English, and indeed it is because it seemed to me so English that I gave my best attention to it. If one is attempting to gather impressions of a people and to learn to know them, everything is interesting that is characteristic, quite apart from its being beautiful. English manners are made up of such a multitude of small details that the portrait a stranger has privately sketched in is always liable to receive new touches. And this indeed is the explanation of his noting a great many small points, on the spot, with a degree of relish and appreciation which must often, to persons who are not in his position, appear exaggerated, if not absurd. He has formed a mental picture of the civilisation of the people he lives among, and whom, when he has a great deal of courage, he makes bold to say he is studying; he has drawn up a kind of tabular view of their manners and customs, their idiosyncrasies, their social institutions, their general features and properties; and when once he has suspended this rough cartoon in the chambers of his imagination he finds a great deal of occupation in touching it up and filling it in. Wherever he goes, whatever he sees, he adds a few strokes. That is how I spent my time at Hastings.

I found it, for instance, a question more interesting than it might superficially appear to choose between the inns—between the Royal Hotel upon the Parade and an ancient hostel, a survival of the posting-days, in a side-street. A friend had described the latter establishment to me as 'mellow', and this epithet complicated the problem. The term mellow, as applied to an inn, is the comparative degree of a state of things of which (say) 'musty' would be the superlative. If you can seize this tendency in its comparative stage you may do very well indeed; the trouble is that, like all tendencies, it contains, even in its earlier phases, the germs of excess. I thought it very possible that the Swan would be over-ripe; but I thought it equally probable that the Royal would be crude. I could claim a certain acquaintance with 'royal' hotels—I knew just how they were constituted. I foresaw the superior young woman sitting at a ledger, in a kind of glass cage, at the bottom of the stairs, and expressing by refined intonations her contempt for a gentleman who should decline to 'require' a sitting-room. The functionary whom in America we know and dread as an hotel-clerk belongs in England to the sex which, at need, is able to look over your head to a still further point. Large hotels here are almost always owned and carried on by companies, and the company is represented by a well-shaped female figure belonging to the class whose members are more particularly known as 'persons'. The chambermaid is a young woman, and the female tourist is a lady; but the occupant of the glass cage, who hands you your key and assigns you your apartment, is designated in the manner I have mentioned. The 'person' has various methods of revenging herself for her shadowy position in the social scale, and I think it was from a vague recollection of having on former occasions felt the weight of her embittered spirit that I determined to seek the hospitality of the humbler inn, where it was probable that one who was himself humble would enjoy a certain consideration. In the event, I was rather oppressed by the feather-bed quality of the welcome extended to me at the Swan. Once established there, in a sitting-room (after all), the whole affair had all the local colour I could desire.

I have sometimes had occasion to repine at the meagreness and mustiness of the old-fashioned English inn, and to feel that in poetry and in fiction these defects had been culpably glossed over. But I said to myself the other evening that there is a kind of venerable decency even in some of its dingiest consistencies, and that in an age in which the conception of good manners is losing most of its ancient firmness one should do justice to an institution that is still more or less of a stronghold of the faded amenities. It is a satisfaction in moving about the world to be treated as a gentleman, and this gratification appears to be more than, in the light of modern science, a Company can profitably undertake to bestow. I have an old friend, a person of admirably conservative instincts, from whom, a short time since, I borrowed a hint of this kind. This lady had been staying at a small inn in the country with her daughter; the daughter, whom we shall call Mrs B., had left the house a few days before the mother. 'Did you like the place?' I asked of my friend; 'was it comfortable?' 'No, it was not comfortable; but I liked it. It was shabby, and I was much overcharged: but it pleased me.' 'What was the mysterious charm?' 'Well, when I was coming away, the landlady—she had cheated me horribly—came to my carriage, and dropped a curtsey, and said: "My duty to Mrs B., ma'am." Que voulez-vous? That pleased me.' There was an old waiter at Hastings who would have been capable of that—an old waiter who had been in the house for forty years and who was not so much an individual waiter as the very spirit and genius, the incarnation and tradition of waiterhood. He was faded and weary and rheumatic, but he had a sort of mixture of the paternal and the deferential, the philosophic and the punctilious, which seemed but grossly requited by a present of a small coin. I am not fond of jugged hare for dinner, either as a light *entrée* or as a *pièce de résistance*; but this accomplished attendant had the art of presenting you such a dish in a manner that persuaded you, for the time, that it was worthy of your serious consideration. The hare, by the way, before being subjected to the mysterious operation of jugging, might have been seen dangling from a hook in the bar of the inn, together with a choice collection of other viands. You might peruse the bill of fare in an elementary form as you passed in and out of the house, and make up your *menu* for the day by poking with your stick at a juicy-looking steak or a promising fowl. The landlord and his spouse were always on the threshold of the bar, polishing a brass candlestick and paying you their respects; the place was pervaded by an aroma of rum-and-water and of commercial travellers' jokes.

This description, however, is lacking in the element of gentility, and I will not pursue it farther, for I should give a very false impression of Hastings if I were to omit so characteristic a feature. It was, I think, the element of gentility that most impressed me. I know that the word I have just ventured to use is under the ban of contemporary taste; so I may as well say outright that I regard it as indispensable in almost any attempt at portraiture of English manners. It is vain for an observer of such things to pretend to get on without it. One may talk of foreign life indefinitely—of the manners and customs of France, Germany, and Italy—and never feel the need of this suggestive, yet mysteriously discredited, epithet. One may survey the remarkable face of American civilisation without finding occasion to strike this particular note. But in England no circumlocution will serve—the note must be definitely struck. To attempt to speak of an English watering-place in winter and yet pass it over in silence would be to forfeit all claims to the analytic spirit. For a stranger, at any rate, the term is invaluable—it is more convenient than I should find easy to say. It is instantly evoked in my mind by long rows of smuttily plastered houses, with a card inscribed 'Apartments' suspended in the window of the ground-floor sitting-room—that portion of the dwelling which is known in lodging-house parlance as 'the parlours'. Everything, indeed, suggests it—the bath-chairs, drawn up for hire in a melancholy row; the innumerable and excellent shops, adorned with the latest photographs of the royal family and of Mrs Langtry; the little reading-room and circulating library on the Parade, where the daily papers, neatly arranged, may be perused for a trifling fee, and the novels of the season are stacked away like the honeycombs in an apiary; the long pier, stretching out into the sea, to which you are admitted by the payment of a penny at a wicket, and where you may enjoy the music of an indefatigable band, the enticements of several little stalls, for the sale of fancy-work, and the personal presence of good local society. It is only the winking, twinkling, easily rippling sea that is not genteel. But, really, I was disposed to say at Hastings that if the sea was not genteel, so much the worse for Neptune; for it was the favourable aspect of the great British proprieties and solemnities that struck me. Hastings and St Leonards, with their long, warm sea-front and their multitude of small, cheap comforts and conveniences, offer a kind of *résumé* of middle-class English civilisation and of advantages of which it would ill become an American to make light. I don't suppose that life at Hastings is the most exciting or the most gratifying in the world, but it must certainly have its advantages. If I were a quiet old lady of modest income and nice habits—or even a quiet old gentleman of the same pattern—I should certainly go to Hastings. There, amid the little shops and the little libraries, the bath-chairs and the German bands, the Parade and the long Pier, with a mild climate, a moderate scale of prices and the consciousness of a high civilisation, I should enjoy a seclusion which would have nothing primitive or crude.

Winchelsea, Rye and 'Denis Duval'

I

I HAVE recently had a literary adventure which, though not followed by the prostration that sometimes ensues on adventures, has nevertheless induced meditation. The adventure itself indeed was not astounding, and I mention it, to be frank, only in the interest of its sequel. It consisted merely, on taking up an old book again for the sake of a certain desired and particular light, of my having found that the light was in fact not there to shine, but was, on the contrary, directly projected *upon* the book from the very subject itself as to which I had invoked assistance. The case, in short, to put it simply, was that Thackeray's charming fragment of 'Denis Duval' proved to have much less than I had supposed to say about the two little old towns with which the few chapters left to us are mainly concerned, but that the two little old towns, on the other hand, unexpectedly quickened reflection on 'Denis Duval'. Reading over Thackeray to help me further to Winchelsea, I became conscious, of a sudden, that Winchelsea—which I already in a manner knew—was helping me further to Thackeray. Reinforced, in this service, by its little sister-city of Rye, it caused a whole question to open, and the question, in turn, added a savour to a sense already, by good-fortune, sharp. Winchelsea and Rye form together a very curious small corner, and the measure, candidly undertaken, of what the unfinished book had done with them, brought me to a nearer view of them—perhaps even to a more jealous one; as well as to some consideration of what books in general, even when finished, may do with curious small corners.

I dare say I speak of 'Denis Duval' as 'old' mainly to make an impression on readers whose age is less. I remember, after all, perfectly, the poetry of its original appearance—there was such a thrill, in those days, even after 'Lovel the Widower' and 'Philip', at any

162

new Thackeray—in the cherished *Cornhill* of the early time, with a drawing of Frederick Walker to its every number and a possibility of its being like 'Esmond' in its embroidered breast. If, moreover, it after a few months broke short off, that really gave it something as well as took something away. It might have been as true of works of art as of men and women, that if the gods loved them they died young. 'Denis Duval' was at any rate beautiful, and was beautiful again on reperusal at a later time. It is all beautiful once more to a final reading, only it is remarkably different: and this is precisely where my story lies. The beauty is particularly the beauty of its being its author's—which is very much, with book after book, what we find ourselves coming to in general, I think, at fifty years. Our appreciation changes—how in the world, with experience always battering away, shouldn't it?—but our feeling, more happily, doesn't. There *are* books, of course, that criticism, when we are fit for it, only consecrates, and then, with association fiddling for the dance, we are in possession of a literary pleasure that is the highest of raptures. But in many a case we drag along a fond indifference, an element of condonation, which is by no means of necessity without its strain of esteem, but which, obviously, is not founded on one of our deeper satisfactions. Each can but speak, at all events, on such a matter, for himself. It is a matter also, doubtless, that belongs to the age of the loss—so far as they quite depart—of illusions at large. The reason for liking a particular book becomes thus a better, or at least a more generous, one than the particular book seems in a position itself at last to supply. Woe to the mere official critic, the critic who has never felt the *man*. You go on liking 'The Antiquary' because it is Scott. You go on liking 'David Copperfield' —I don't say you go on reading it, which is a very different matter —because it is Dickens. So you go on liking 'Denis Duval' because it is Thackeray—which, in this last case, is the logic of the charm I alluded to.

The recital here, as every one remembers, is autobiographic; the old battered, but considerably enriched, world-worn, but finely sharpened Denis looks back upon a troubled life from the winter fireside and places you, in his talkative and contagious way—he is a practised literary artist—in possession of the story. We see him in a

placid port after many voyages, and have that amount of evidence
—the most, after all, that the most artless reader needs—as to the
'happy' side of the business. The evidence indeed is, for curiosity,
almost excessive, or at least premature; as he again and again puts
it before us that the companion of his later time, the admirable
wife seated there beside him, is nobody else at all, any hopes of a
more tangled skein notwithstanding, than the object of his infant
passion, the little French orphan, slightly younger than himself,
who is brought so promptly on the scene. The way in which this
affects us as undermining the 'love-interest' bears remarkably on
the specific question of the subject of the book as the author would
have expressed this subject to his own mind. We get, to the moment
the work drops, not a glimpse of his central idea; nothing, if such
had been his intention, was in fact ever more triumphantly con-
cealed. The darkness therefore is intensified by our seeming to gather
that, like the love-interest, at all events, the 'female interest' was
not to have been largely invoked. The narrator is in general, from
the first, full of friendly hints, in Thackeray's way, of what is to
come; but the chapters completed deal only with his childish years,
his wondrous boy-life at Winchelsea and Rye, the public and private
conditions of which—practically, in the last century, the same for
the two places—form the background for this exposition. The
south-eastern counties, comparatively at hand, were enriched at
that period by a considerable French immigration, the accession of
Huguenot fugitives too firm in their faith to have bent their necks
to the dire rigours with which the revocation of the Edict of Nantes
was followed up. This corner of Sussex received—as it had received
in previous centuries—its forlorn contingent; to the interesting
origin of which many Sussex family names—losing, as it were, their
drawing but not their colour—still sufficiently testify. Portions of
the stranger race suffered, struggled, sank; other portions resisted,
took root and put forth branches, and Thackeray, clearly, had found
his rough material in some sketchy vision of one of these obscure
cases of troubled adjustment, which must often have been, for difficulty and complexity, of the stuff of dramas. Such a case, for the
informed fancy, might indeed overflow with possibilities of character, character reinforced, in especial, by the impression, gathered

and matured on the spot, of the two small ghosts of the Cinque Ports family, the pair of blighted hill-towns that were once sea-towns and that now draw out their days in the dim after-sense of a mere indulged and encouraged picturesqueness. 'Denis Duval' could only, it would seem, have been conceived as a 'picturesque' affair; but that may serve exactly as a reason for the attempt to refigure it.

Little hilltop communities sensibly even yet, with the memory of their tight walls and stiff gates not wholly extinct, Rye and Winchelsea hold fast to the faint identity which remains their least fragile support, their estate as 'Antient Towns' involved (with the distincter Five and raising the number to seven) in that nominal, though still occasionally pompous, Wardenship, the image—for our time—of the most famous assignment of which is preserved in Longfellow's fine verses on the death of the Duke of Wellington. The sea, in previous times half friend, half foe, began long since to fight, in each character, shy of them, and now, in wrinkled wistfulness, they look across at the straight blue band, two miles or so away, that tells of the services they rendered, the illusions they cherished—illusions in the case of poor Winchelsea especially absurd—and the extreme inconvenience they repeatedly suffered. They were again and again harried and hacked by the French, and might have had, it would seem, small appetite for the company, however reduced and disarmed, of these immemorial neighbours. The retreating waters, however, had even two centuries ago already placed such dangers on a very different footing, and the recovery and evocation of some of the old processes of actual absorption may well have presented themselves to Thackeray as a problem of the sort that tempts the lover of human histories. Happy and enviable always the first trepidation of the artist who lights on a setting that 'meets' his subject or on a subject that meets his setting. The editorial notes to 'Denis Duval' yield unfortunately no indication of whether Winchelsea put into his head the idea of this study, or of whether he carried it about till he happened judiciously to drop it there. Appearances point, in truth, to a connection of the latter kind, for the fragment itself contains no positive evidence that Thackeray ever, with the mere eye of sense, beheld the place; which is precisely one of the ambiguities that challenge the critic and an item in the unexpectedness that I spoke of at the beginning of these remarks. What—in the light, at least, of later fashions—the place has to offer the actual observer is the effect of an object seen, a thing of aspect and suggestion, situation and colour; but what had it to offer Thackeray—or the taste of forty years ago—that he so oddly forbore to give us a tangled clue to? The impression of to-day's reader is that the chapters we possess might really have been written without the author's having stood on the spot; and that is just why they have, as I began by saying, so much less to contribute to our personal vision than this influence, for its part, has to suggest in respect to the book itself.

Evidently, none the less, the setting, little as it has got itself 'rendered', did somehow come into the painter's ken; we know this, moreover, independently, and we make out that he had his inner mysteries and his reasons. The little house of Duval, faring forth from the stress of the Alsatian fatherland, seeks safety and finds business in the shrunken city, scarce at last more than a hamlet, of Edward the First's defeated design, where, in three generations, well on into the century, it grinds and sleeps, smuggles and spends, according to the fashions of the place and time. These communities appear to have had, in their long decline, little industry but their clandestine traffic with other coasts, in the course of which they quite mastered the art of going, as we say, 'one better' than the officers of the revenue. It is to this hour a part of the small romance of Rye that you may fondly fancy such scant opulence as rears its head to have had its roots in the malpractice of forefathers not too rude for much cunning—in nightly plots and snares and flurries, a hurrying, shuffling, hiding, that might at any time have put a noose about most necks. Some of those of the small gentry who were not smugglers were recorded highwaymen, flourishing about in masks and with pistols; and indeed in the general scene, as rendered by the supposed chronicler, these appear the principal features. The only others are those of his personal and private situation, which in fact, however, strikes me as best expressed in the fact that the extremely talkative, discursive, ejaculatory and moralising Denis was possessed in perfection of his master's maturest style. He writes, almost to the life, the language of 'The Roundabout Papers'; so that if the third person had been exchanged, throughout, for his first, and his occasional present tense been superseded by the past, the rest of the text would have needed little rearrangement. This imperfect unity was more or less inevitable—the difficulty of projecting yourself as somebody else is never so great as when you retain the *form* of being yourself; but another of the many reflections suggested by reperusal is as to whether the speaker is not guilty of a slight abuse. Of course it may be said that what really has happened was that Thackeray had, on his side, anticipated his hero in the use of his hero's natural idiom. It may thus have been less that Denis had come to write highly 'evolved' nineteenth-century English than that his creator had arrived, in 'The Roundabout Papers' and elsewhere, at writing excellent reconstructed eighteenth. It would not, however, were the inquiry to be pushed, be only on the autobiographer's personal and grammatical, but on his moral and sentimental accent, as it were, that criticism would probably most bear. His manner of thinking and feeling is quite as 'Roundabout' as his manner of saying.

A dozen wonderments rise here, and a dozen curiosities and speculations; as to which, in truth, I am painfully divided between the attraction of such appeals and a certain other aspect of my subject to which I shall attempt presently to do justice. The superior stroke, I remind myself—possibly not in vain—would be to deal handsomely with both solicitations. The almost irresistible fascination, critically speaking, of the questions thus abruptly, after long years, thrust forth by the book, lies in their having reference to this very opposition of times and tastes. The thing is not forty years old, but it points already—and that is above all the amusement of it—to a general *poetic* that, both on its positive and its negative sides, we have left well behind. Can the author perhaps have had in mind, misguidedly, some idea of what his public 'wanted' or didn't want? The public is really, to a straight vision, I think, not a capacity for wanting, at all, but only an unlimited capacity for *taking*—taking that (whatever it is) which will, in effect, make it open its mouth. It goes to the expense of few preconceptions, and even on the question of opening its mouth has a consciousness limited to the suspicion that in a given case this orifice *has*—or had not—gaped. We are therefore to imagine Thackeray as perfectly conscious that

he himself, working by his own fine light, constituted the public
he had most to reckon with. On the other hand, his time, in its degree, had helped to shape him, and a part of the consequence of this
shaping, apparently, was his extraordinary avoidance of picture.
This is the mystery that drives us to the hypothesis of his having
tried to pay, in some uncanny quarter, some deluded deference.
Was he under the fear that, even as *he* could do it, 'description'
would not, in the early sixties, be welcome? It is impossible to stand
to-day in the high, loose, sunny, haunted square of Winchelsea
without wondering what he could have been thinking of. There are
ladies in view with easels, sun-bonnets, and white umbrellas—often
perceptibly, too, with nothing else that makes for successful representation; but I doubt if it were these apparitions that took the
bloom from his vision, for they were much less frequent in those
looser days, and moreover would have formed much more a reason
for not touching the place at all than for taking it up indifferently.
Of any impulse to make the reader see it with seeing eyes his page,
at all events, gives no sign. We must presently look at it for ourselves, even at the cost, or with the consequence, of a certain loyal
resentment. For Winchelsea is strange, individual, charming. What
could he—yes—have been thinking of? We are wound up for saying
that he has given his subject away, until we suddenly remember
that, to this hour, we have never really made out what his subject
was to have been.

Never was a secret more impenetrably kept. Read over the fragment itself—which reaches, after all, to some two hundred and fifty
pages; read over, at the end of the volume, the interesting editorial
notes; address yourself, above all, in the charming series of intro-
ductions lately prepared by Mrs Richmond Ritchie for a new and,
so far as possible, biographical edition of her father's works, to the
reminiscences briefly bearing on Denis, and you will remain in each
case equally distant from a clue. It is the most puzzling thing in the
world, but there *is* no clue. There are indications, in respect to the
book, from Thackeray's hand, memoranda on matters of detail, and
there is in especial a highly curious letter to his publisher; yet the
clue that his own mind must have held never shows the tip of its
tail. The letter to his publisher, in which, according to the editor

of the fragment, he 'sketches his plot for the information of' that gentleman, reads like a mystification by which the gentleman was to be temporarily kept quiet. With an air of telling him a good deal, Thackeray really tells him nothing—nothing, I mean, by which he himself would have been committed to (any more than deterred from) any idea kept up his sleeve. If he were holding this card back, to be played at his own time, he could not have proceeded in the least differently; and one can construct to-day, with a free hand, one's picture of his private amusement at the success of his diplomacy. All the while, what *was* the card? The production of a novel finds perhaps its nearest analogy in the ride across country; the competent novelist—that is, the novelist with the real seat—presses his subject, in spite of hedges and ditches, as hard as the keen fox-hunter presses the game that has been started for his day with the hounds. The fox is the novelist's idea, and when he rides straight he rides, regardless of danger, in whatever direction that animal takes. As we lay down 'Denis Duval', however, we feel not only that we are off the scent, but that we never really have been, with the author, on it. The fox has got quite away. For it carries us no further, surely, to say—as may possibly be objected—that the author's subject was to have been neither more or less than the adventures of his hero; inasmuch as, turn the thing as we will, these 'adventures' could at the best have constituted nothing more than its *form*. It is an affront to the memory of a great writer to pretend that they were to have been arbitrary and unselected, that there was nothing in his mind to determine them. The book was, obviously, to have been, as boys say, 'about' them. But what were *they* to have been about? Thackeray carried the mystery to his grave.

II

If I spoke just now of Winchelsea as haunted, let this somewhat overworked word stand as an ineffectual tribute to the small, sad, civic history that the place appeals to us to reconstruct as we gaze vaguely about. I have a little ancient and most decorative map of Sussex—testifying remarkably to the changes of relation between sea and land in this corner of the coast—in which 'Old Winchelsey

Drowned' figures as the melancholy indication of a small circular spot quite out at sea. If new Winchelsea is old, the earlier town is to-day but the dim ghost of a tradition, with its very site—distant several miles from that of its successor—rendered uncertain by the endless mutation of the shore. After suffering, all through the thirteenth century, much stress of wind and weather, it was practically destroyed in 1287 by a great storm which cast up masses of beach, altered the course of a river and roughly handled the face of many things. The reconstruction of the town in another place was thereupon decreed by a great English king, and we need but a little fuller chronicle to help us to assist at one of those migrations of a whole city of which antiquity so often gives us the picture. The survivors of Winchelsea were colonised, and colonised in much state. The 'new' community, whose life was also to be so brief, sits on the pleasant table of a great cliff-like hill which, in the days of the Plantagenets, was an admirable promontory washed by the waves. The sea surrounded its base, came up past it to the east and north in a long inlet, and stretched away, across the level where the sheep now graze, to stout little neighbouring Rye, perched—in doubtless not quite equal pride—on an eminence more humble, but which must have counted then even for more than to-day in the pretty figure made, as you stand off, by the small, compact, pyramidal port. The 'Antient Towns' looked at each other then across the water, which made almost an island of the rock of huddled, church-crowned Rye—which had too much to say to them alike, on evil days, at their best time, but which was too soon to begin to have too little. If the early Winchelsea was to suffer by 'drowning', its successor was to bear the stroke of remaining high and dry. The haven on the hill-top—a bold and extraordinary conception—had hardly had time to get, as we should now say, 'started', before it began to see its days numbered. The sea and the shore were never at peace together, and it was, most remarkably, not the sea that got the best of it. Winchelsea had only time to dream a great dream— the dream of a scant pair of centuries—before its hopes were turned to bitterness and its boasts to lamentation. It had literally, during its short career, put in a claim to rivalship with the port of London.

The irony of fate now sits in its empty lap; but the port of London had never suggested even a frustrate 'Denis Duval'.

While Winchelsea dreamed, at any rate, she worked, and the noble fragment of her great church, rising solid from the abortive symmetry of her great square, helps us to put our hand on her deep good faith. She built at least as she believed—she planned as she fondly imagined. The huge ivy-covered choir and transepts of St Thomas of Canterbury—to whom the structure was addressed—represent to us a great intention. They are not so mighty, but they are almost as brave, as the wondrous fragment of Beauvais. Walled and closed on their unfinished side, they form at present all the church, and, with its grand lines of arch and window, its beautiful Gothic tombs and general hugeness and height, the church—mercifully exempt as yet from restoration—is wonderful for the place. You may at this hour—if you are given to such emotions—feel a mild thrill, not be unaware even of the approach of tears, as you measure the scale on which the building had been planned and the ground that the nave and aisles would have covered. You murmur, in the summer twilight, a soft 'Bravo!' across the ages—to the ears of heaven knows what poor nameless ghosts. The square—apparently one of many—was to have been worthy of New York or of Turin; for the queerest, quaintest, most touching thing of all is that the reinstated city was to have been laid out on the most approved modern lines. Nothing is more interesting—to the mooning, sketching spectator—than this evidence that the great Edward had anticipated us all in the convenient chess-board pattern. It is true—attention has been called to the fact—that Pompeii had anticipated *him*; but I doubt if he knew much about Pompeii. His abstract avenues and cross-streets straggle away, through the summer twilight, into mere legend and mystery. In speaking awhile since of the gates of these shattered strongholds as 'stiff', I also spoke of their walls as 'tight'; but the scheme of Winchelsea must have involved, after all, a certain looseness of cincture. The old vague girdle is lost to-day in the fields where the sheep browse, in the parkish acres where the great trees cluster. The Sussex oak is mighty—it was of the Sussex oak that, in the old time, the king's ships were built; it was, in particular, to her command of this material that Rye owed the burdensome honour of supplying vessels, on constant call, to the royal navy. Strange is this record, in Holloway's History of that town, and in presence of the small things of to-day; so perpetual, under stress, appears to have been the demand and so free the supply and the service.

Rye continued indeed, under her old brown south cliff, to build big boats till this industry was smitten by the adoption of iron. That was the last stroke; though even now you may see things as you stand on the edge of the cliff: best of all on the open, sunny terrace of a dear little old garden—a garden brown-walled, red-walled, rose-covered on its other sides, divided by the width of a quiet street of grass-grown cobbles from the house of its master, and possessed of a little old glass-fronted, panelled pavilion which I hold to be the special spot in the world where Thackeray might most fitly have figured out his story. There is not much room in the pavilion, but there is room for the hard-pressed table and the tilted chair—there is room for a novelist and his friends. The panels have a queer paint and a venerable slant; the small chimney-place is at your back; the south window is perfect, the privacy bright and open. How can I tell what old—what young—visions of visions and memories of images come back to me under the influence of this quaint receptacle, into which, by kind permission, I occasionally peep, and still more under the charm of the air and the view that, as I just said, you may enjoy, close at hand, from the small terrace? How can I tell why I always keep remembering and losing there the particular passages of some far-away foolish fiction, absorbed in extreme youth, which haunt me, yet escape me, like the echo of an old premonition? I seem to myself to have lain on the grass somewhere, as a boy, poring over an English novel of the period, presumably quite bad—for they were pretty bad then too—and losing myself in the idea of just such another scene as this. But even could I rediscover the novel I wouldn't go back to it. It couldn't have been so good as this; for this—all concrete and doomed and minimised as it is—is the real thing. The other little gardens, other little odds and ends of crooked brown wall and supported terrace and glazed winter sun-trap, lean over the cliff that still, after centuries, keeps its rude drop; they have beneath them the river, a tide that comes and goes, and the mile or more of grudging desert level, beyond it, which now throws the sea to the near horizon, where, on summer days, with a depth of blue and a scattered gleam of sails, it looks forgiving and resigned. The little old shipyards at the base of the rock are for the most part quite empty, with only vague piles of brown timber and the deposit of generations of chips; yet a fishing-boat or two are still on the stocks—an 'output' of three or four a year!—and the ring of the hammer on the wood, a sound, in such places, rare to the contemporary ear, comes up, through the sunny stillness, to your meditative perch.

The tidal river, on the left, wanders away to Rye Harbour and its bar, where the black fishing-boats, half the time at lop-sided rest in the mud, make a cluster of slanting spears against the sky. When the river is full we are proud of its wide light and many curves; when it is empty we call it, for vague reasons, 'rather Dutch'; and empty or full we sketch it in the fine weather as hard as ever we can. When I say 'we' I mean *they* do—it is to speak with hospitality. They mostly wear, as I have hinted, large sun-bonnets, and they crouch on low camp-stools; they put in, as they would say, a bit of white, in places often the least likely. Rye is in truth a rudimentary drawing-lesson, and you quite embrace the question when you have fairly seized the formula. Nothing so 'quaint' was ever so easy— nothing so easy was ever so quaint. Much more to be loved than feared, she has not, alas, a scrap of 'style', and she may be effectively rendered without the obligation of subtlety. At favoured seasons there appear within her precinct sundry slouch-hatted gentlemen who study her humble charms through a small telescope formed by their curved fingers and thumb, and who are not unliable to define themselves as French artists leading a train of English and American lady pupils. They distribute their disciples over the place, at selected points, where the master, going his round from hour to hour, re- minds you of nothing so much as a busy *chef* with many saucepans on the stove and periodically lifting their covers for a sniff and a stir. There are ancient doorsteps that are fairly haunted, for their con- venience of view, by the 'class', and where the fond proprietor, going and coming, has to pick his way among paraphernalia or to take flying leaps over genius and industry. If Winchelsea is, as I gather, less beset, it is simply that Winchelsea enjoys the immunity of her greater distinction. She is full of that and must be even more difficult than she at first appears. But I forsook her and her distinction, just now, and I must return to them; though the right moment would quite have been as we stood, at Rye, on the terrace of the little old south-garden, to which she presents herself, beyond two or three miles of flat Dutch-looking interval, from the extreme right, her few red roofs almost lost on her wooded hill and her general presence masking, for this view, the headland of Hastings, ten miles by the coast, westward.

It was about her spacious solitude that we had already begun to stroll; for the purpose, however, mainly, of measuring the stretch, south and north, to the two more crumbled of her three old gates. They are very far gone, each but the ruin of a ruin; but it is their actual countrified state that speaks of the circuit—one hundred and fifty acres—they were supposed to defend. Under one of them you may pass, much round about, by high-seated villages and in constant sight of the sea, toward Hastings; from the other, slightly the less dilapidated, you may gather, if much so minded, the suggestion of some illustration or tail-piece in a volume of Italian travel. The steep white road plunges crookedly down to where the poor arches that once were massive straddle across it, while a spreading chestnut, beside them, plays exactly the part desired—prepares you, that is, for the crack of the whip of the *vetturino* trudging up beside his travelling-carriage. With a bare-legged urchin and a browsing goat the whole thing would be there. But we turn, at that point, to mount again and cross the idle square and come back to the east gate, which is the aspect of Winchelsea that presents itself most— and in fact quite admirably—as the front. Yet by what is it that, at the end of summer afternoons, my sense of an obliterated history is fed? There is little but the church really to testify, for the extraordinary groined vaults and crypts that are part of the actual pride of the place—treasure-houses of old merchants, foundations of upper solidities that now are dust—count for nothing, naturally, in the immediate effect. The early houses passed away long ago, and the present ones speak, in broken accents and scant and shabby signs, but of the last hundred, the last couple of hundred, years. Everything that ever happened is gone, and, for that matter, nothing very eminent, only a dim mediocrity of life, ever did happen. Rye has Fletcher the dramatist, the Fletcher of Beaumont, whom it brought to birth; but Winchelsea has only the last preachment, under a tree still shown, of John Wesley. The third Edward and the Black Prince, in 1350, overcame the Spaniards in a stout sea-fight within sight of the walls; but I am bound to confess that I do not at all focus that performance, am unable, in the changed conditions, to 'place' anything so pompous. In the same way I fail to 'visualise', thank goodness, either of the several French inroads that left their mark of massacre and ruin. What I do see, on the other hand, very comfortably, is the little undistinguished picture of a nearer anti-quity, the antiquity for a glimpse of which I reopened 'Denis Duval'. Where please, was the barber's shop of the family of that hero, and where the apartments, where the preferred resorts, the particular scenes of occupation and diversion of the dark Chevalier de la Motte? Where did this subtle son of another civilisation, with whom Madame de Saverne had eloped from France, *en plein ancien régime*, without the occurrence between them of the least impro-priety, spend his time for so long a period; where had he his little habits and his numerous indispensable conveniences? What was the general geography, to express it synthetically, of the state of life of the orphaned Clarisse, quartered with a family of which one of the sons, furiously desirous of the girl, was, at his lost moments, a high-wayman stopping coaches in the dead of night? Over nothing in the whole fragment does such vagueness hover as over the domestic situation, in her tender years, of the future Madame Denis. Yet these are just the things I should have liked to know—the things, above all, I should have liked most to tell. Into a vision of *them*, at least, we can work ourselves; it is exactly the sort of vision into which Rye and Winchelsea, and all the land about, full of lurking hints and modest memories, most throws us back. I should, in truth, have liked to lock up our novelist in our little pavilion of inspiration, the gazebo at Rye, not letting him out till he should quite have satisfied us.

Close beside the east gate, so close that one of its battered towers leans heavily on the little garden, is a wonderfully perched cottage, of which the mistress is a very celebrated lady who resorts to the place in the intervals of an exacting profession—the scene of her renown, I may go so far as to mention, is the theatre—for refreshment and rest. The small grounds of this refuge, supported by the old town-wall and the steep plunge of the great hill, have a rare position and view. The narrow garden stretches away in the manner of a terrace to which the top of the wall forms a low parapet; and here it is that, when the summer days are long, the sweet old soul of all the land seems most to hang in the air. It is almost a question indeed whether this fine Winchelsea front, all silver-gray and ivy-green, is not even better when making a picture itself from below than when giving you one, with much immensity, from its brow. This picture is always your great effect, artfully prepared by an absence of prediction, when you take a friend over from Rye; and it would appear quite to settle the small discussion—that may be said to come up among us so often—of which is the happier abode. The great thing is that if you live at Rye you have Winchelsea to show; whereas if you live at Winchelsea you have nothing but Rye. This latter privilege I should be sorry to cry down; but nothing can alter the fact that, to begin with, the pedestal of Winchelsea has twice the height, by a rough measure, of that of its neighbour; and we all know the value of an inch at the end of a nose. Almost directly under the Winchelsea hill, crossing the little bridge of the Brede, you pass beyond a screen of trees and take in, at the top of the ascent, the two round towers and arch, ivied and mutilated, but still erect, of the old main gate. The road either way is long and abrupt, so that people kind to their beasts alight at the foot, and cyclists careful of their necks alight at the head. The brooding spectator, moreover, who forms a class by himself, pauses, infallibly, as he goes, to admire the way the great trees cluster and compose on the high slope, always striking, for him, as day gathers in and the whole thing melts together, a classic, academic note, the note of Turner and Claude. From the garden of the distinguished cottage, at any rate, it is a large, melancholy view—a view that an occasional perverse person whom it fails to touch finds easy, I admit, to speak of as dreary; so that those who love it and are well advised will ever,

at the outset, carry the war into the enemy's country by announcing
it, with glee, as sad. Just this it must be that nourishes the sense of
obliterated history as to which I a moment ago wondered. The air
is like that of a room through which something has been carried
that you are aware of without having seen it. There is a vast deal of
level in the prospect, but, though much depends on the day and
still more on the hour, it is, at the worst, all too delicate to be ugly.
The best hour is that at which the compact little pyramid of Rye,
crowned with its big but stunted church and quite covered by the
westering sun, gives out the full measure of its old browns that
turn to red and its old reds that turn to purple. These tones of
evening are now pretty much all that Rye has left to give, but there
are truly, sometimes, conditions of atmosphere in which I have
seen the effect as fantastic. I sigh when I think, however, what it
might have been if, perfectly placed as it is, the church tower—
which in its more perverse moods only resembles a big central
button, a knob on a pin-cushion—had had the grace of a few more
feet of stature. But that way depression lies, and the humiliation of
those moments at which the brooding spectator says to himself that
both tower and hill *would* have been higher if the place had only been
French or Italian. Its whole pleasant little pathos, in point of fact,
is just that it is homely English. And even with this, after all, the
imagination can play. The wide, ambiguous flat that stretches eastward from Winchelsea hill, and on the monotone of whose bosom,
seen at sunset from a friendly eminence that stands nearer, Rye takes
the form of a huge floating boat, its water-line sharp and its bulk
defined from stem to stern—this dim expanse is the great Romney
Marsh, no longer a marsh to-day, but, at the end of long years,
drained and ordered, a wide pastoral of grazing, with 'new' Romney
town, a Port no more—not the least of the shrunken Five—mel-
lowed to mere russet at the far end, and other obscure charms, revealed best to the slow cyclist, scattered over its breast: little old
'bits' that are not to be described, yet are known, with a small thrill,
when seen; little lonely farms, red and gray; little mouse-coloured
churches; little villages that seem made only for long shadows and
summer afternoons. Brookland, Old Romney, Ivychurch, Dym-
church, Lydd—they have positively the prettiest names. But the

point to be made is that, comparing small things with great—which may always be done when the small things are amiable—if Rye and its rock and its church are a miniature Mont-Saint-Michel, so, when the summer deepens, the shadows fall, and the mounted shepherds and their dogs pass before you in the grassy desert, you find in the mild English 'marsh' a recall of the Roman Campagna.

Old Suffolk

I AM not sure that before entering the county of Suffolk in the early part of August, I had been conscious of any personal relation to it save my share in what we all inevitably feel for a province enshrining the birthplace of a Copperfield. The opening lines of David's history offered in this particular an easy perch to my young imagination; and to recall them to-day, though with a memory long unrefreshed, is to wonder once more at the depth to which early impressions strike down. This one in especial indeed has been the privilege of those millions of readers who owe to Dickens the glow of the prime response to the romantic, that first bite of the apple of knowledge which leaves a taste for ever on the tongue. The great initiators give such a colour to mere names that the things they represent have often, before contact, been a lively part of experience. It is hard therefore for an undefended victim of this kind of emotion to measure, when contact arrives, the quantity of picture already stored up, to point to the nucleus of the gallery or trace the history of the acquaintance. It is true that for the divine plant of sensibility in youth the watering need never have been lavish. It flowered, at all events, at the right moment, in a certain case, into the branching image of Blunderstone—which, by the way, I am sorry to see figure as 'Blunderston' in gazetteers of recent date and more than questionable tact. Dickens took his Rookery exactly where he found it, and simply fixed it for ever; he left the cradle of the Copperfields the benefit of its delightful name; or I should say better, perhaps, left the delightful name and the obscure nook the benefit of an association ineffaceable: all of which makes me the more ashamed not as yet to have found the right afternoon —it would have in truth to be abnormally long—for a pious pilgrimage to the distracting little church where, on David's sleepy Sundays, one used to lose one's self with the sketchy Phiz. One of the reasons of this omission, so profane on a prior view, is doubt-

less that everything, in England, in old-time corners, has the con-
necting touch and the quality of illustration, and that, in a particularly golden August, with an impression in every bush, the immediate vision, wherever one meets it, easily attaches and suffices.
Another must have been, I confess, the somewhat depressed memory
of a visit paid a few years since to the ancient home of the Peggottys,
supposedly so 'sympathetic', but with little left, to-day, as the event
then proved, of the glamour it had worn to the fancy. Great Yarmouth, it will be remembered, was a convenient drive from Blunderstone; but Great Yarmouth, with its mile of cockneyfied sea-front
and its overflow of nigger minstrelsy, now strikes the wrong note
so continuously that I, for my part, became conscious, on the spot,
of a chill to the spirit of research.

This time, therefore, I have allowed that spirit its ease; and I
may perhaps intelligibly make the point I desire if I contrive to express somehow that I have found myself, most of the month, none
the less abundantly occupied in reading a fuller sense into the lingering sound given out, for a candid mind, by my superscription and
watching whatever it may stand for gradually flush with a stronger
infusion. It takes, in England, for that matter, no wonderful corner
of the land to make the fiddle-string vibrate. The old usual rural
things do this enough, and a part of the charm of one's exposure to
them is that they ask one to rise to no heroics. What is the charm,
after all, but just the abyss of the familiar? The peopled fancy, the
haunted memory are themselves what pay the bill. The game can
accordingly be played with delightful economy, a thrift involving
the cost of little more than a good bicycle. The bicycle indeed, since
I fall back on that admission, may perhaps, without difficulty, be
too good for the roads. Those of the more devious kind often engender hereabouts, like the Aristotelian tragedy, pity and terror;
but almost equally with others they lead, on many a chance, to the
ruddiest, greenest hamlets. What this comes to is saying that I have
had, for many a day, the sweet sense of living, aesthetically, at
really high pressure without, as it were, drawing on the great fund.
By the great fund I mean the public show, the show for admission
to which you are charged and overcharged, made to taste of the tree
of possible disappointment. The beauty of old Suffolk in general,

and above all of the desperate depth of it from which I write, is that these things whisk you straight out of conceivable relation to that last danger.

I defy any one, at desolate, exquisite Dunwich, to be disappointed in anything. The minor key is struck here with a felicity that leaves no sigh to be breathed, no loss to be suffered; a month of the place is a real education to the patient, the inner vision. The explanation of this is, appreciably, that the conditions give you to deal with not, in the manner of some quiet countries, what is meagre and thin, but what has literally, in a large degree, ceased to be at all. Dunwich is not even the ghost of its dead self; almost all you can say of it is that it consists of the mere letters of its old name. The coast, up and down, for miles, has been, for more centuries than I presume to count, gnawed away by the sea. All the grossness of its positive life is now at the bottom of the German Ocean, which moves for ever, like a ruminating beast, an insatiable, indefatigable lip. Few things are so melancholy—and so redeemed from mere ugliness by sadness—as this long, artificial straightness that the monster has impartially maintained. If at low tide you walk on the shore, the cliffs, of little height, show you a defence picked as bare as a bone; and you can say nothing kinder of the general humility and general sweetness of the land than that this sawlike action gives it, for the fancy, an interest, a sort of mystery, that more than makes up for what it may have surrendered. It stretched, within historic times, out into towns and promontories for which there is now no more to show than the empty eye-holes of a skull; and half the effect of the whole thing, half the secret of the impression, and what I may really call, I think, the source of the distinction, is this very visibility of the mutilation. Such at any rate is the case for a mind that can properly brood. There is a presence in what is missing— there is history in there being so little. It is so little, to-day, that every item of the handful counts.

The biggest items are of course the two ruins, the great church and its tall tower, now quite on the verge of the cliff, and the crumbled, ivied wall of the immense cincture of the Priory. These things have parted with almost every grace, but they still keep up the work that they have been engaged in for centuries and that can-

not better be described than as the adding of mystery to mystery.
This accumulation, at present prodigious, is, to the brooding mind,
unconscious as the shrunken little Dunwich of to-day may be of it,
the beginning and the end of the matter. I hasten to add that it is
to the brooding mind only, and from it, that I speak. The mystery
sounds for ever in the hard, straight tide, and hangs, through the
long, still summer days and over the low, diked fields, in the soft,
thick light. We play with it as with the answerless question, the
question of the spirit and attitude, never again to be recovered, of
the little city submerged. For it *was* a city, the main port of Suffolk,
as even its poor relics show; with a fleet of its own on the North
Sea, and a big religious house on the hill. We wonder what were
the apparent conditions of security, and on what rough calculation
a community could so build itself out to meet its fate. It keeps one
easy company here to-day to think of the whole business as a magnificent mistake. But Mr Swinburne, in verses of an extraordinary
poetic eloquence, quite brave enough for whatever there may have
been, glances in the right direction much further than I can do.
Read moreover, for other glances, the 'Letters of Edward Fitzgerald', Suffolk worthy and whimsical subject, who, living hard
by at Woodbridge, haunted these regions during most of his life,
and has left, in delightful pages, at the service of the emulous
visitor, the echo of every odd, quaint air they could draw from his
cracked, sweet instrument. He has paid his tribute, I seem to remember, to the particular delicate flower—the pale Dunwich rose
—that blooms on the walls of the Priory. The emulous visitor,
only yesterday, on the most vulgar of vehicles—which, however, he
is quite aware he must choose between using and abusing—followed, in the mellow afternoon, one of these faint hints across the
land and as far as the old, old town of Aldeburgh, the birth-place
and the commemorated 'Borough' of the poet Crabbe.

Fitzgerald, devoted to Crabbe, was apparently not less so to this
small break in the wide, low, heathery bareness that brings the
sweet Suffolk commons—rare purple and gold when I arrived—
nearly to the edge of the sea. We don't, none the less, always gather
the particular impression we bravely go forth to seek. We doubtless
gather another indeed that will serve as well any such turn as here

may wait for it; so that if it was somehow not easy to work Fitzgerald into the small gentility of the sea-front, the little 'marina', as
of a fourth-rate watering-place, that has elbowed away, evidently in
recent years, the old handful of character, one could at least, to
make up for that, fall back either on the general sense of the happy
trickery of genius or on the special beauty of the mixture, in the
singer of Omar Kháyyám, that, giving him such a place for a setting,
could yet feed his fancy so full. Crabbe, at Aldeburgh, for that
matter, is perhaps even more wonderful—in the light, I mean, of
what is left of the place by one's conjuring away the little modern
vulgar accumulation. What is left is just the stony beach and the big
gales and the cluster of fishermen's huts and the small, wide, short
street of decent, homely, shoppy houses. These are the private emotions of the historic sense—glimpses in which we recover for an
hour, or rather perhaps, with an intensity, but for the glimmer of
a minute, the conditions that, grimly enough, could engender
masterpieces, or at all events classics. What a mere pinch of manners
and customs in the midst of winds and waves! Yet if it was a feature
of these to return a member to Parliament, what wonder that, up
to the Reform Bill, dead Dunwich should have returned two?

The glimpses I speak of are, in all directions, the constant company of the afternoon 'spin'. Beginning, modestly enough, at Dunwich itself, they end, for intensity, as far inland as you have time to
go; far enough—this is the great point—to have shown you, in
their quiet vividness of type, a placid series of the things into which
you may most read the old story of what is softest in the English
complexity. I scarce know what murmur has been for weeks in my
ears if it be not that of the constant word that, as a recall of the
story, may serve to be put under the vignette. And yet this word is
in its last form nothing more eloquent than the mere admonition
to be pleased. Well, so you are, even as I was yesterday at Wesselton
with the characteristic 'value' that expressed itself, however shyly,
in the dear old red inn at which I halted for the queer restorative—
I thus discharge my debt to it—of a bottle of lemonade with a 'dash'.
The dash was only of beer, but the refreshment was immense. So
even was that of the sight of a dim, draped, sphinx-like figure that
loomed, at the end of a polished passage, out of a little dusky back

parlour which had a windowful of the choked light of a small
green garden—a figure proving to be an old woman desirous to
dilate on all the years she had sat there with rheumatism 'most
cruel'. So, inveterately—and in these cases without the after-taste—
is that of the pretty little park gates you pass to skirt the walls and
hedges beyond which the great affair, the greatest of all, the deep,
still home, sits in the midst of its acres and strikes you all the more
for being, precisely, so unrenowned. It is the charming repeated
lesson that the amenity of the famous seats in this country is
nothing to that of the lost and buried ones. This impression in particular may bring you round again harmoniously to Dunwich and
above all perhaps to where the Priory, laid, as I may say flat on its
back, rests its large outline on what was once the high ground,
with the inevitable 'big' house, beyond and a little above, folded,
for privacy, in a neat, impenetrable wood. Here as elsewhere the
cluster offers without complication just the signs of the type. At
the base of the hill are the dozen cottages to which the village has
been reduced, and one of which contains, to my hearing, though
by no means, alas, to his own, a very ancient man who will count
for you on his fingers, till they fail, the grand acres that, in his day,
he has seen go the way of the rest. He likes to figure that he ploughed
of old where only the sea ploughs now. Dunwich, however, will
still last his time; and that of as many other as—to repeat my hint
—may yet be drawn here (though not, I hope, on the instance of
these prudent lines) to judge for themselves into how many mean-
ings a few elements can compose. One never need be bored, after
all, when 'composition' really rules. It rules in the way the brown
hamlet disposes itself, and the gray square tower of the church, in
just the right relation, peeps out of trees that remind me exactly of
those which, in the frontispiece of Birket Foster, offered to my
childish credulity the very essence of England. Let me put it directly
for old Suffolk that this credulity finds itself here, at the end of
time, more than ever justified. Let me put it perhaps also that the
very essence of England has a way of presenting itself with completeness in almost any fortuitous combination of rural objects at
all, so that, wherever you may be, you get, reduced and simplified,
the whole of the scale. The big house and its woods are always at

hand; with a 'party' always, in the intervals of shooting, to bring
down to the rustic sports that keep up the tradition of the village
green. The russet, low-browed inn, the 'ale-house' of Shakespeare,
the immemorial fountain of beer, looking over that expanse, swings,
with an old-time story-telling creak, the sign of the Marquis of
Carabas. The pretty girls, within sight of it, alight from the Marquis's wagonette; the young men with the one eye-glass and the
new hat sit beside them on the benches supplied for their sole
accommodation, and thanks to which the meditator on manners
has, a little, the image, gathered from faded fictions by female hands,
of the company brought over, for the triumph of the heroine, to
the hunt or the county ball. And it is always Hodge and Gaffer
that, at bottom, *font les frais*—always the mild children of the glebe
on whom, in the last resort, the complex superstructure rests.

The discovery, in the twilight of time, of the merits, as a building-
site, of Hodge's broad bent back remains surely one of the most
sagacious strokes of the race from which the squire and the parson
were to be evolved. He is there in force—at the rustic sports—in
force or in feebleness, with Mrs Hodge and the Miss Hodges, who
participate with a silent glee in the chase, over fields where their
shadows are long, of a pig with a greased tail. He pulls his forelock
in the tent in which, after the pig is caught, the rewards of valour
are dispensed by the squire's lady, and if he be in favour for respectability and not behind with rent, he penetrates later to the
lawn within the wood, where he is awaited by a band of music and
a collation of beer, buns, and tobacco.

I mention these things as some of the light notes, but the picture
is never too empty for a stronger one not to sound. The strongest,
at Dunwich, is indeed one that, without in the least falsifying the
scale, counts immensely for filling in. The palm in the rustic sports
is for the bluejackets; as, in England, of course, nothing is easier
than for the village green to alternate with the element that Bri-
tannia still more admirably rules. I had often dreamed that the ideal
refuge for a man of letters was a cottage so placed on the coast as
to be circled, as it were, by the protecting arm of the Admiralty. I
remember to have heard it said in the old country—in New York
and Boston—that the best place to live in is next to an engine-house,

and it is on this analogy that, at Dunwich, I have looked for ministering peace in near neighbourhood to one of those stations of the coastguard that, round all the edge of England, at short intervals, on rock and sand and heath, make, with shining whitewash and tar, clean as a great State is at least theoretically clean, each its own little image of the reach of the empire. It is in each case an image that, for one reason and another, you respond to with a sort of thrill; and the thing becomes as concrete as you can wish on your discovering in the three or four individual members of the simple staff of the establishment all sorts of educated decency and many sorts of beguilement to intercourse. Prime among the latter, in truth, is the great yarn-spinning gift. It differs from man to man, but here and there it glows like a cut ruby. May the last darkness close before I cease to care for sea-folk!—though this, I hasten to add, is not the private predilection at which, in these incoherent notes, I proposed most to glance. Let me have mentioned it merely as a sign that the fault is all my own if, this summer, the arm of the Admiralty has not, in the full measure of my theory, represented the protection under which the long literary morning may know— abyss of delusion!—nothing but itself.

Index